Medusa

Michael John Dibdin was born in Wolverhampton in
1947. His mother was a nurse and his father a
Cambridge-educated physicist with a passionate
enthusiasm for folk music. The family travelled exten-
sively around Britain until Michael turned seven, when
they settled in Northern Ireland.

After graduating with an English degree from Sussex
University he took a Master's Degree at the University
of Alberta, Canada. Dibdin's first published novel,
The Last Sherlock Holmes Story, his self-proclaimed
'pastiche', appeared in 1978. Shortly afterwards he
moved to Italy to teach for a number of years at the
University of Perugia where he was inspired to write
a second novel, *A Rich Full Death*, set in Victorian
Florence. In 1988 he wrote *Ratking*, the first of the
famous crime series featuring the Italian detective
Aurelio Zen. The novel won the Crime Writers'
Association Gold Dagger award. Other books in this
series include three of his best received titles, *Cabal*
(1992), which was awarded the French Grand Prix du
Roman Policier, *Dead Lagoon* (1994), and finally *End*

Games, published posthumously in 2007. Amongst his best-received non-Zen novels were *The Dying of the Light*, an Agatha Christie pastiche, and the darkly comic *Dirty Tricks*.

While Dibdin travelled frequently to Italy, he lived in Seattle with his wife the novelist Kathrine Beck, from where he wrote all but the first three Zen novels. The city also provided a new location for his other detect-ive novels, including *Dark Spectre* (1995) and *Thanksgiving* (2000), the story of a British journalist's obsession with his recently dead American wife.

Michael Dibdin died in 2007 at the age of 60.

MICHAEL DIBDIN

Medusa

faber and faber

First published in 2003
by Faber and Faber Limited
Bloomsbury House
74–77 Great Russell Street
London WCIB 3DA
First published in paperback in 2004
This paperback edition first published in 2011

Typeset by RefineCatch Ltd, Bungay, Suffolk
Printed in England by CPI Bookmarque, Croydon

A CIP record for this book
is available from the British Library

ISBN 978–0–571–27087–3

2 4 6 8 10 9 7 5 3 1

Pulchra es amica mea suavis et decora sicut Hierusalem terribilis ut castrorum acies ordinata. Averte oculos tuos a me quia ipsi me avolare fecerunt.

You are beautiful my love, sweet and graceful like Jerusalem, terrible as an army drawn up for battle. Avert your eyes from me, for they put me to flight.

The Song of Songs 6:3

I

An oily fog had mystified the streets, sheathing the façades to either side, estranging familiar landmarks and coating the windows with a skein of liquid seemingly denser than water. Gabriele tried to edge away from the fat woman in the next seat, who was phoning in a gruesomely detailed account of some elderly relative's colostomy, but her bulk still left him no room to open his newspaper in comfort. The only thing he could read with any ease was the headline, which referred to hostilities in progress in some distant land where young men were killing and being killed. Outside, the stalled traffic snarled and yelped. The tram rumbled along its dedicated right-of-way through the shrouded city, the bell clanging intermittently in warning of its approach.

'God knows!' the fat woman was saying. 'First I have to pick up the car from Pia, assuming she's there yet, which I doubt, and after that it's anyone's guess with this damned fog.'

Gabriele hugged the window, turning up the collar of his green loden coat in a symbolic attempt to screen the woman out. He liked the fog, the world quietened down and closed in. Glossy turned to matt, every stridency was muted, substance leached out of the brute matter all around. Things became notions, the brash present a vague memory.

By some parallel process of slippage, his innumerable childhood memories of foggy days morphed into other memories. The fog of illness, real or feigned, of fevers and flu and febrility. 'I don't feel well, Mamma.' She was always eager to believe him, and knowing that he was giving her pleasure alleviated whatever slight guilt he might have felt in faking or exaggerating his symptoms. His mother liked him to be ill. It made her feel needed. Sometimes he had even suspected that she knew he was malingering, but forgave him, perhaps even encouraged him.

Fog to Gabriele also meant the feather duvet that his mother fluffed up and floated down over him while the impotent clock insisted that he should be in school, with its horde of bullies and swots. 'My cloud,' he'd called it. Weightless and warm, flung back as soon as his mother had left the room so that he could run to the bookcase and pick out a selection of novels to take back to bed, folding the cloud over him again. Books were another form of fog, dipping down to infiltrate and insidiously undermine the authoritative, official version, showing it up for the sham it was. He knew the stories were all made up, the characters puppets, the outcome predetermined, so why did they seem more real than reality? And why was no one else shocked by this gleeful scandal?

The tram squealed to a halt and the fat woman got up, still talking continuously on her mobile, stepped out into the street and instantly evaporated. The doors closed again and the tram lumbered into motion. With the seat next to him now empty, Gabriele spread out his paper and briefly skimmed the ongoing international and political stories. As usual, they reminded him of his mother's dictum regarding left-over food: 'Just add one new ingredient, and you can serve it up again and again.'

Here in the old centre of the city, the fog seemed even thicker, far more real than the transient hints of stone and glass formed and dissolved in the opaque vistas it offered. Gabriele turned to the *Cronaca* pages and read about a domestic homicide in Genoa, a drug death in Turin, and the discovery of a corpse in an abandoned military tunnel high up in the Dolomites.

The tram slowed to its next stop, the one before his. Gabriele closed the paper and folded it vertically so that it formed a tight short baton, then thrust it into his pocket and got off along with seven other people. He waited by the stop, feigning a coughing fit, until they had dispersed in the fog. The tram rolled away with its cargo of light, leaving him purblind in the miasma.

He crossed to the pavement, hurrying to avoid the lights of a car which turned out to be much closer than it had appeared, then stumbled along in the direction the tram had taken, stopping every so often to look and listen and to sniff the laden air. After a few blocks a café appeared, botched together at the last moment from fragments of gleam and glow. Gabriele paused for a moment, then pushed open the door.

He had never got off the tram at this stop before, and never been in this café, so it was only natural that he should take a vivid interest in every detail of the layout, décor, and above all the clientele. He inspected the other customers carefully, paying particular attention to those who entered after him. When his cappuccino and brioche arrived, he took them to the very end of the marble bar, where it curved around to meet the wall. From there he had a view of the entire room, and of the only entrance. The patrons appeared to be just the sort of people you would expect to find in that sort of café in that area of Milan at that time in the morning: solid, professional, well-heeled and preoccupied with their own concerns. They all stood in couples or larger groups and none of them paid him the slightest attention.

Gabriele took the newspaper out of his pocket,

unfolded it furtively and read through the article again. Then he tossed it into the waste bin and wiped his hands on a paper napkin drawn from the metal dispenser on the counter. Whoever would have thought it? After all these years.

If it hadn't been for the postcards, he himself might have succeeded in forgetting by now. Apart from that time some Communist journalist had come around asking about Leonardo under the pretext of wanting to buy a book. But Gabriele had got rid of him in short order.

The series of postcards had begun the year after Gabriele had resigned his commission. Since then, they had arrived annually wherever he happened to be living at the time, all sent from Rome and postmarked on the anniversary of the day Leonardo had died. Since 1993, they had arrived at the shop. They were always the same, a cheap tourist postcard of the Loggia dei Lanzi in Florence showing Cellini's bronze statue of Perseus holding the severed head of Medusa. Gabriele's name and address were printed on the right-hand side of the reverse. The space intended for the message had been left blank.

'We'd better get going,' said one of the men at the bar. 'They'll be waiting for us.'

And they would be waiting for him, thought Gabriele. If not today, then tomorrow. If not at work, then at home. What made it worse was that he had no idea who 'they' were. Medusa was something he had put behind him long ago. He had even had the tattoo removed, a surgical intervention which had cost him quite a lot of money and some minor discomfort. All he had ever known about the organization had been the other three names in his cell, but there must of course have been many more besides theirs, and above all an overarching command structure which no doubt reached up very far indeed into the military and political hierarchy. He had learned from an article in the press some years before that Alberto – now Colonel – Guerrazzi was now someone very high up in the secret services. Those people had unimaginable powers. If they felt threatened, as they undoubtedly must, by the potential disclosure of the truth behind Leonardo's death, their response was likely to be immediate, pre-emptive, and totally unpredictable.

Outside, the fog was as persistent as ever. Gabriele dodged into the first doorway he came to and glanced back. No one emerged from the café he had just left. He walked slowly on, head down, seemingly intent on keeping his footing and avoiding obstacles. A chirpy clanging announced the arrival of another tram. It ground to a halt at the stop where he normally got off every morning. He waited until the group of commuters had dispersed and then inspected the street carefully. The row of shops on the ground floor of the big eighteenth-century *palazzo* was beginning to open. They were mainly fashion and accessory outlets, with a jeweller's, a hair salon and his own antiquarian bookshop interspersed. There were very few people about, and no conspicuous watchers, but he knew that that meant nothing. Realizing that he was rapidly becoming conspicuous himself, he turned left and started to walk around the block.

I'm no good at this, he thought. Never had been, never would be. He'd tried hard, he really had, but do what he might he'd never been a natural like Alberto, Nestore and poor Leonardo. 'Not really officer material.' He'd never forgotten that comment. It had stung, even though an officer was the last thing he'd wanted to be, if he'd been honest with himself. And it had made no difference. Strings were pulled and buttons pushed, and he got his commission just the same, thanks to the influence of his father, who of course had never let him forget the fact.

But that martinet at the military academy had been right. He wasn't officer material. He could follow orders as faithfully as a dog, but he couldn't give them in such a way as to inspire the same unthinking obedience in others. Or even in himself. Above all, he lacked the initiative to improvise successfully when things got tough and there was no superior around to tell him what to do. Such as now.

What was he to do? Where was he to go? He hadn't spoken to his sister for months, and anyway they'd find him there easily enough. The same went for his few close friends, even supposing he could impose on them without explanation. A trip abroad was tempting, but that meant credit cards and identification and all the rest of it, a paper trail that could be traced. What he really needed to do was just disappear until the situation resolved itself.

He strode on with fake purposefulness through the eddying currents. When another café loomed up, he turned into it blindly and ordered a whisky. Gabriele rarely drank, and never before lunch. He knocked the foul-tasting spirit back like medicine, staring at his image in the mirror behind the bar, surprised as always by his sturdy, wiry body and determined gaze. He always thought of himself as tiny, weedy, frail and terminally inadequate. The joke that life had played on him was putting such a personality inside the body of a professional welter-weight boxer. It had saved him from getting beaten up at school, and later at the academy, but even those victories felt hollow, won by deceit. And the women in his life, unlike the men, had never been fooled. On the contrary, they had loved him, those few who had lasted longer than a week or two, precisely for the weakness they had so perceptively diagnosed. For a while it had seemed sweet to be mothered again, but in the end it felt like another defeat.

Besides, they had all wanted to be real mothers, and he had no intention of collaborating in a re-run of that sad sorry farce. Hippolyte Taine, whose collected works Gabriele was currently reading, had as usual got it ruthlessly right: 'Three weeks flirting, three months loving, three years squabbling, thirty years making do, and then the kids start again.' He wasn't going to let that happen to him. Besides, it might turn out to be a boy. He'd had enough of father-and-son routines to last him several lifetimes. The women had sensed this and moved on, and by now Gabriele had lost all interest in the whole business. If you didn't want children, what was the point? At his age, sex seemed a bit disgusting and stupid, and the present cultural obsession with it depressing and sick. According to various comments that his mother had let slip from time to time, this was at least one thing that he had in common with his father.

The café was starting to fill up now. It was small and rather seedy for this area, and the clientele was very different from that at the previous establishment: tradesmen, street sweepers, delivery drivers, city cops, pensioners, janitors . . .

It took another moment before the penny dropped, and when it did Gabriele had enough sense not to use his mobile. The café's pay phone was at the rear of the establishment, in an overflow zone where the tables and chairs began to peter out and be replaced by stacks of mineral water cases, cardboard boxes of crisps, unused advertising materials and a broken ice-cream freezer with its lid up. On the wall nearby hung a framed black-and-white aerial photograph of a small town somewhere in the alluvial flatlands to the south, Crema or Lodi perhaps. It must have been taken shortly after the war, for there was still little extensive development outside the walls, just a few suburban villas and the railway station. After that the vast plains spread away, faintly lined with dirt roads and dotted at intervals with isolated *cascine*, the rectangular complexes of clustered farm buildings characteristic of the Po valley.

He stood there, phone in hand, staring up at the photograph. Eventually the dialling tone changed to an angry whine. Gabriele hung up, fed in a coin and redialled. He knew what to do now, and it could be done.

'*Pronto.*'

'Fulvio, it's Gabriele Passarini.'

'*Salve, dottore.*'

'Listen, you remember that time, years ago, when I locked myself out of the shop?'

A brief laugh.

'It's happened again?'

'It's happened again. And I want you to do the same thing you did last time. Do you understand?'

'You mean go down to . . .'

'Yes, yes! Exactly what you did last time. I'll be waiting.'

There was a pause. When Fulvio finally spoke, he sounded flustered, perhaps by the intensity in Gabriele's voice.

'Very well, *dottore*. I'm up to my ears with work this morning, but . . .'

'I'll make it worth your while.'

He hung up, wiped his palms on his coat and returned to the bar, where he ordered and downed a coffee and then paid his bill before leaving the café.

Fulvio was waiting for him just inside the doorway. The janitor was a lean, stooping man whose perpetual expression of amazement, due to the loss of his eyebrows in an industrial accident, gave him a slightly gormless air. In fact, Fulvio was the intermediary, when not the instigator, behind everything that happened in the building. Gabriele had recognized this early on, and had always taken good care to ensure that Fulvio was aware that he both understood and appreciated the situation: a *panettone* from one of the city's best pastry shops every Christmas, some chocolates for his wife on her birthday, the occasional but satisfyingly large tip now and again.

The janitor beckoned Gabriele in, then pulled the rusty iron door to and locked it again. A dim bulb showed the steep stairway down into the cellarage.

'Any new developments?' Gabriele asked casually, using the stock phrase they had evolved for this conversation.

Fulvio sighed profoundly. After the evident and excessive emotion in Gabriele's voice on the phone, he sounded relieved to return to this well-worn topic.

'Eh, what can I tell you? Signora Nicolai had another mild heart attack last week, but she's recovered now and will probably see us all out. Pasquino and Indovina are much the same as ever, and the Gambetta family are still arguing over who gets what from their uncle's will. But I promise you, *dottore*, an apartment here will become vacant sooner or later.'

'But probably not during my lifetime.'

'Eh, eh, eh!'

They walked down the steps and along a narrow passageway that led into a cavernous space filled with dim hulks kept vague by the thin whey of light from open barred windows at pavement level above. Selecting another key from the bunch he carried, Fulvio unlocked a door in the end wall. He switched on a feeble light and they passed through into another subterranean vault, similar in shape and size to the previous one but this time smelling strongly of coal. The floor crunched beneath them as they crossed towards a set of steps in the corner leading back up into the building above.

They were about halfway there when the light went out. The intolerable memory of the shrieks and pleas and curses surged up in Gabriele's mind. 'You'd scream like that if it was happening to you,' he'd thought at the time. That had been the worst aspect of it, the way they had reduced Leonardo – 'the young priest', Nestore had jokingly dubbed him, because of his seeming lack of interest in women – to the lowest common denominator of the human animal. People could be destroyed even before they were killed, and he had been an accomplice to such a destruction, as well as to the killing itself. There had never been any hiding from that horror, only forgetting. But forgetting was no longer an option, for the others involved would not forget.

'*Dottore?*'

The echoes lent Fulvio's voice an unwonted authority, but the only reply was a wheezing respiration which reminded the janitor of the bellows they'd used to blast the furnace back when he'd started as an apprentice at the foundry. He groped around in his pocket, found his cigarette lighter and clicked a flame.

'*Dottore?*'

With an effort, Gabriele got the attack under control. The screams faded, the grisly details vanished, the naked rock walls became dressed stone again.

'I'm all right,' he said.

'The steps are just here. Follow me.'

They climbed the stairs and walked along a short passage. After some fumbling with his lighter and keys at the dead end, Fulvio unlocked yet another door, and promptly fell over.

'*Porca Madonna!*'

The lighter went out and the interior behind the door was dark, but Gabriele advanced confidently, getting out his keys. He knew where he was now. Stepping over the recumbent janitor, as well as the cleaning mop and bucket he had tripped over, he unlocked and opened the inner door. The lattice steel grill protecting the shop windows gave just enough light to see by. Behind him, Fulvio had got to his feet and was groping for the switch inside the door. Gabriele's hand grasped his arm.

'No!'

The janitor gazed at him with a look of astonishment which had nothing to do with the absence of eyebrows.

'No lights?' he breathed.

Gabriele shook his head.

'But why? What's all this about, anyway?'

Bruised and humiliated by his fall, Fulvio sounded angry now.

'You had your keys all along! So why all this fooling about? What's going on?'

Gabriele had stepped forward into the centre of the room and stood looking round at the serried spines. Their discreet but sumptuous tones seemed to fill the air like gentle organ music.

Fingers yanked at his sleeve.

'I demand an explanation, *dottore*!'

Gabriele placed one forefinger on his closed lips.

'All in good time, Fulvio.'

He felt calm and strong and safe now. He knew each volume by heart, could name the title, author, edition, date and publisher from where he stood. If only he could just stay here, with a nice apartment upstairs so that he could get some sleep and have a shower and change once in a while, but still be able to come down and commune with his books at any time of the day or night!

He went over to the safe located behind the desk where he normally presided over the ceremonies of the shop. The janitor shuffled about awkwardly, mumbling something under his breath. Gabriele spun the dial the requisite number of times and eased the heavy door open. Turning his back on Fulvio, he rapidly pocketed a bundle of banknotes.

'This is most irregular,' the janitor repeated in an aggrieved tone. 'With all due respect, *dottore*, you owe me an explanation.'

Gabriele relocked the safe, then perched over his desk and wrote rapidly on a card. With a last look round, he stood up and walked back to Fulvio. He extracted two of the notes from the bundle in his pocket and held them out.

'Here's your explanation,' he said. 'I may be away for some time. When I get back, I'll pay you the same again for each week I've been gone. In return, I want you to keep a sharp eye on the shop, and particularly on anyone who comes round asking after me. Keep a note of dates, descriptions and names, if they give any, and above all of what they say. Finally, please fasten this to the window at the front of the shop once I've left.'

He handed the janitor the card he had written. Under the name and logo of the bookshop was printed *Chiuso per Lutto*. Fulvio looked at him with a new understanding, sympathy and respect.

'You're in mourning, *dottore*? A death in the family?'

Gabriele very faintly smiled.

'Yes,' he said. 'Yes, I suppose that's what it amounts to.'

II

'I suppose you've heard about that terrible thing.'

Riccardo was standing just inside the kitchen, the piled plates in his hand, looking about him sheepishly as he always did.

'What thing?' Claudia asked, relieving him of his burden.

He didn't answer at once. Instead, he turned back and closed the door to the living room. That was something he had never done before. For a moment she wondered . . .

But that was silly. It was only Ricco, and besides those days were over. She set the plates down on the counter and looked at him with a touch of asperity. These sociable afternoons with the Zuccottis had a fixed, reassuring rhythm that nothing ever disturbed. The fall of the cards was the only invariable permitted, and even there she and Danilo virtually always won.

'What are you talking about?'

The question seemed to confuse poor Riccardo still further. And when the answer came, it was in a disjointed stutter, like a terrified declaration of love.

'That body. Corpse, I mean. In the mountains . . . What a terrible business.'

He rubbed his hands together helplessly.

'It had been there thirty years, they say.'

Claudia wrinkled her nose in disgust.

'There was something about it on the news. Yes, of course, terrible. So why bring it up?'

Riccardo looked at the floor, at the sink, then out of the window at the roofs of Verona, anywhere but at her. It looked almost as if he was going to cry, and the answer to her heartless question was suddenly obvious. He must of course have known the victim, or at least the family. Lightly burdened by remorse, she stepped over and took his hand, rubbing it gently.

'I'm so sorry,' she said.

It was at this moment that the door opened and Raffaela walked in.

'Oh!'

She set down the coffee pot she had carried in as a pretext. This too was new. When they met at the Zuccottis' home, Raffaela served and Danilo helped her clear up. Here at Claudia's, she and Riccardo did the work. As at cards, they never cut for partners.

'I do hope I'm not interrupting anything!' Raffaela went on archly.

'Of course not!' her husband snapped, his fit of nervous hesitancy quite dispelled. 'I was simply . . .'

18

He broke off.

'Ricco was just telling me about that terrible business of the climber they found dead in that cave near Cortina. I didn't know you two were personally concerned. I'm so sorry.'

Raffaela Zuccotti gave her a look which was clearly intended to convey that if she, Claudia, thought for a moment that she, Raffaela, was going to fall for such a transparently flimsy excuse as that, then she had another think coming. She turned to her husband and very forcefully said nothing.

'I thought it was someone Claudia might have known,' Riccardo said feebly.

'A dead climber?' his wife queried acidly.

'No one knows who he was. He was found by some Austrian climbers. Well, they were cavers, actually.'

Thirty years of teaching at a *liceo classico* had left Raffaela well prepared for such badinage as this.

'Whether their explorations concerned peaks or grottoes,' she said with a pointed glance at Claudia's ample figure, 'I fail to see why any of this is of such personal concern to either of you.'

Claudia laughed effortlessly.

'For God's sake, Raffaela! The whole thing was just a misunderstanding. Ricco mentioned the news item, and I thought for some reason that he knew the poor man. I was just being sympathetic, that's all.'

Abandoning them abruptly, she returned to the living room, where Danilo was sitting at the coffee table idly shuffling the pack of cards. Claudia subsided on to the sofa beside him and started an intense monologue about the celebrity scandal of the moment. It was conducted in an almost inaudible undertone, and she paid not the slightest attention to the Zuccotti couple when they emerged from the kitchen.

'Thank you so much, *cara*!' cried Raffaela, taking charge of the situation as always. 'Everything was perfect. We have so enjoyed ourselves, but we really must be going. It looks like rain, doesn't it? Come on, Ricco.'

Her husband presented the most extraordinary spectacle, staring at Danilo with a mute fixity that Claudia found completely inexplicable.

'Riccardo!' his wife admonished.

'*Certo, sì. Arrivo. Anzi, andiamo. Cioè . . .*'

Claudia vaguely waved and smiled.

When the front door finally closed behind her guests, she rose from the sofa.

'I'm going to slip into something more comfortable,' she said, turning her back but not moving.

Danilo obediently stood up and unzipped her dress. Claudia walked off into the hallway leading to her bedroom, the garment already tumbling off her shoulders and down to her waist. Leaving the door open, she unhooked her brassiere and breathed a soft sigh as it fell to the floor. She kicked off her shoes and wriggled out of the dress, then stripped off her stockings and unlatched the hateful corset. With a lilt she stepped across the ruins and slipped silk on like a younger skin.

'So what was all that about?' she remarked, returning to the living room.

Danilo was now standing by the sideboard stacked with photographs of Claudia's son Naldo at every age from birth to twenty years. He was still nervously shuffling the cards.

'Raffaela seems to be taking life terribly hard, *poverina*. Not that maturing is easy for any of us, but imagine a steady diet of four decades with the ghastly Riccardo, and then realizing that the clock has run out. It must be like being confined to one's bed with some terminal illness when one's never done anything or travelled anywhere.'

'Whereas you've travelled from bed to bed, done everything and never been confined anywhere.'

Claudia wound the ankle-length robe loosely about her and uttered a practised laugh.

'Honestly, the things you say! I always behaved perfectly while Gaetano was alive.'

Danilo raised an ironic eyebrow.

'I mean I never screwed anyone in our social set,' Claudia retorted. 'What more can you ask?'

Danilo didn't seem inclined to ask, or to say, anything. But he didn't leave either. Another little anomaly. They were piling up this afternoon.

'Would you like a pastry?' Claudia asked him pointedly. 'Some more coffee?'

Danilo put the cards down and turned to face her. He seemed about to say something, then gave one of his trade-mark boyish guffaws which always charmed Claudia, even though she knew he could produce them on demand as and when it suited him.

'Why do you laugh?' she asked.

'Oh, I just remembered what Gaetano used to say about cards. You know that our pack is different from the one used in every other country? Not just the suits of swords and cups, but the fact that there are only forty cards, because the ten, nine and eight are missing. Gaetano claimed that this symbolized everything that was wrong with the Italian military. Almost a third of the total force consisted of senior officers while the rest were cannon fodder. The former weren't always stupid and the latter were often brave, but what was missing was a solid, dependable corps of *sottufficiali* to pull the whole unit together and get things done on the ground. That's what kept the Germans in the war, ever after Stalingrad and Normandy. Their NCOs were the best in the world.'

'Yes, Gaetano could be quite boring on military matters,' Claudia replied languidly. 'But I had to put up with it from him. He was my husband. I don't have to put up with it from you.'

Danilo's glance seemed to be trying to spare her something. An uneasy silence fell.

'Well, I think I'll have a bath,' Claudia announced briskly, heading for the inner hallway of the apartment. 'Feel free to let yourself out when you're ready.'

Danilo strode across, gripping her wrist and pulling her back into the room. Astounded, almost excited, Claudia let herself be drawn. Danilo was her casual companion and card partner, an endless source of scurrilous gossip, a creature of varied charms and indeterminate sexuality. The one thing he never had been was physical.

'There's something I have to tell you,' he told her. 'Sit down. Let me get you a drink.'

'I don't drink.'

'Yes, you do, *cara*. I can smell it from here. Vermouth, I'd say. The sweet variety.'

Her shoulders sagged. She was aware that her robe was hanging open in an unseemly manner, showing half her bosom, but that was the last thing on her mind. Danilo was busily opening and closing the doors of the sideboard.

'In the kitchen,' she told him. 'Above the sink.'

Opening a silver box which looked entirely decorative, Claudia helped herself to one of her rare cigarettes as Danilo returned bearing a tumbler filled almost to the brim with Cinzano Rosso. He handed it to her and, in what he managed to make appear the same smooth gesture, proffered a flame from his lighter.

'Well?' she asked with marked sarcasm. Whatever was going on had already gone on much too long.

There was no reply. Danilo just stood there, gazing into space. Claudia took a gulp of the red liquid, which tasted even more sickly than usual. But Cinzano was a ladylike drink. She could name some women who had moved on to gin and vodka and never found their way back.

'Danilo, over the years you've made me laugh, you've made me cry and you've made me angry. Once or twice you've even made me think. Now you're beginning to bore me. I never thought you'd do that. If you've got something to say, for God's sake say it!'

Danilo smiled nervously.

'Sorry, I'm just not sure how to start. Riccardo was supposed to do this, you see. He's had time to think the whole thing through, work out the best way to put it. But Raffaela interrupted and then hauled him off, so I've had to step into the breach. Anyway, basically it's about that body they found in the mountains last week.'

'So I gather. What about it, for the love of heaven?'

He made three futile attempts to begin, then spread out his hands in appeal.

'How much did Ricco tell you?'

'Nothing. He was just getting to the point when Raffaela marched in on marital patrol duty.'

With evident relief, Danilo seized the opportunity to laugh.

'Ah yes, I see! Well, the point is that while the body hasn't been officially identified as yet, sources in Rome close to the regiment have informally advised various people here as to certain relevant facts. Some of them in turn informed Riccardo, who told me, and we both agreed that it would be better if you heard it from us first.'

'Heard what, for God's sake?'

Danilo faltered again for a moment, then plunged on like a horse taking a fence.

'Leonardo Ferrero.'

Claudia didn't move or speak, didn't react at all for at least a minute. Shock has its uses, and comes in various forms. Hearing that name on Danilo's lips was like hearing a poodle pronounce the secret name of God.

She reached forward to flick the ash off her cigarette, then slowly stood up, looking around her with the startled expression of someone who has fallen asleep on the bus home from work and awakened to find herself in a foreign country.

Danilo coughed.

'You knew him, I believe.'

Claudia smiled brightly, as though putting two and two together at last.

'Lieutenant Ferrero? Certainly we knew him. He was one of Gaetano's favourites. But that was all a long time ago.'

She finally seemed to become aware of Danilo's silence.

'So why bring it up now?'

'Because on the basis of the information that we have received, and I must stress that this is strictly confidential, the preliminary identification of the corpse that has been found in those tunnels up in the mountains appears to indicate that it is his.'

Claudia went over to the window giving on to the courtyard of the building. The woman in the apartment opposite had opened her shutters, a thing she only did when she was entertaining one of her many younger lovers that evening. Later, just before the crucial moment, she would teasingly close them again. At least I've never sunk that low, thought Claudia abstractly. Flaunting one's romantic triumphs was vulgar. She finished her cigarette, opened the window and tossed it out.

'That's absurd,' she said, turning back to face Danilo. 'Lieutenant Ferrero died thirty years ago in a plane crash. An explosion in the fuel tank. Gaetano and I attended the funeral.'

'So did I. And that's what we all believed, of course. But it seems that we were wrong.'

'So what did happen?'

Danilo made a wide, open-handed gesture.

'That's what the authorities are trying to find out now. The point is that sooner or later they may come here, wanting to question you. It would therefore be best for you to prepare yourself.'

Claudia walked back to her drink, downing half of it at a gulp.

'But what on earth has it got to do with me?'

Danilo looked her in the eyes in a way he had never done before.

'I don't think you really want me to address that question, Claudia. We both know the answer, and to discuss it would be unnecessarily painful for both of us. At our age one wants to avoid pain as much as possible, don't you agree?'

The telephone rang, and for once she was eager to answer it. It turned out to be Naldo, making his usual weekly duty call.

'*Ciao*, Naldino! How are you, darling? And how's the restaurant going? Really? Oh dear! Well, I'm sure things will pick up once spring comes.'

She carried on in this vein for several minutes, deliberately overdoing the maternal gushiness in hopes that Danilo might take the point and leave. But he showed no signs of doing so. Eventually the conversational flow began to dry up and Naldo even started to sound slightly alarmed, as though he suspected that his mother was drunk. And perhaps she was ever so slightly tipsy, for she had a sudden urge to tell Naldo that his father's body had been recovered. Only Danilo's presence saved her.

The drawback was that when she hung up, Danilo was still there. Claudia regarded him with the air of someone who has just noticed a very bad smell in the room and is speculating as to its origin.

'Do forgive me if I'm being dim,' she said, 'but I still haven't the remotest idea what you're talking about.'

Danilo walked over and took her hands in his. More physicality. Not wanting to meet his eyes, Claudia looked down at the white, perfectly manicured fingers grasping hers. Not the hands of a soldier, one would have said, although Danilo had served for almost thirty years. He had handled guns, knives, shells, bombs, and perhaps a select number of the young recruits who had passed through the Verona barracks at one time or another, but none of this had left a trace. Then she looked at her own hands, and remembered what they had done.

'*Cara*, you cannot be unaware of the rumours that circulated at the time of Gaetano's death . . .'

She snatched her hands away.

'What rumours? I don't understand. I refuse to understand!'

Danilo sighed deeply.

'You understand perfectly well.'

He gestured towards the window.

'And there are plenty of people out there who understand too, or think they do. You know what this town is like. They'll be all too ready to gossip to some snooping cop. And this will be an investigation by the *polizia di stato*, not the *carabinieri*. They've been squared away, but apparently the Ministry of the Interior is now launching its own enquiry. Some political battle I don't understand. Anyway, the crucial thing is that you're prepared. Spend a little time thinking over what you want to tell them. Go through your papers to make quite sure that there aren't any things you'd prefer not to fall into the hands of the judicial authorities. They may have a search warrant, you see.'

'To search this house? Why on earth would they want to do that?'

'Well, that rather depends on what they may have learned in the course of their earlier investigations. At all events, Riccardo and I feel very strongly that it would be better to take no chances. Both for your sake, and for the honour of the regiment.'

This last phrase was spoken with a peculiar emphasis. Danilo nodded once, jerkily, turned on his heel and walked out, almost slamming the door behind him.

Claudia stood there for a full minute after he left. Then she went through to the kitchen and refilled her glass from the open bottle of Cinzano Rosso on the counter. Danilo had never spoken to her in such a tone of voice before, like a parade-ground sergeant bawling out some raw recruit. What in the name of God was going on? If the body that had been found really was Leonardo's, it was she who should be going mad. Instead, everyone else was.

'For the honour of the regiment'! She'd never thought to hear that cliché again since Gaetano's death. But once again, apparently, the ranks were closing, and this time against her. No wonder Danilo had wanted his friend to bring the matter up with her. Riccardo was a gentleman through and through, thoroughly decent even if stupendously boring, and given a little more time would have found a way to make her understand what had happened and what needed to be done while respecting her feelings and freedom of action.

She had thought that Danilo was much the same, but she realized now how mistaken she had been. He wasn't kind; he was a sentimentalist, a very different thing. And like all sentimentalists, he could turn vicious in a moment if thwarted. But how had she thwarted him? What did he want? How much did he know? He'd hinted at this and that, but was it out of tactful discretion, as he'd claimed, or just out of ignorance? He had been playing some sort of game with her, of that she felt sure, but she didn't know the nature, still less the purpose, of the game. In fact she really didn't know anything much about Danilo at all, she realized.

On the other hand, she thought, returning to the living room for an unheard-of second cigarette, he didn't know anything much about her. So there was really nothing to worry about, except of course for those concerned with 'the honour of the regiment'. They must have been shitting their neatly starched knickers, she thought, using an Austrian expression occasionally voiced by her bilingual mother. If this investigator for the Ministry of the Interior ever found out even a fraction of what had really occurred all those years ago, the honour of the regiment would resemble a pair of those soiled knickers for the foreseeable future. It would be the scandal to end all scandals.

But those in power would of course take steps to prevent this happening, hence the discreetly menacing tone of Danilo's parting shot. She was to be careful how she handled herself with the police, not just because of her own involvement in the matter, but because if she said the wrong thing and became a lia-bility to those who had even more to lose they would not hesitate to sacrifice her in order to save themselves. Yes, that had been the message: a crude threat wrapped in a thin layer of superficial concern.

She swallowed another gulp of Cinzano, reeling from this revelation but pleased and proud that she still had the wit to work it out. Very well, the situation was clear. Now she had to decide what to do, a much harder matter, and one she certainly didn't feel up to tackling now. She needed a bit of time to come to terms with what had happened and to work out a course of action. The best way would be to go to the garden and consult The Book. That would help her get things in perspective, as it had so often in the past. And then she might take one of her periodic trips to Lugano and just wait for the whole affair to blow over. She knew from experience that these things always did in the end.

III

The kick-turn perfectly executed, he emerged from the depths and gasped in air, then powered forward again, cleaving the wavelets set up by his previous passage. Three, four, five, six . . . The powerful arms thrashed the water that streamed down his hairy shoulders and back, ending in a dense twist like the tail of some small parasite seeking refuge down the crack in the man's buttocks.

Eight, nine, ten . . . Sighting the wall ahead, he swivelled and kicked off again, torpedoing a good two metres underwater before breaking surface again. Forty-eight lengths already, and he was feeling fine. In fact he was feeling great. His arms and legs were still solid, enjoying their work, and even the edgy warming pain from the lactic acid build-up merely served as a stimulant. But above all his *voglia* was back, his will to win. The idea had been to break fifty laps for the first time, to celebrate his birthday, and now he knew that he could.

Seen from the road running up the hillside above, had there been an observer there, the house, the swimming pool and the surrounding terraces resembled a section of tessera unearthed from a once larger antique inlaid floor: an azure rectangle contrasting with the russet dash of the roof tiles, both keyed to the blocks and wedges of ochre paving and the surrounding array of silvery olive trees. As for the shadows cast by the potted shrubs lining the driveway leading up to the house, they might have been explained away as ancient stains; wine, perhaps, or blood.

Eight, nine, ten . . . Another perfect flip-over and once again he was caroming up through the depths and hitting his stride for the final length. It was as he rose to breathe after the initial battery of strokes that he heard the sound for the first time. At first he ignored it as an aural aberration, some tinnitus brought on by a combination of water in the ear canals and his extraordinary exertions. The second time he spouted, he knew the sound was real, but it was only after the third that he realized what it was. Well, they could wait, whoever they were.

His fingers touched the tiled wall. He rose triumphantly to his feet and surveyed the scene. A large white cloud was sliding over the tremulous sun. Beneath the veranda of the house, a heavy white plastic table with its yellow parasol supported a newspaper, a glossy news magazine, a bottle of mineral water, a glass with a slice of lemon and a mobile phone.

Nestore felt a crawling sensation on his right arm, and looked down to see a butterfly exploring the undergrowth of wet hairs just above the small black tattoo of a woman's head. Its huge wings were a miraculous pattern of rusty orange and cobalt blue dots and dashes on an ochre ground while its head was festooned with delicate antennae like a radio aerial. With a careless swipe of his hand he crushed the creature, which fell like limp ashen paper into the chlorinated water of the pool.

The sound which had interrupted him continued without interruption, a series of high nagging whines. He strode over to the side of the pool, thrusting the water aside with his powerful thighs, placed his hands in the trough at the edge, then leapt up on to the tiles and strode briskly over to pick up the phone.

No sooner had he grasped it than it stopped ringing. He was about to close the cover again when he noticed the text message light blinking. It must have been Irene. Damn. If he'd told her once, he'd told her a hundred times never to contact him at the weekend. Presumably the temptation to send him birthday greetings had proved too strong. 'We'll celebrate my twentieth on Monday,' he'd said when they parted. She'd frowned. 'Your twentieth?' '*Certo, amore.* Whenever I'm with you I feel thirty years younger.' Which was true. Dark, short and skinny, Irene was no one's idea of a pin-up, but she had a dirty, driven quality that he found extremely sexy. Just the same, that wouldn't stop him doubling the usual ration of precoital welts to her buttocks as punishment for this indiscretion. *Gli ordini vanno rispettati*. Rules were rules. Andreina's astounding inability to learn Italian had got him off the hook on several occasions, but if she had happened to see this particular message, he'd have had the hell of a time trying to talk his way out of it.

But the message wasn't from Irene. Water crawled coldly down the man's back as he read it. *348 393 9028: MEDUSA*. After the heated pool, the air was distinctly cool, even down here in the sheltered terraces above Lake Lugano. He keyed in the number, then turned to face the hillside behind the villa. The land rose precipitously, the contours marked by the looping line of Via Totone and its accompanying homes and gardens. There was no one in sight.

The distant phone answered. Nestore remembered those curt, peremptory tones all too well.

'We need to talk. Drive to Capolago and take the little train up Monte Generoso. Get off at Bellavista. Tell no one. Come immediately and alone.'

He was suddenly furious.

'Don't give me orders, Alberto! I'm not in the army any more.'

'You still are when it comes to this. We all are, all three of us.'

'What the hell are you talking about?'

'They've found Leonardo.'

The only upside to the whole business was that Andreina was predictably furious. 'But what about lunch? I've got a table for fifteen booked at Da Candida! Everyone's coming! You can't just change your plans at the last moment like this!'

In his wife's domestic theology, changing one's plans at the last moment was a mortal sin on a par with not noticing when she'd had her hair done or forgetting their wedding anniversary. Nestore used his invariable formula for dealing with these outbursts.

'It's a matter of business, *cara*.'

The none-too-subtle implication being, 'Where the hell do you think the money for all this comes from?'

Once dressed, he went to his study. It was a blatantly masculine room, the tone immediately given by the odour of leather and cigar smoke, the rosewood cabinet filled with shotguns and the two mounted ibex heads on the wall above the fireplace. He removed the one to the left and tapped an eight-digit code into the keypad of the metal door inside. From the recess behind he removed a Glock 32 pistol, checked it carefully, then placed it in his coat pocket.

'I only have to go to Capolago,' he told Andreina after pecking her on the cheek. 'I should be back in plenty of time, but if for some reason I'm delayed just go on down without me and I'll meet you and the others there. Tell Bernard I'm having the *controfiletto di cervo* and let him pick the wine.'

He climbed into his new BMW Mini Cooper S – 163 hp at 6000 rpm, 0–100 kph in 7.4 seconds, top speed 220 kph, alloy wheels with run-flat tyres, and the Getrag 6-speed manual box – and drove down the steep twisting street, past the old casino and the construction area for the new one, down into the original town square on the shore of the lake, when the place had been a fishing village. A pair of huge birds were circling on the thermals high above the glassy waters of the lake. Nestore had often observed them from the patio of the villa, but had never been able to identify them. They were obviously raptors of some kind, yet they never seemed to stoop to prey.

He drove round the tight bends by the old church, then out along the suburban street leading to the elegant Fascist-era boxed arch of black and white stone marking the confines of this tiny Italian enclave in the Ticino; 'a tiny bubble of Italian air trapped in the thick Swiss ice', as Nestore thought of it.

No formalities of any sort at the border, of course. You simply drove across an invisible line and were, equally invisibly, in Switzerland. Politically Italian, financially Swiss, but to all intents and purposes off-shore, Campione was a useful anomaly which attracted many sophisticated and wealthy foreign residents such as himself. The principal amenity it had to offer, although not to Italian citizens, was its negligible rate of income tax, the assessment for which was at the discretion of the local authorities, but almost equally important to Nestore was the fact that Lugano was just a short drive or ferryboat ride away across an unsupervised frontier. That made various things so much easier, notably banking.

There were many fine establishments in Lugano, but he favoured the UBS, partly for the discretion and professionalism of their staff, and partly because it came *raccomandata* by no less a figure than Roberto Calvi, who before being found hanged under Blackfriars Bridge in London had paid a seven million dollar backhander to the Socialist party leader Bettino Craxi through that very bank. Nestore reckoned that what had been good enough for the late lamented Dr Calvi would be good enough for him.

Despite its international flavour, due not least to the casino whose profits provided all the municipal income, thereby abolishing all other rates and taxes, Campione was geographically a dead end, almost forty kilometres from the country of which it was nominally a part. The one way out reflected this, a narrow unimproved country road running between nineteenth-century villas set in huge walled gardens above the lake, then ducking underneath the huge swathe of the *autostrada* up to the San Bernardino and Gotthard tunnels, before trickling into the insignificant village at the head of the lake.

He left his Mini Cooper – a personal toy that Andreina didn't appreciate, but which Irene certainly did – in the Swiss Federal Railways car park and went off to feed the machine at the entrance. The Swiss might be happy to let the residents of Campione pay virtually no taxes whatever, but God forbid you shouldn't pay for your parking ticket.

A thickset man with a spectacularly broken nose was sitting on a bench at the end of the mainline station. A huge jaw, ratty eyes set too close together, jug ears, shaven head. Black suit, narrow rectangular shades. Not Swiss, Nestore thought idly, returning to place the ticket on the dashboard of the Mini. He prided himself on being able to spot people's nationality at a glance, sometimes even their profession.

He walked across the metre-gauge rails embedded in the roadway to the bar opposite, with its typical lakeside array of lindens, palms and dwarf pines. Here he checked the timetable for the mountain railway and then ordered a large espresso and a glass of kirsch. He was going to need a bit of fortification before his appointment with Alberto. Amazing, he thought. Of all the stupid things he'd done, and there had been plenty, this was the last that he had ever imagined would come back to haunt him. On the very rare occasions when he thought about it at all, he'd always imagined it to be as dead and buried as Leonardo himself.

Anyway, apparently the corpse had turned up. So now what? 'We need to talk.' Meaning of course that Alberto needed to talk. And what would the talk amount to? That they were all in this together, a chain is only as strong as its weakest link, all for one and one for all, etc, etc. That would be about the extent of it, and it was all perfectly obvious, but it was only too much like Alberto to seize this heaven-sent opportunity to bore him to death.

Not to mention insisting on this absurd secret rendezvous! As if anyone cared about Operation Medusa any more. Those days were long over, far longer indeed than the intervening three decades of calendar time. The innovative ideas of that period were now accepted and its various political causes were all lost. Obsessed as always with the conspiracies and counter-conspiracies which went with his fanatical half-baked patriotism, Alberto was probably the only person left in the country who didn't realize this.

A blue and orange two-coach electric unit came to rest in the road opposite, pushing a small wagon filled with two large metal rubbish bins and plastic-wrapped cases of mineral water destined for the hotel at the summit of the mountain. Nestore tossed back the rest of his kirsch, crossed the road and took a seat at the very end of the rear carriage. From there he could keep an eye on anyone who boarded after him. They all seemed to be the expected crew of sightseers and hikers. The ugly pug had left his bench and was now taking something from the boot of a red Fiat Panda in the parking lot. It had Italian number-plates, quite unusual here. The minute hand of the station clock clicked to a vertical position and the train jolted into motion.

Nestore leaned back in his seat as the train rumbled across the mainline tracks, under the concrete cliff of the *autostrada*, gripped the rack rails and hauled itself through a thick growth of elder trees up the steep lower flank of the mountain, then through a sharply curving tunnel almost as narrow as the one to which they'd taken Leonardo and out on to the eastern slopes of the ridge in a ravine of dense beeches. There was no undergrowth here, just the tall erectile trees, most of them retaining their dead leaves, and the brown mulch of beech nut casings below. The air-brake system exhausted its excess pressure with a loud hiss. The thug down at the station could have been Alberto's companion or driver, thought Nestore idly. Alberto himself would have taken an earlier train, and return by a later one. The old fart always had been a stickler for security procedures, not to say obsessed with conspiracies and plots of every kind.

Bellavista station was a passing loop set in a level clearing in the beeches before the railway started its final climb towards the summit. There was a small buffet and booking office, both closed at this time of year. A sign above the door stated that the altitude was 1223 metres, while another on a pole nearby indicated that the walking time to Scudellate and Maggio was two hours, and to Castel San Pietro two and a half. The air was distinctly colder and sharper than down by the lake.

Nestore waited by the station building, apparently short-sightedly peering at the timetable, until various hearty types in brightly coloured hiking gear had dispersed along their respective paths. Once they were out of sight and the train had continued on its way, he looked around him. There was no one in view, and the only sound was the soughing of the breeze through the beeches, which were mostly bare in this more exposed spot. The ballast between the tracks was thickly covered in their crisp umber leaves.

It was beginning to look as though he had been stood up. And there was nothing he could do except wait for the next train down to Capolago. Another and very nasty thought crossed his mind, namely that Alberto's call had just been a ruse to draw him away from his home. The hood at the station had been there to check that he did indeed board the train, and as soon as it left he had driven to join Alberto in Campione and force an entrance to the villa. They could be going through his papers right now, noting down all the secrets of his business and financial dealings with a view to blackmailing him. Andreina might even be in peril! Dream on, he thought cynically.

Then he heard a low whistle. He turned and saw a figure standing at the edge of the trees on the other side of the tracks. After a moment's hesitation he started towards him.

'Alberto,' he said neutrally when he drew close enough.

The other man had been inspecting him closely as he walked towards him. Now he nodded once, as if to confirm the resulting identification.

'Nestore.'

He gestured towards the path from which he had emerged, a narrow ribbon of bare earth winding off into the forest.

'Shall we?'

Alberto seemed to have changed only in the sense that left-over fondue changes from a bubbly sauce to a compact, grey, gelatinous mass. He had lost some hair and put on a bit of weight, but both his physique and his peremptory manner were essentially unaltered.

'You'd already heard, I take it.'

'Heard?'

'About Leonardo.'

'No, actually.'

Alberto gave him one of his trademark coded looks, which might be decrypted roughly as 'Obviously I don't believe you, but equally obviously you don't intend or expect me to. Honour is therefore satisfied, and we're back where we started, only one level up.'

'I don't bother any more,' Nestore said.

'Bother?'

'With the news.'

Alberto laughed indulgently.

'No, of course not! Neither do I. If those media clowns have heard of it, it isn't news. But I thought you might . . .'

The winding path, proceeding gently in ascent, had brought them to a viewpoint with a slatted wooden bench overlooking the lake. The gnarled roots of the huge beeches showed above ground between outcrops of rock covered in lichen and some patchy grass. Alberto extracted a pair of small binoculars from his pocket and looked down through them to the terminus of the railway far below. Nestore subsided on to the bench.

'So you haven't?' Alberto remarked, replacing the binoculars in his pocket.

Another unaltered trait: picking up some apparently discarded conversational thread as though it were one among dozens of chess games he was playing simultaneously and with equal mastery. For a vertiginous moment, Nestore felt twenty again, not in the conventional jokey sense in which he'd said it to his mistress, but with a kind of terror. We always misremember youth, he thought. The fact is that it was scary and demanding. He was happy being the age he now was, with the various perks and comforts that age had brought. He wasn't up to youth any more, and he certainly wasn't prepared to be dicked around by Alberto.

'Haven't what?' he demanded in a tone that reflected this feeling.

'Any inside channels. Contacts from the old days, perhaps.'

'Like who?'

Alberto's casual, almost irritated shrug struck the first false note in their encounter.

'Oh, I don't know!'

A small lizard sped across the rocky ledge between them.

'Gabriele, for instance.'

'Why should I?'

'Why shouldn't you?'

'Passarini was a wimp, even back then. I don't associate with wimps.'

Alberto nodded, as though evaluating some important and complex piece of data.

'So you're no longer in touch with Gabriele.'

Nestore got to his feet.

'I'm no longer in touch with anyone from those days, Alberto. And the only reason I'm talking to you is because you dragged me up here with an urgent summons that made it all sound vitally important, a matter of life and death. I don't get it. All right, Leonardo's body has been found. So what?'

Alberto slipped immediately into another of the roles that Nestore knew so well, but had forgotten; in this instance, that of the great professor indulging a promising student by deliberately misinterpreting his ploddingly literal question for a more suggestively meaningful one.

'Before the Viminale moved, I would absolutely have agreed with you,' he replied, nodding slowly. 'The investigation was initially being handled by the Brothers-in-Law, and the combination of their own ineptitude and a little judicious guidance orchestrated by yours truly promised to bring the whole unfortunate business to a speedy and discreet conclusion.'

This is how women must feel, thought Nestore, listening to some bore droning on, trying to impress them. Except that they at least know what he wants. But what did Alberto want?

'What day is it?'

He was pleased to note the momentary flash of startled confusion before the reply came.

'Why, Sunday.'

'Correct. It also happens to be my birthday, and I'm celebrating by having lunch out with my friends, none of whom would know you from the Romanian guest worker who washes the dishes at the very exclusive restaurant where I am due in just under an hour. I am no longer Nestore Soldani. My name is Nestor Machado Solorzano and I am a Venezuelan citizen living a blameless life in a quietly luxurious tax haven in southern Switzerland. I am grateful for the help that you provided in the past over those oil contracts and arms deals, but you got your cut at the time. In short, Alberto, unless you can demonstrate in the next thirty seconds that what happened all those years ago is of the slightest consequence to me now, then with all due respect I invite you to stick your Italian intrigues up your arse and leave me in peace.'

He had been expecting fury and fireworks, but to his astonishment – disappointment even – Alberto just crumpled.

'Of course, of course!' he murmured. 'I'm sorry. Let's start back to the station. The train will be along soon and you'll be back in Campione in good time for your lunch. I had no idea that it was your birthday and I apologize for intruding. Only I had to be sure, do you see?'

When there was no answer, he repeated the apparently rhetorical question in an even more emphatically anguished tone.

'Do you see?'

I was completely wrong about him, thought Nestore. The old boy's gone to pieces. It's all front, bluster and bluff, and the generalized paranoia of the old.

'See what?' he demanded roughly.

'That I had to be sure.'

'Sure of what?'

Alberto paused for a moment, holding his companion by the arm. He gave a brief laugh to signal an upcoming joke.

'That I'd "secured my flanks". Remember that pedant Oddone in his lecture on Cannae? "Aemilius Paullus had imprudently neglected to secure his flanks." At which Andrea promptly pipes up, "And his rear was wide open too." Ah, happy days!'

Nestore pointedly consulted his watch, and Alberto hastened to lead the way along the path again.

'Anyway, that's rather my position just now, you see.'

' "Securing your flanks". Meaning me and Gabriele?'

There was no reply.

'What's become of Gabriele, anyway?'

Not that he gave a toss. This was just a social chat now, a question of finding some topic in common to keep the embarrassment of silence at bay.

'He runs a bookshop in Milan,' Alberto murmured. Nestore nodded.

'I can imagine him doing that.'

'Only he doesn't seem to be there at the moment. Or at his house either. In fact he seems to have disappeared. It's all a bit worrying. Are you sure you have no idea where he might be?'

'We haven't been in touch for over twenty years.'

'Ah, right. Well, we're looking into it. We'll find him sooner or later. It's just that time is of the essence.'

' "We"?'

Alberto's demeanour changed in some indefinable way.

'I moved over to intelligence work about the same time that you went off to South America.'

'The *servizi*?'

Alberto acknowledged the point with a self-satisfied bow.

'SISMI, the *Servizio Informazioni e Sicurezza Militare*. Better promotion prospects, not to mention the possibility of assisting you in your business ventures, but above all a real opportunity to serve my country. There's little chance of Italy being involved in open warfare in the immediate future, but there's no end to the covert wars. The post offers me superior challenges and superior resources. That's how I've been able to maintain up-to-date records on you and Gabriele, just in case the need should ever arise.'

'The need for what?'

'To meet and talk frankly about the situation. Above all, to ensure that our secret remains ours, and will not become a public scandal which could compromise public trust in our armed forces in the most disastrous way, as well as reopening the terrible scars left on our body politic by the events of the seventies.'

Pompous prick, thought Nestore.

'Well, I'm glad I've been able to reassure you,' he said affably.

'Indeed. Now it's just a question of tracking down Gabriele and having the same conversation with him. I'm sure the outcome will be the same too. I hear the train coming. Many thanks for your cooperation, Nestore, and profound apologies for the disturbance. But I did have to be sure. You understand that, don't you? I did have to be sure.'

Nestore shrugged wearily.

'No problem, Alberto. Only next time, not on my birthday, all right?'

Alberto regarded him with a look which Nestore found impossible to decipher.

'There won't be a next time.'

He turned and walked away into the surrounding forest of beeches. Nestore headed off across the tracks to the station building.

So what the hell had all that been about, apart from the loss to him of the fifty-franc fare and a quiet Sunday morning at home? All this secret service stuff! Alberto must have gone gaga in his sealed world of spooks, where the only people you could discuss your work with were as crazy as you. And all he'd wanted had been the reassurance that Nestore wouldn't blab about Leonardo's death. As though he would! They could have met at one of the cafés in the main square of Campione, for God's sake. It would have taken a fraction of the time, and the end result would have been exactly the same.

The journey back down the mountainside, at a steady fourteen kilometres an hour, seemed to take an eternity. When they finally arrived, Nestore got out and glanced around the car park. The Italian car had gone and there was no sign of the broken-nosed bouncer. Probably some mummy's boy from Como who'd come up to Switzerland for the day to give himself a thrill.

He unlocked the Mini Cooper and climbed in. It felt cramped somehow. Reaching down under the seat, he pulled the lever up and pushed back. The seat slotted into its most extended position. Nestore sighed and started up the engine. He always had that problem when Andreina had been using one of their cars. She moved the driving seat forwards so she could reach the pedals, then forgot to return it to its original position. It was one of many sloppy traits of hers that he no longer found charming. But Andreina never drove the Mini, and anyway if the seat had been moved, surely he would have noticed it on the way there? He shrugged and gunned the car out of town and back along the lake, delighting in its superb acceleration and sure-footedness. One of these days he must take it up into the mountains and give it a real thrash.

The bells of Santa Maria del Ghirli started ringing noon as he re-entered Italian territory. Perfect. Just time to go home, change into something more fashionable and then head out to the restaurant. He would stick with venison for the main course, but what to start with? The ravioli with meat and truffles were hard to beat at this time of year, but then so was everything else on the menu. Maybe the best thing would be to get Bernard to serve a selection of first courses so that people could sample them all. He drew up in front of the steel gates of the villa, took the *telecomando* from the glove compartment and depressed the green button at the top.

IV

The torch acted as the *genius loci*, its scope and sway strictly limited but within that ambit omnipotent, calling a myriad objects and vistas into being before dismissing them back into latency with a flick of its narrow beam.

The world was made of rock, and always hemming in, but lately it had become more disorganized. The bounds had burst somewhere, allowing massive lumps and clusters to fall, or in some cases erupt upwards, almost blocking their path. But at the last moment the torch would always find a way. Some slit or aperture would appear, and they would crawl or squeeze through, mindful of the jagged edges all around, and patch together from disjunctive glimpses an impression of yet more rectangular tunnel strewn with debris.

'Now we must be careful,' announced Anton in his stalkily precise Italian. 'This is the pitch head.'

The beam of the squat orange torch dashed about, speedily brushing in their notional surroundings like a manic cartoon sequence, and then, unaccountably, its power ceased. The darkness in front of them, just a few metres distant, seemed no different or more intense than that which had surrounded them ever since they entered the tunnels, but the playful minor divinity of the place, out of his depth here, could get no grip on it.

'Rudi wanted to go down and take a look, so we fixed an eight-millimetre self-drilling expansion bolt over here as a primary belay.'

He pointed the torch at the wall of the tunnel, picking out a glinting metal ring.

'Then we ran a secondary to the natural anchor point on that boulder over there.'

The torch briefly illumined the chunk of raw rock.

'We didn't really count on much in the way of horizontal work when we planned the expedition,' the young Austrian went on. 'Nevertheless, we brought about fifty metres of static nylon rope, a harness and a minimum of other gear, just in case. What we didn't have was any rope-protector, since we were thinking that if there were possible descents then they will be free hangs, with no rub points. But as soon as Rudi went over the edge he spotted a sharp protrusion. There was no way to belay around it so he carried on. It was safe enough for a single descent and ascent, but anything more than that would have been risky.'

His voice boomed around the confined space, evacuated only by the gulf that had opened up at their feet.

'Rudi rappelled down as far as he could, until he came to the knot marking the end of the rope. And he was shouting something we couldn't make out, and we were shouting too, you know, because we were excited, and also feeling a little foolish because we had got lost. Then there were a few flashes when he took the pictures, and after that he prusiked back up the pitch and we hauled him over the edge and he told us that there was a body down there.'

Anton gestured in an embarrassed way. 'Been there, done that' was the motto of him and his pals at the University of Innsbruck Speleology Club. That meant the Stellerweg and Kaninchenhöhle, of course, but also the Trave and the Piedra de San Martin, two of the longest and deepest systems in Northern Spain, not to mention various expeditions to Slovenia, Mexico, Norway and even Jamaica. And then to spend a weekend break exploring a network of military tunnels dating from the First World War and get lost in a man-made shaft in what had used to be part of their own country? The indignity, the disgrace, and . . . well, yes, a certain amount of fear had come into it, even before they'd found the body.

'Let me take a look,' said Zen.

'All right, but on your hands and knees, please. Then on your stomach when I do. Your clothing will get dirty, but it's perfectly dry here and it will brush off after. But we don't want another accident.'

It seemed to Zen that ghostly quotation marks seemed to hover around the last word, but he made no comment. They both proceeded in the prescribed manner until they reached the brink of the chasm. Anton leant out and shone his torch down, but there was little to see except occasional hints of the sheer scale of the pit beneath. Somewhere very far below – Zen found it impossible to estimate the depth even roughly – a wild chaos of rocks was dimly visible.

'Is this a natural formation?' asked Zen.

'No, no. The Dolomites are formed out of the rock that gives them their name. It's a crystalline form of limestone and virtually impervious to erosion, even by acidic water. So there's no caving here, although further north, where the limestone is softer, the situation is quite different. This was man-made. We're now in one of the Austrian tunnels. The Italians countermined it in 1917. Over thirty thousand kilos of explosives. This is the result.'

He moved the torch beam closer to the edge.

'You can see the overhang down there, about two metres below,' Anton went on in his slightly pedantic manner. 'It is this which prevented us seeing the body from here, of course. But when Rudi reached the end of the rope, he illuminated his torch so that he could see how far there is to go and where he will land, and . . .'

'And then he saw the corpse.'

'Yes. Of course we were anxious to inform the authorities, but we were also lost in this maze of tunnels, so Rudi took some photographs to confirm and then we started back, this time keeping a sketch map for reference. After two hours and many false starts we found another way out, not the one by which we had entered. From there I called to the *carabinieri* on my mobile phone and then we waited some time for them to arrive. Quite a long time, actually.'

He crawled back a metre or so before standing up.

'So, I think that is all there is to show you. Shall we go back?'

'We won't get lost?'

'No, after returning with the police I know the way well now.'

Back in its element, the torch became their guide and saviour again, pointing out the crooks and crannies they had to negotiate, the low-hanging clumps of rock in the roughhewn tunnel, the subterranean barracks and storerooms, and the various junctions and steep flights of spiral steps which at long last led them back out into the cold wan twilight.

They emerged on to a broad track cut as a supply route into the rock face of a cliff overlooking the valley almost a thousand metres below. With relief, Zen removed the additional skull of the helmet that Anton had insisted he wear. Underground, he had had to follow his guide, and the noise of their feet on the broken rock, as well as the constant need to pay attention to their surroundings, had made silence at once necessary and easy. Now that they could walk side by side, and the only sound was the whine of the unpredictable squally breeze with fistfuls of sleet in its folds, that silence became oppressive. Invisible behind the clouds, the sun had already set.

'The case is being treated as an accident?' Anton asked at length.

'Apparently.'

'So who was he? What happened? And when?'

'That's still unclear.'

They walked on along the rock road marked by the ruts carved almost a century before by the metal wheels of carts and gun carriages.

'Strange,' remarked Anton. 'Of course, this is also what we thought when we found the body. Someone who had tried to do what we were doing, only badly equipped and alone. But there was no sign of any rope at the top of the pitch. Or at the bottom, I think. Even if it had frayed and broken on that rub point, the upper length should still be there attached to the belay and the rest should be with the body. Unless he was one of those free-style alpine climbers, and tried to descend without aids. But he wasn't dressed correctly for this, or even for walking at such an altitude, still less exploring those tunnels, which are cold, as you know. In fact, from what the photographs show, he didn't seem to be wearing any shoes or boots.'

'He was barefoot?'

'Apparently, yes. Of course, people who come alone into the mountains for adventures are often a little bit strange, but I have never heard of this before. Besides, if he was going to do something extreme in this way, he would surely have informed a relative or the hotel keeper of his intentions and estimated time of return. If someone goes missing, there's always a search and an enquiry, at least in my country. Even if they don't find him, the police keep an open file in case a body turns up. We get a few up in the Alps once in a while, particularly now that the glaciers are receding so fast. Those bodies are often chewed up by the ice, but even then they are almost always identified, even if they have been there fifty or more years. In this case the corpse was not so badly decayed, because of the cool stable air in the tunnels. You would think it would not be so difficult to put a name to this person.'

'You would, wouldn't you?'

At the point where the path up the face of the massif crossed the old military road, they turned right and started zigzagging down the way they had ascended over four hours earlier, Anton effortlessly, Zen taking frequent pauses to admire the view.

'You mentioned some photographs,' Zen said as they picked their way down the steep, rock-strewn track.

'Yes, Rudi was carrying a camera on his belt, and he took a few shots of the scene just to prove that we hadn't touched anything or interfered in any way. In the event we forgot all about them, but it didn't matter. The officers who answered our call weren't interested. They just took our names and addresses and a brief statement and then said we could go. And of course we were only too happy to do so, and still perhaps a little in shock from this experience. So it was only when we got back to Innsbruck that Rudi remembered the photos.'

'Where are they now?'

'I have a set with me. I'll give them to you when we get back to the *rifugio*, if you like. But these are just amateur snapshots, taken in a moment of some stress and anxiety. The quality isn't that good, and of course you'll have access to the official photographic record taken when the body was removed.'

'Yes, of course. Still, it would be interesting to see them, if you don't mind.'

'Not a problem. I brought them just for that.'

The path narrowed to wind over the shoulder of a rocky bluff, followed by an even more precipitous descent, and silence once more became an acceptable option.

It was pitch-dark by the time they reached the small hostel in the bleak, rock-strewn plain where the road crossed the pass towards Cortina and the valleys to the east. Once through the double set of doors, the smoke-laden fug was initially overwhelming after the icy air outside. Bruno was propped up in a booth at the far end, pointedly ignoring the fact that he was being pointedly ignored by everyone else in the bar. Catching sight of his superior, he hurriedly straightened his uniform, replaced his cap and stood up, but Zen waved to him to stay put. The young patrolman nodded, sat down again and picked up the crossword puzzle magazine he had been working on.

The bar was crowded with a gang of German motor-cyclists of both sexes, all sheathed in garish leather suits, as well as a smattering of elderly people who looked local, although where they could have come from was a mystery. Zen led Anton into the restaurant area at the side of the building. There were the same red and white checked curtains over the tiny windows, the same glossily varnished wooden chairs and tables, the same dim lighting from elaborate brass fixtures with frosted glass bowls, but this space was unoccupied and much quieter, apart from a muttered news bulletin from the inevitable television set mounted on a cabinet at the end of the room.

A blank-looking girl of perhaps fifteen came over, a note-book in her hand. After a brief discussion, they settled on a selection of cheese and *salumi*, a bottle of red wine and two large bowls of soup. Out of sheer habit, Zen initially ordered minestrone, until Anton sensibly pointed out that to be worth eating this required fresh vegetables and high-quality olive oil and parmesan, none of which was likely to be available at this remote spot. Instead they both opted for lentil soup made with chunks of smoked bacon.

'So, I hope you feel that your visit has been worthwhile,' said Anton.

It took Zen a moment to realize the oddity of the question. Anton had spoken German to the waitress, who had replied in the same language. Everyone else in the room was speaking either German or, like the TV newscaster, Ladino, the archaic dialect of Latin which had survived only in this isolated mountain range. There wasn't a word of Italian to be heard or seen anywhere in the place. Zen felt very much as if it were he, and not Anton Redel, who had travelled to a foreign country.

'Indeed,' he replied. 'You too, I trust.'

The Austrian laughed.

'Oh yes! It is always a pleasure to come down here to our former transalpine provinces. Everything is so cheap, too. But this is the first time I've had the additional pleasure of doing so at the expense of the Italian government.'

When their food arrived, Anton's choice proved to have been inspired. The lentils and bacon were a thick, unctuous, rib-sticking delight, more stew than soup. The cold cuts, too, were subtly different from their southern cousins, darker and smokier in flavour and texture. The wine was from the Adige valley where they had both started their journey that morning. It was a very young light red with a tart raspberry taste and a slight prickle of spritz. It was utterly delicious, and cut the rich, heavy food perfectly.

When they had eaten, Anton lit a small cheroot.

'So, the photographs.'

He got up and went over to the stairs leading to the bedrooms. Zen's driver appeared at the table.

'Ready when you are, *capo*.'

Zen relaxed into Italian as if into a warm lavender-scented bath. He dug out his battered pack of Nazionali and lit up.

'Calm down, Bruno. I'm not quite finished yet.'

'*Benissimo*. Only it's just starting to snow. We should be able to make it down the mountain if we start soon, otherwise . . .'

He shrugged expressively.

'I'll be as quick as possible,' Zen told him.

'I'll go and get the car warmed up.'

Bruno walked off back to his table as Anton reappeared, holding an envelope which he placed on the table between them. It contained four colour prints which Zen looked through one by one without saying anything. Indeed, it was difficult to find anything to say. The pictures looked like reproductions of modern art, all blobs and scurries, masses and evasions of colour and form whose presumed significance could only be their apparent lack thereof.

'Rudi didn't have much time, and his camera is not so good,' Anton explained through a cloud of cigar smoke. 'But it is digital, so I've enclosed a diskette with the files.'

'Files?'

'In case you want to do an enhancement. They're compressed, of course. You'll need to unzip them.'

Zen extracted a black plastic rectangle from the envelope. He nodded sagely and puffed on his cigarette. Yet another foreign language. Compression and unzipping he could more or less understand, but what sort of magic was involved in an enhancement?

'This one, for instance,' the Austrian added, selecting one of the prints and turning it the right way up. Zen suddenly realized that it showed the outflung wreck of the corpse lying broken on the floor of the blast pit. It was dressed only in a shirt and slacks. The feet appeared to be bare. The face was turned away, but the right arm lay outstretched across the jagged rocks. Anton pointed to some markings just above the elbow.

'It might be significant to know exactly what this is,' he said. 'But such details will naturally have emerged during the post-mortem examination.'

Was there a hint of irony in his tone? It was hard to tell with the Austrians. They liked to present themselves as slow, cosy, complacent country bumpkins, but their empire had produced some of the most incisive thinkers and artists in Europe. Zen called the waitress and settled the bill.

'Well, thank you for your cooperation, Herr Redel. I hope you have good walking tomorrow.'

'It looks like it will be cross-country skiing with this weather. But they rent *langenlauf* equipment here, so either way I shall enjoy myself.'

The two men shook hands. Then Zen looked his guest straight in the eye.

'What do you think really happened?'

Anton Redel looked understandably confused by this question.

'Well, of course I am not a policeman. But if this had occurred somewhere else, say in the elevator shaft of an abandoned city warehouse, I'd probably suspect that others were involved.'

'Others?'

'Some gangsters, perhaps. Drugs or some such thing. They kill the man and then hide his body in the shaft. Or they just throw him down. Maybe the corpse

66

will never be found. Even if it is, it may be too late to identify him.'

He gave Zen a charming, thick-lipped Austrian smile.

'But of course this is ridiculous! There are many dangers up here in the mountains, but criminal organizations are not among them.'

Outside the insulating double doors, the snow was now descending in earnest frothy flakes that were deceptively insubstantial as they floated into the lights of the hostel, but already lay several centimetres deep on its concrete forecourt. Bruno had drawn the marked police Alfa right up to the entrance. Zen got into the back seat and they set off.

To Zen's relief, Bruno was not one of those police drivers for whom the point of the exercise was to validate their virility. Indeed, for the first thirty minutes or so, when the snow was still heavy and the road treacherous, he was almost excessively cautious as they negotiated the frequent reverse curves and steep gradients in very poor visibility. After that, the snow gradually turned to sleet and eventually a slushy rain, the surface reverted to a reliable shiny black, and they were able to speed up.

In the back, Zen relaxed, dozy after so much unaccustomed exercise and fresh air, but also taunted by the question which Anton Redel had no doubt intended merely as a courtesy. *Did* he feel that his visit had been worthwhile? The honest answer was 'No', but this was in keeping with every other aspect of this case which had been tossed into his lap, he suspected, more than anything else as a sop to give him the illusion of being gainfully employed.

'You might want to take a look at these,' was how the departmental head had put it when he handed Zen a bunch of files at the termination of his weekly briefing at the headquarters of the Interior Ministry on the Viminale hill in Rome. 'They're mostly quite routine, I think, but it would be valuable to have any input or suggestions you might have to offer.'

Zen had accepted the files in the same spirit, and taken them back that evening to the apartment in Lucca that he shared with Gemma, the new woman in his life. There were eight in all, the very number confirming Zen's suspicions that none of this was intended to be taken too seriously. Most of the cases indeed appeared to be fairly routine. The exception was the one that he had brought with him to the Alto Adige.

This already had a certain curiosity value based on its provenance. Rather than being forwarded to police headquarters in Rome by one of the Ministry's provincial *questure*, it had been obtained 'through channels' from the *carabinieri*, who were handling the case. When Zen made a few phone calls to query various aspects of the report, his interest immediately quickened. He had done this often enough in the past, and was familiar with the standard response: a mixture of obscurantism, grudging disclosures and resentful passing off of the intruder to subordinates, the officer who had been called having more pressing matters to attend to. This was standard procedure, and he had frequently employed it himself when the boot was on the other foot.

This time, though, things went quite differently. Zen's call was immediately transferred to the officer in charge, a Colonel Miccoli, who evinced an almost embarrassing readiness to address any and all questions that his esteemed colleague might have. Of course Zen wasn't wasting his time! Full disclosure and cooperation between the two forces of order was of the essence to effective law enforcement in a modern democracy. '*Mi casa es su casa*,' quoted the colonel, adding that he had spent several months liaising with the Spanish anti-terrorist squad back in the nineties over some Basque suspects who had allegedly spent several years in hiding in Sardinia.

He had some interesting and amusing anecdotes to tell about that episode, but almost nothing to say about the case concerning which Zen had called. Everything was in limbo at the moment and it would be injudicious to draw any premature conclusions. The body had been removed from the tunnel complex and flown by helicopter to the central hospital in Bolzano. Yes, a post-mortem examination had been performed, but the results appeared to be inconclusive. No, it had not been possible to positively identify the victim as yet. Misadventure seemed the most likely cause of death, but foul play had not entirely been ruled out. In short, it was a question of time, and at worst the affair might turn out to be one of those minor mysteries associated with a mountainous district whose rugged remoteness naturally attracted – how should he put it? – amateurs of extreme sports and thrill-seekers of all kinds. He would of course pass on any further details should they become available. It had been a pleasure to have the opportunity of discussing the case with Dottor Zen. Not at all, on the contrary, the pleasure had all been his.

Zen had by now become accustomed to the wide-spread effects of what his friend Giorgio De Angelis termed 'Italia Lite': the new culture of empty slogans, insincere smiles and hollow promises overlaying the authentic adversarial asperity of public life. He was somewhat surprised to find that the rot had tainted a military body such as the *carabinieri*, with its long traditions and strong esprit de corps, but no more than that. It was none of his business anyway. He had duly 'reviewed' and returned the file. No one would thank him for exerting himself any further.

Nevertheless, he was left with a nagging feeling, based on decades of experience of how these things were handled, that something wasn't quite right. After a few days, it became strong enough to nudge him into contacting the Questura in Bolzano and asking them to obtain a copy of the post-mortem report direct from the hospital. Their reply had been more than enough to confirm his doubts. '*The official response of the hospital authorities is that such a request can only be considered if routed through the Ministry of Defence, which has been designated the competent State agency in this matter. According to our sources, however, the post-mortem report and the photographs taken in the course of the examination, together with the cadaver itself and all clothing and objects appertaining thereto, are no longer in the possession of the hospital, having been taken in charge by officers of the* carabinieri *on the morning of the 15th inst.*'

It was at this point that Zen had decided that there was a case to be made for him to travel north. Much as he liked Lucca, he was in a mood to leave for a few days, and was particularly looking forward to meeting Colonel Miccoli, given that their telephone conversation had taken place three days after the developments noted in the Questura's fax. He had therefore booked a first-class sleeper on the night train which passed through Florence just before midnight and stopped at Bolzano about four hours later.

On his arrival at the *carabinieri* headquarters later that morning, he had been told that Colonel Miccoli was 'out of town'. Not only that, but his adjunct claimed never to have heard of Zen, and to have no personal knowledge of the case in question.

Fortunately Zen had arranged a fallback position. One of the few substantive facts in the *carabinieri* report he had been given concerned the three young Austrians who had discovered the body. Their names, addresses and home telephone numbers had all been noted down as a matter of routine, and with a sense that he had nothing to lose Zen had taken the long shot of calling one of them. Initially this turned out to be abortive due to language difficulties, but on the third attempt Zen reached Anton Redel, who had been born and raised in the Alto Adige and spoke serviceable Italian. He had readily agreed to return to the scene of the tragedy and explain what had happened, in exchange for a reasonable sum to cover the expense of the journey down from Innsbruck, where he was now at university.

A straggle of low buildings appeared at a sharp bend in the road ahead, seemingly propped up against the precipitous slope of the mountainside. Most were abandoned, but a few showed lights, and in the centre of the village there was a bar and shop with petrol pumps outside. Bruno turned off and parked outside.

'Need to pee, *capo*,' he explained.

The air inside the bar was as suffocatingly thick and hot as it had been at the establishment up at the pass, but when the half-dozen clients inside noticed Bruno's uniform, the temperature immediately seemed to drop by several degrees.

Zen went up to the counter and asked for two coffees and a glass of an interesting-looking homemade liqueur in a litre bottle on the bar. He had to repeat the order several times before the woman who was serving finally nodded and shuffled off without the slightest acknowledgement. While he waited, Zen skimmed through a story in the German-language newspaper lying on the counter, something about a rich Venezuelan who'd been killed when his car exploded outside the gates of his villa in Campione d'Italia. Good, he thought. The sooner this dead-end case he had mistakenly got involved with ceased to be national news, the better.

Bruno reappeared, ostentatiously zipping up his flies and checking the positioning of their contents. Their coffees and Zen's liqueur arrived without a word being spoken. In fact no word had been spoken by anyone in the bar since they had entered.

'Quiet, isn't it?' remarked Bruno.

Zen lit a cigarette but made no reply.

'On the face of it,' the patrolman went on loudly, leaning back against the bar and gazing round the room. 'But appearances can be deceptive. In fact, every-one in this village suffers from a rare and ultimately fatal condition whose inexorable progress can only be delayed by drinking the blood of a live human being.'

He nodded solemnly.

'That's the price you pay for centuries of incest. Poor things. There are few of them left now, because of course once in a while, when pickings from the passing trade are slim, they get desperate and draw lots among themselves. But their normal practice is to lure travel-lers in here with the promise of a hot drink or some petrol for the car. This dump used to be a mining com-munity and there's still a warren of shafts going back into the mountains. They stack the husks in there and resell the cars to the Mafia. Once in a while some tour-ist goes missing somewhere on the road to Cortina. No one can prove anything.'

He pointed to the floor.

'That's the trapdoor, right there where you're stand-ing, *dottore*. Lucky you didn't come in alone. Next thing you knew, you'd be lying down in the cellar with a broken leg and these creatures pouring down the stairs, giggling and squealing and knocking each other aside in their eagerness to open up an artery so that they could feast.'

Bruno swivelled round and stabbed a finger at one of the other drinkers, a man of diminutive stature.

'You dwarf!' he roared. 'How many litres have you downed over the years, eh? Sucking the rich red curd down like mother's milk! And that swine next to you, nuzzling his snout into the still-living entrails in hopes of finding a last drop of the good stuff clinging to some gizzard!'

Zen laid some money on the counter, took Bruno by the elbow and steered him outside. It was starting to snow, even at this lower level.

'Are you out of your mind?' Zen asked the patrolman once they were back in the car. 'You know the problems we have in this territory! What are you trying to do, start another terrorist movement up here?'

'Sorry about that, *capo*. I just lost it for a moment. But it's all right, they don't speak Italian.'

'They understand it.'

'Of course, but they'd never admit that. It would be letting the side down. Hence my little game. Must be maddening for them.'

Zen sighed massively and lit a cigarette, cranking the window down slightly. Tufts of snow landed on his face like flies.

'Where are you from?' he asked in a subdued voice.

'Bologna. I used to be bored there when I was growing up, but now I can't wait to go back. It's like being separated from your wife. And you, *capo*, if you don't mind my asking?'

'Venice.'

They drove on in silence for a while.

'I hate the mountains,' said Bruno.

'So do I.'

'And I hate the people who live here. Not because they're foreigners. It's their country and as far as I'm concerned they're welcome to it. But all the bright, enterprising, intelligent people left long ago, because they hated the mountains too. I mean, who'd want to live up here? So the only people left are the scum. The village idiots, the child and wife abusers, the no-brain losers and retards of every variety.'

Another silence.

'How long have you got to go?' asked Zen.

'Three months and thirteen days.'

Zen nodded.

'From a professional point of view, I think it might be advisable to make a special exception in your case.'

Bruno peered back at him in the rear-view mirror.

'You can do that?'

'I'll try. Provided you get me back to the valley, safe and sound, and by nine at the latest.'

'You want the station, right?'

'No, I've changed my mind. Drop me at the hospital. I'll take a cab from there.'

V

Night slipped past the open window at a steady one hundred and forty kilometres per hour. Chips and shards of light, some isolated, others roughly clustered, were borne past on its current at an apparent speed relative to their distance from the train. Parallax, thought Zen, although his immediate memory was of twirled sparklers, wire with a fizzy firework coating that created illusionary circles and whorls of solid light in the darkness. That and fireflies. Whatever had happened to fireflies?

By now they were quite far down the valley, past Rovereto. The snow had finally petered out at about the same point as the everyday use of the German language, but early that evening in Bolzano it had at once been clear that Bruno's warning about getting down from the mountains in time had not been just a pretext for cutting short a long day. When they finally reached the city, after one distinctly scary moment involving an uncontrolled skid and an oncoming truck, the streets were already lightly covered, while huge but seemingly weightless flakes were falling so densely as to make driving almost as difficult as in fog. In the end, Bruno had insisted on remaining at the hospital while Zen did his business there and then driving him to the station, on the basis that taxis would be impossible to find and that it was too far to walk.

'I can't wait to get out of here,' he'd added, seemingly casually. 'And you shouldn't hang around either, *dottore*. They'll get the snowploughs out on the main streets, but it all takes time and you have that train down south to catch . . .'

'What's your surname, Bruno?' Zen had remarked equally casually.

'Nanni, *capo*.'

'I'll see what I can do.'

In the event he was back at the car in just over forty minutes, and they reached the station with almost an hour to spare. The train on which Zen had a reserved sleeper was waiting on one of the central platforms, but the locomotive had not yet been coupled up and the carriages were all dark and locked. He went to the station buffet and ate a toasted cheese and ham sandwich with some excellent beer, followed by a glass of local kirsch that was so good that he bought a small bottle as a souvenir for Gemma. Then he walked along the station building to the door marked *Servizio*.

In the dense warmth within, half a dozen men in railway uniform were smoking, chatting and playing cards. By a combination of implied threat, backed up by his police identification, and overt bribery, backed up by his wallet, he persuaded one of the sleeping-car attendants to walk with him across the tracks. The snow had not yet started to settle here, but it was now falling more thickly than ever.

'Do you think we'll get away on time?' Zen asked the attendant as he unlocked one of the blue sleeping cars.

'No question, *dottore*. The whole crew's from Rome. It would take the worst blizzard these krauts have ever seen to keep us banged up here overnight. Sorry about the cold inside. The heating'll come on as soon as the engine hooks up.'

Once in his chilly compartment, Zen lay down fully clothed on the bunk bed, bone-weary and dispirited, and immediately fell asleep.

He surfaced briefly when something nudged the train heavily and the lights came to glaring life, then dozed again for a while, lulled by the complex and comforting sounds and motion. But for the last half-hour or so he had been on his feet at the open window, wide awake and seemingly for good. The slightly rumpled bed beckoned, the night-light glowed cosily, but sleep wouldn't come.

He opened the bottle of kirsch he had bought for Gemma at the station, took a satisfying slug and lit a cigarette. After the day he'd had, not to mention only four hours' sleep the previous night, he should have been exhausted. Indeed, he *was* exhausted. It just so happened that he was also wide awake.

This normally only happened to him when he was in the grip of a case, deeply involved and yet unable for the moment to understand what needed to be done, or how to go about it. He hadn't previously imagined that this was the situation here. On the contrary, everything had seemed to suggest that this case had been shunted off in his direction, among a sheaf of others, as a sop to his professional pride, a transparent excuse to look busy. It seemed, however, that various supposedly subordinate departments of his mind – down in the basement, where the real work got done – were not convinced. Perhaps it had been Anton Redel's oddly insinuating remarks, or perhaps the reception he had been given by the *carabinieri* in Bolzano, or the information he had gathered earlier that evening at the local hospital.

In any event, it was all nonsense. He was in charge, for God's sake, his rational, waking self, and he had decided to go home, file his report and make an end of it. It was as home that he now thought of Lucca. He knew that few of its inhabitants would ever return the compliment, but that was their business. As far as he was concerned, he had settled in, and with the only woman he had ever met who accepted him without question just as he was. That was no little thing, and all the rest seemed to naturally follow. One of the few differences between them, which Gemma had also accepted without comment or suggestions for a cure, was that after some days there he began to feel restless.

It was in this spirit that Zen had accepted the assignment dangled before him by his superior Brugnoli in Rome. It would give him a chance to get out and about a bit, he had thought, to exercise his professional skills, spend some time away, and then return home refreshed and ready to enjoy the quiet pleasures of life in a small town so far off the beaten track that he would have to kill a good few hours of the early morning in Florence before the first connection left on the single-track branch line that ran through Pistoia and Lucca to Viareggio. Gemma had offered to come and pick him up when he had called her from Bolzano, but he had of course refused. It was humiliating enough not to own a car, and have still less desire to acquire one, without forcing your lover out of bed in the middle of the night to drive a hundred and fifty kilometres to save you from the consequences of your own inadequacy.

He took another drink from the bottle and lit another cigarette. Standing to the left-hand side of the window, he was protected from the surging air. The light of a skittish moon, constantly dodging behind rafts of cloud, provided the only sense of place, and when it came, it was dramatic: towering cliffs of raw jagged rock, densely wooded slopes, the swathe of destruction on either bank, and then of course the Adige itself, surging and boiling in the shallow stretches, sinisterly calm and muscular where the channel deepened.

Battlements clustered like birds' nests appeared on a crag across the river, some medieval lordling's lair perched above the highways he'd taken toll on, a previous version of the military works which Zen had viewed earlier in the day. The thought of the labour that had gone into those ingenious constructions, erected by sheer human sweat in the harshest of environments, not to mention the constant risk of being shot or blown up, was astonishing and humiliating. Depressing too, because in the end it had all been for nothing, both for the robber baron and for the young men who had died in the barren peaks Zen had visited earlier. The former had been replaced by more organized and democratic forms of extortion, while the Italian army had lost both its honour and the war at the *disfatta storica* of Caporetto, the battle which had wiped out all the earlier gains. Despite their heroic sacrifices and sufferings, the Alpini had been forced to withdraw.

True, at the end of the war the nation had got the whole territory back, as well as the Austrian cisalpine provinces of the Südtirol, the valleys south of the Brennero, as a gracious crumb let fall from the grand table of the Versailles peace conference. The fact remained that young men had died in their hundreds of thousands, most of them farm labourers from the centre and south of the country who had not the slightest idea of who they were fighting, let alone why.

The train seemed to have speeded up. They were going too fast, he thought, and in the same instant involuntarily recalled a passage from a French novel he'd read, probably while he was at university. He had perhaps remembered it because it was about railways, and his father had been a railwayman. In any event, he had now forgotten everything about the book except the demonic ending featuring a troop train hurtling through a featureless landscape towards the front in some forgotten war. The conscripts, numbed with exhaustion and booze, chanted and sang, unaware of the fact that the driver had fallen from the footplate of the locomotive, that the uncontrolled machine itself was driving them towards their inevitable destruction.

La storia. Le storie. History. Stories. The two senses of the word were coming together in his mind. Despite being of a generation that had never had to go to war, Zen – like every Italian, directly or indirectly – had had his appointments both with history and the infinite stories, true and false, which had been woven around it. In his case, they had usually come in the form of official cases that he had been charged with investigating, or helping to investigate, or more cynically hindering. How many had there been? How many stories had he worked on? Unless of course, as some said, they were all the same story, whose author and outcome would never be known.

Certainly this latest addition to the list did not seem very promising, even discounting the difficulties due to the fact that he had practically been operating in a foreign country. When Mussolini's Fascists came to power after the First World War, exploiting the internal contradictions of the former regime's hollow victory, they had exercised their absolute power to the utmost in the newly-named Alto Adige, forbidding the use of German, encouraging internal immigration from Sicily and the South, and generally grinding down the Austrian population in a blatant attempt to persuade them to head home across the Brennero Pass and not come back.

It was small wonder that resentment against the Italians still smouldered in the area. Since the granting of regional autonomy, this largely manifested itself on the personal level to which Bruno had taken exception in the mountain bar, but back in the seventies Zen had been at the sharp end of separatist terrorism during his 'hardship years' in the police, the obligatory posting to either Sicily, Sardinia or the Alto Adige, the nation's three most troubled and dangerous areas. Now, though, the terrorists had all retired and written their memoirs, while the locals were doing very nicely thank you off their status as nominally Italian but in practice self-regulating in all the issues that really mattered. They might still flaunt their cultural and linguistic diversity, but when push came to shove they were happier dealing with a remote and largely indifferent government in Rome than coming under the thumb of their own people to the north and having to do everything by the book.

Certainly Werner Haberl, the junior doctor whom Zen had interviewed at the hospital in Bolzano, showed no traces of resentment at all. On the contrary, he had handled the occasion with an urbane, amused, slightly patronizing ease, treating Zen as if dealing with a promising exchange student from some developing country such as Ethiopia. The body found in the old *Minenkriegstollenlage*? A memorable case, even before the *carabinieri* had staged their midnight raid and whisked everything away without a word of explanation. It wasn't every day that you got a partially mummified unidentified body of indeterminate age on the slab. The last one had been that Ice Age corpse they'd found up in the Alps, about a hundred metres on the Austrian side of the border as it turned out in the end. But Ötzi too had been there for a while, while the political aspects got sorted out.

Yes, he'd been present at the autopsy. They all had. Staff, students, even people from outside the department. It was a unique case, after all; none of your run-of-the-mill car crashes, drug overdoses, suicides and cardiac arrests. They'd all hovered around while the professor did the business, describing his procedures and findings minutely for the benefit of the assembled company, as well as the voice recorder from which he would subsequently transcribe his notes before writing up the official report. That had of course been taken, along with everything else, in the course of the *carabinieri*'s intervention last week. At four in the morning. Ten of them in two jeeps, with a military ambulance to take the cadaver and all the effects. Protests had been made, but all in vain.

Sensing an opening, Zen had immediately moved in.

'They've been pretty high-handed with us too. We made a request to see the post-mortem report – purely routine matter, in order to keep the bureaucratic record straight – and they just turned us down flat. Without even the courtesy of an excuse! For some unknown reason they seem to feel that they own this case. I would dearly love to prove them wrong about that, and if there's anything you can do to help me, I'll be most grateful. What was the cause of death, for example?'

'Impossible to establish definitively. There were extensive lacerations and contusions, as was to be expected in the circumstances, but the body was so decomposed that the initial post-mortem examination was inconclusive. We were about to order further forensic tests when the *Aktion* occurred.'

'What about identification?'

'Again, inconclusive. The face was very badly damaged, but a search of dental records might have yielded some results, if we'd had a chance to make one.'

'And his clothing?'

Werner Haberl nodded.

'That was perhaps the most interesting feature we discovered. It was not, for example, military uniform. That was important to establish, as the dry, cold conditions in those tunnels inhibit putrefaction, and our first thought was obviously that this might be one of our glorious dead. Or perhaps of yours.'

'So the corpse had been there for some time?'

'Judging by the condition of the flesh and organs, the pathologist conservatively estimated a period of at least twenty years and perhaps much longer. However, he could not have been a war victim. The clothes were of synthetic fabric and a more modern cut, certainly not dating from the period of the Great War, and consisted entirely of a pair of trousers, a shirt and underclothes and socks. No footwear, no jacket. Moreover, all the makers' marks had been removed and there were no personal items in the victim's pockets or at the scene where the body was discovered.'

'In other words . . .'

'In other words, we were apparently faced with the scenario of a young man – the pathologist's provisional estimate is that he was aged between twenty and twenty-five when he died – entering those tunnels alone, wearing light summer clothing from which all identifying tags had been removed, without shoes or boots, and then falling to his death.'

'Did you happen to notice any sort of marking on the man's right arm?'

'There was lots of superficial damage. The cadaver was in a very bad condition, as I've said.'

'No, I mean something artificial. A tattoo, for example.'

Harberl paused a moment.

'I believe there was something of the sort, now that you mention it. We didn't pay much attention to such superficial details at the preliminary stage, but of course they would be apparent on the video of the autopsy.'

'And where is that?'

Werner Haberl sighed wearily and rolled his eyes for an answer.

'That's very interesting,' said Zen, laying one of his cards on the desk between them. 'Here's my number, in case you remember anything else about the events we have discussed, or if there are any further developments.'

Werner Haberl looked at the card but did not touch it.

'I have the feeling that if there are any further developments, they will take place in Rome. Where, I note from your card, you are based, *dottore*.'

The honorary title emerged like sausage meat from a grinder.

'You may well be right,' Zen had replied, getting to his feet. '*Aber man kann nie wissen.*'

One never knows. A safe folk precept. Right now, for instance, he himself did not remotely know where he was. The stations dodged by so quickly, their lights all extinguished, that he couldn't read their names. But they had left the high ravines of the Adige, that much was clear. As was the moon. The weather was improving, the landscape was gentler and more cultivated, the economy productive rather than extractive. Distances sprang out, roads were straight, lights abounded, and there was traffic on the roads they crossed. Life was returning. Zen could smell its heady presence, stuffed with promise and challenge, in the mild air surging in through the window.

The train slowed slightly, clattered over a set of points and then dipped into a concrete underpass beneath another set of lines running at ninety degrees to its course. Leaving his compartment, Zen went out into the corridor. Yes, there were the lights of Verona, a city he had always irrationally loathed and never visited. *Una città bianca*, a fiefdom of the priests and the army, of soulless entrepreneurs and all the loutish scum of the Venetian hinterland who had inherited the worst qualities of both their ancestors and their Austro-Hungarian invaders, without any of the redeeming features of either. And the feeling was mutual. The *veronesi* had always hated the lordly Venetians too.

Now they were moving out into the vast desolation of the Po flatlands. Zen returned to his compartment for another dose of kirsch and a fresh cigarette. The railway line had narrowed to a single track, as though to emphasize the precarious hold of civilization on these reclaimed swamps, while the moonlight, filtered down through a layer of mist, evoked a dimensionless landscape punctuated by the squat, rectangular outlines of the *cascine*; agricultural barracks, now largely abandoned, where generations of crop-sharing farmhands had been born, grown up, married, laboured and died, all within one isolated and self-sufficient community lost in this featureless plain plagued by suffocating heat in summer and clammy cold in winter.

'In case you want to do an enhancement,' Anton had said about the black plastic thing that came with the photographs now packed away in Zen's overnight bag on the rack above. What was that supposed to mean?

The train rolled resonantly over a series of long metal spans laid out across the monstrous obesity of the lower

Po. Its lights showed the skeletal remains of the former brick and stone structure, the central arches gutted by bombs. Another war, another battleground, another failure. Mussolini's Chief of Staff, Marshal Badoglio, had allegedly deserted his unit at Caporetto and sought safety behind the lines. A quarter of a century later, after the Duce's downfall, he had dithered and prevaricated about the handover to the Allies just long enough to allow the Germans to occupy all but the extreme south of the peninsula, thereby ensuring the destruction of much of the nation's heritage and infrastructure, including the bridge they had just crossed.

A station flitted by. The train was going more slowly now, and he could just make out the name. Mirandola. A couple of houses on a minor road. He would never know anything more about Mirandola, just as he would never know anything more about the case he had been assigned. This was perfectly normal. Stories were one thing, history another. The first abounded, the second was unknowable. Despite Italy's economic prosperity and impeccable European credentials, not to mention the glitzy 'open government' stance of the current regime, its public history remained riddled with the secret network of events collectively dubbed the *misteri d'Italia*. The wormholes pervading the body politic remained, but the worms had never been identified, still less charged or convicted.

That was the way it was. Reasons existed, but reason itself, discredited by the excesses committed in its name, had been abandoned. Even reality was little more than a designer tag for whatever tissue of lies was being worn that year. But this too was normal. None of the ways we experience the world corresponds even remotely to the scientific truths about it. Not only are our intuitions invariably wrong, it is impossible to imagine what they would be like if they were right.

I should have joined the *magistratura*, he thought. Antonio Di Pietro, the inspirational investigating judge who had almost single-handedly brought about the fall of the former regime, the so-called First Republic, had formerly been a policeman. Then he had studied at night for a qualification to the judiciary, having realized that only that independent body could give him the power he needed to solve at least some of the more egregious 'mysteries of Italy'. I've never been that ambitious, Zen conceded gloomily. I've just carried on in my little rut, always taking the path of least resistance, trying to do the best I can, and then wondering why my work never amounts to anything in the end.

A clatter of points recalled him to the present. The line had now doubled again and the train was approaching a mass of orange lights, squishy in the light mist rising from the far shore of the swamplands. A cigarette and a final glug of kirsch later, they were trundling through Bologna station, past the rebuilt waiting room with the plaque commemorating yet another of those impenetrable mysteries: the bomb of 2 August 1980, which had killed eighty-four people and left over two hundred others scarred for life. Both the right and left wings of political opinion had blamed extremists of the opposing faction. There had been a flurry of investigations and a few charges had been brought, but nothing had come of it. It was as if that everyday atrocity had been an Act of God, like a hurricane or an earthquake. Shame, of course, shocking tragedy, but nothing to be done.

Now feeling tired for the first time, Zen lay down on the bed. The window was still open, and as the train entered a valley in the Apennine foothills he caught a momentary whiff of sweet wood smoke. Then there was nothing but the hammering of the wheels reverberating off the walls of the tunnels, increasingly frequent and long. Here at last he dozed off, only to be awakened by the sleeping car attendant he had bribed earlier, who told him that they were passing through Prato. He had just time to collect his things and make himself look more or less presentable before the train arrived in Florence.

He stepped wearily down on to the platform, still only half-awake, and wondering how on earth he was to fill the long hours before his connection to Lucca left. Then a lithe form emerged from the shadows and kissed him.

'You're looking very well. The mountain air must suit you.'

He stared at Gemma.

'What are you doing here?' he said irritably. 'I told you not to bother.'

'Well, I did. The car's outside. Give me your bag.'

'I can manage perfectly well. You're not my mother!'

'No, I'm not.'

'Anyway, thank you for coming. Sorry I'm so tetchy. I'm completely exhausted. God, it's good to be home.'

'Make the most of it, because the Ministry's been in touch. Someone named Brugnoli. He wants to see you in Rome tomorrow.'

'I don't want to go to Rome.'

'Well, I do. And you have to. I've booked us both seats on the nine o'clock.'

'What have you got to do with it? You don't work for Brugnoli. Or do you? Is that it? He planted you on me at the beach back in the summer to . . .'

'Calm down. I just want to do some shopping.'

'Fine, but I have to work. You can't just expect me to drop everything, escort you round the shops and then take you to lunch.'

'I prefer to shop alone, and I'm lunching with a friend.'

'A friend?'

'Her name's Fulvia. We were at school together. We'll take the train down together in the morning and then back again in the evening, leaving the car at the station here in Florence.'

'But . . .'

'You're just tired. And a bit drunk, I think. It'll all make sense in the morning.'

'No, it won't.'

'All right, then it won't. Is getting worked up about it now going to change that?'

'Why do you always have to be right?'

'Why do you always have to be wrong?'

'I'm *not* always wrong!'

'No, but you think you are. You even want to be. Well, I want to be right. And I usually am. I took a chance on you, don't forget. A very big chance. Was I wrong about that?'

'No, you were right.'

'I rest my case. Now you rest, and I'll drive.'

VI

Once the sun had set into a distant bank of clouds to the south-west, Gabriele opened the trap-door in the floor, lowered the ladder and clambered down. After that it was easy: the precipitous sets of stairs leading to the second floor, then the much grander and gentler stone sweep to ground level and the stately entrance hall of the *bocchirale* running the entire length of the building, its wasted space and elaborately frescoed ceiling proclaiming the status of the landlord.

He opened the front door to the vast courtyard, with its slightly raised and cambered threshing floor framed by shallow drainage channels, and walked diagonally across to the last of the seven arched openings of the cloister-like *barches-sale*, where the farm machinery and equipment had once been stored. As a child, he had kept his bicycle here, and that was where he kept it now, well out of sight of any casual – or not so casual – visitors.

Ten minutes later he was pedalling steadily along the dead flat, dead straight lane that passed the property, flanked by deep ditches on either side, the desolate flatness of the landscape making the lines of poplars, pollarded to break the wind, stand out like architecture. Timing was crucial to the success of this outing. There was still enough light for him to see, but little enough to make it unlikely that he would be seen. Apart from the invariable ground mist that was already starting to creep up, the nights had been consistently clear, and the moon would rise just in time to light his way back. When he was a boy, there had been no electricity at the *cascina*. During the many summers he had spent here, he had been keenly aware of the rising and setting times of the sun and moon, and of the latter's phases. It was a form of respectful attention which he had now effortlessly regained.

The trip was still a risk, of course, but a minimal and necessary one. He would be taking back roads to his destination. Given the massive depopulation of the whole area, these were almost unused, particularly after dark. With any luck, the shopkeeper would be the only person to see his face, and with his newly grown beard and dark glasses even his sister would have had difficulty in recognizing him. Besides, the batteries for the camping lantern that he had brought with him from Milan had almost run out, and without that substitute for the oil and acetylene lamps of his boyhood, he wouldn't be able to function at all during the hours of darkness.

To be honest, he would have had to get out, however briefly, in any case. The rectangular block of the *cascina*, totally sealed off from the outside world except for its two gateways, and surrounded by a wide drainage ditch like the moat of a medieval castle, had an overwhelming sense of being cut off from the outside world. This had initially seemed comforting, but by now Gabriele was starting to suffer from what he and his friends in the army had used to call 'barracks fever'.

And there was another factor. He was starting to feel a bit of a ninny. That's how his father had sometimes referred to him in a tone of contemptuous affection – *il babbione* – and as so often in the past it was beginning to look as though he had been right. Ten days gone, and nothing whatever had happened. More to the point, it was getting difficult to see what could happen to justify his panicked flight to the family's former rural property.

He remembered having read somewhere that the difference between a theory and a belief rested not on proof but on the possibility of disproof. No matter how many observations appeared to corroborate the theory of relativity, for example, it could never conclusively be proved to be true. Its scientific respectability rested on the fact that it could instantly be proven false should contradictory evidence come to light. The same did not apply to the idea that God had created the world in six days and then faked the fossil record to suggest otherwise, which is why this amounted to nothing more than a belief. As did his fears about his own safety, he now realized. They weren't rational, and therefore could not be dispelled. What would have to happen to prove that he had been wrong, that in fact there was no threat, nothing whatever to fear?

Not that he wasn't quite comfortable where he was. Indeed, that was part of the problem. The nights were still quite mild for the time of year, and the camping gear he had bought before leaving Milan – for cash, in case anyone was tracing his credit card records – was perfectly adequate to his needs. He lived as simply as he did at home, on pasta, parmesan, oil, *salumi* and dried soups, occasionally supplemented by a hare or pigeon he had trapped and prepared using his army training for living off the land. His only other purchase, before slipping on to a train bound for Cremona from the suburban station of Lambrate, had been this second-hand bicycle, on which he had invisibly arrived at his refuge, and which was always available for trips like this. The water from the well was better than what came out of the tap in Milan and he had brought plenty of books from the shop to keep him amused.

Best of all, absolutely no one knew where he was! Not just his enemies, but his friends, acquaintances and associates, not to mention his sister Paola and her thirty-something, live-at-home son. To think of all the time and affection he had lavished on the idle cipher that his nephew, so charming and intelligent when young, had turned out to be as an adult. But it had been his own fault. People always let you down. You were better off without them. Another of the things he had realized here – there had been plenty of time to think – was that he had always secretly dreamed of disappearing, of becoming invisible, wholly a subject to himself but in no way an object for others. That was what he had always wanted, and now, to all intents and purposes, he had it.

The bike rolled easily along, with an endearing little squeak from the rear axle. It was an old-fashioned ladies' model, the black-painted frame elegantly bowed like a harp. There were three gears, two brakes and no gadgets. Gabriele had fallen in love with it at first sight, a cotton print frock amidst the massed acrylic sports gear of the ATBs, and the price had been absurdly low.

The light was fading fast now, but he would almost have known his way blindfold. All he needed was a glimmer to keep him from falling into one of the deep ditches that lined every road and track in this territory reclaimed centuries ago from the monstrous Po. He had covered them all as a boy, often walking and cycling for ten or twelve hours a day, and sometimes sleeping rough if he got lost or the bike broke down. No one had worried if he didn't return by night-fall. In those days, the world had been hard but benign; now it was soft and malevolent.

He swung left on to the slightly wider road that curved along the bank of the river into which all this land drained, and which in turn drained into a minor tributary of the Po. Two cars passed him, one in each direction, but each travelling at such a speed that Gabriele could have figured to the occupants as no more than a hazardous blur to be avoided if possible. The remaining locals all drove like maniacs, as though taking revenge for the years when their forebears had had to trudge endless distances each day of their lives, under a blazing sun or pouring rain, to or from their work in the fields.

The road eventually curved around to join the main *strada statale* at the triple-arched medieval bridge leading up into the small town perched on its ledge safely above the flood level of the plains all around. Gabriele dismounted, hid the bicycle away in a grove of poplars near the junction and then continued on foot.

Within the walls, all was as quiet as a tomb. He turned left, off the main road, and then right into a street of low, two-storey brick terraces. The town had a name, but on a deeper level it was generic; one of a thousand or more almost indistinguishable communities dotted across the Po valley and delta, low and modest in appearance, built of plastered brick, and originally serving as a market and shopping centre for the surrounding area. Since the flight to the cities of the sixties and seventies, such places had a sad air of living in enforced retirement. This suited Gabriele's plans perfectly. Three-quarters of the population had left, and those who remained stayed within doors of an evening and went to bed early. There was no one about on the street, and his rubber-soled sports shoes made no sound as he walked towards the central piazza. Apart from the lack of people about, everything was as he remembered it from forty years earlier. More parked cars, of course, and the odd bit of repainting or remodelling here and there, but basically the same old stale loaf of a town.

The shop was still there too, although with a new sign and plate-glass window, and presided over not by Ubaldo and Eugenia, but by a menopausal woman whom Gabriele finally recognized with a shock as their daughter Pinuccia, about whom he used to have wet dreams. He had put on his dark glasses before entering the shop and he now put on his thickest Milanese accent and asked if they sold batteries, in a tone suggesting that hicks like them probably wouldn't know what batteries were, never mind have any.

While Pinuccia was searching through a mass of cardboard boxes stacked on a shelf in a dim recess of the shop, Gabriele's eye was caught by a large black skeleton printed on transparent plastic which was hanging from a hook behind the counter. A witch with a pointed hat and broomstick dangled on the other side of the cash register. Of course, Halloween was approaching. When he had last been interested in such things, the importation of exotic items such as this had not yet been thought of. The church would have banned it, for that matter, or at least fulminated against it. All Saints' Day was a religious festival, and the superstitious legends and old wives' tales surrounding the preceding evening something to be ridiculed or ignored.

Pinuccia returned with a selection of batteries, of which Gabriele purchased six. He paid and left, removing his dark glasses so that he could see his way. The almost full moon peeked over the roofs of the houses on the main road. He had timed his journey perfectly.

The light of the town's one public telephone box gleamed dully from the far side of the pompous *rinascimentale* piazza. It would probably be broken, or of the almost obsolete variety that only took tokens. Maintaining public phones cost the company a lot of money, and even the beggars had mobiles these days. So did janitors, on the other hand.

The interior of the box was a bit of a mess – cigarette butts on the floor, a heavily used copy of *Il Giornale* replacing the missing phone book, a tang of urine in the air – but the machine accepted his phone card and connected him to Fulvio's mobile. Gabriele was well aware that making this call also involved an element of risk, but he had assessed it at length over several days and had decided that it was acceptable.

'*Pronto!*'

As always, Fulvio answered the phone as if making a declaration of war.

'It's Passarini.'

'*Dottore*! How have you been? Where have you been?'

'I'm fine. I'm just calling to find out whether anyone has been trying get in touch with me. Do you understand?'

Although unprepossessing in manner, the janitor was remarkably quick on the uptake.

'*Certo, certo!*'

'Well?'

'Actually there has been someone. Was, I should say. I haven't seen him for a few days.'

'What happened?'

'He came to my cubicle in the front hall and asked if I was responsible for the building. I said that I was, and he asked if that included the . . .'

He was however, Gabriele remembered, long-winded.

'Yes, yes. And the upshot?'

'He asked about the bookshop, your shop. I said I didn't know, I understood that there had been a death in the family and that you'd decided to take some time off. He asked how long, I said I had no idea. He said he had a very important business matter to discuss with you – huge amount of money at stake, something that couldn't wait, all the rest of it. But he wouldn't leave a name or number. I simply told him I had no idea where you were, which is true apart from anything else, and I was sorry but I couldn't help. Basically just stone-walled him out of there, but he didn't want to go, I can tell you that.'

Gabriele was silent for so long that the janitor thought they'd been cut off and started going '*Pronto? Pronto?*'

'I'm still here, Fulvio. Anything else?'

'Just the usual post and casual callers. That professor from the university dropped by while I was taking out the garbage. He wanted to know if the plates he'd ordered had arrived. From some atlas.'

Jansson's *Atlas Novus*, thought Gabriele. A few loose sheets from one of the Latin editions, possibly 1647. He had acquired them very reasonably in Leipzig, but now he had a buyer in the United States interested, so the professor would have to wait and see what the market price turned out to be.

'That man who came asking after me. What did he look like?'

'Thick-set, average height, brown eyes set close together, bald, prominent ears. Oh, and a broken nose.

Really splayed out, like a boxer or rugby player. What more can I say? He had a sense of power about him, as if he was someone, or thought he was. That's about it.'

'Very good, Fulvio. Thanks for your help.'

'But when will you be back, *dottore*?'

'I can't really say. It may be some time. Anyway, just keep on as you have been doing and I'll make it up to you as soon as I return.'

He hung up, retrieved his phone card and then, as a final thought, rolled up the copy of *Il Giornale* and stuck it in his coat pocket. It might be mildly interesting to find out what had been going on in the world since he had left it.

He was about to start back to his bicycle when an idea struck him. He returned to the shop and asked Pinuccia if she had any fireworks. It was only when she looked at him in a way suggesting a certain confused recognition that he realized that he had forgotten to put his stage shades back on.

'Fireworks?' she said.

'*Certo*,' he replied in his pushy Milanese accent. 'For Halloween. Firecrackers. Bangers. Light blue touch-paper and retire immediately. Boom. Big thrill for the kiddies. You understand?'

For a moment he was worried that she'd understood only too well, but in the end the dullness in her eyes subdued that momentary spark of intelligent interest and they concluded the transaction without further incident. Still, the spark had been there, if only for a second, he thought as he walked back down the street leading to the bridge.

Had Pinuccia ever had fantasies about him? He had been one of the local landowner's sons, after all. This was an aspect of the situation which had never occurred to him at the time. He had been far too busy becoming himself to give a moment's thought to who he actually was, but others might not have been so dim. And his once-beloved's failure to recognize him, although a blessing given the circumstances, nevertheless felt like a loss. She was no longer she and he was no longer he. Alone in the familiar environs of the *cascina*, he had grown accustomed to thinking of himself as a boy again, but that boy was as dead as poor Leonardo.

The ride back was calm and uneventful, a magic adventure in the moonlight-soaked landscape. The only problem was the mist, which had curdled in patches now in that unpredictable way it had, so that one moved from almost total transparency to opacity in a second, and for no apparent reason at all. And then out again, from a clump so thick he had to dismount and walk, watching his way carefully, only to stumble suddenly into a clarity so perfect it made mock of his caution. Passing one of the places where an irrigation canal ran over the drainage ditches on a slender stone aqueduct, he recalled his childish fascination with this physical oxymoron: water flowing over water.

Back at his base, he checked the fine cotton thread he had strung across the door set in the main gateway, its green-painted slatted planks faded now to a gentle blue. The tell-tale was unbroken. He bent under it and stepped through into the echoing *aia*, looking around the space which was so familiar to him that it was almost invisible behind its panoply of memories. He kept expecting a door or window to open and a voice to shout, 'Gabriele! Welcome home!' But those voices were all dead. How much work had been done here, how many lives lived out! Like a battlefield, he thought; an endless, indecisive engagement in a meaningless war fought with outdated equipment for reasons that no one could now remember.

Back in his eyrie, as he had named it when he first moved there at the age of fifteen, he carefully lowered and secured the light-proof blinds he had cut from an oilskin tablecloth, before replacing the batteries of the camping lantern and turning it on. Despite the wind-breaks of elms and poplars around the house, in this level landscape any light might show for miles, and would immediately attract interest.

He filled the saucepan with water from the bucket in the corner, set it on the butane stove and settled down to read the paper he had brought back. Most of the articles didn't interest him – the usual exaggerated fuss about some impending cabinet reshuffle in Rome – but his eye was caught by one of the headlines on the *Cronaca* page, about a killing in some town called Campione d'Italia. There was a photograph of the victim, who was identified as Nestor Machado Solorzano, a citizen of Venezuela. To Gabriele's eye, he very much resembled a slightly older Nestore Soldani.

He skimmed rapidly through the article, then reread it several times with close attention. According to his wife Andreina, speaking through an interpreter, the victim had been phoned at home on his birthday and had driven out to an impromptu appointment with a person or persons unknown in Capolago, just across the Swiss border. On his return, the BMW Mini Cooper which he was driving had blown up at the entrance to their villa in Campione. The explosion had utterly destroyed the car and gates, and shattered the windows of the surrounding houses. Virtually no trace of the victim's body had been recovered.

Gabriele quickly worked out the dates. The murder had occurred the day after he had left Milan, having read about the discovery of Leonardo's body.

The pasta water boiled over. He removed the saucepan from the stove with trembling hands. To think that only an hour or so earlier he had been jeering at himself for having panicked unnecessarily, and raising philosophical questions about the nature of the proof that would be required to justify his having fled into hiding here. Here was his proof! So far as he was aware, only three men knew for sure what had happened to Leonardo Ferrero, and one of them was now dead, killed by a bomb in his car two days after the discovery of the body.

That left only him and Alberto. He was loath to contact Alberto – indeed, he half-suspected him of being behind the series of mute, implicitly menacing postcards that arrived every year around the anniversary of Leonardo's death – but now he felt he had no choice. Whoever had killed Nestore would have his name next on their list. This was no longer a game of hide-and-seek but of life-and-death. He couldn't hide out at here at the *cascina* for ever, but neither did he wish to live in perpetual terror back in Milan, or to emigrate and eke out a miserable existence in some foreign country where they would still be able to reach him sooner or later.

In short, he had no choice but to force the issue, and Alberto was the only person he could turn to. It would have to be drafted carefully, of course, giving nothing away about his present location, still less his fears. He must sound confident and assertive, even a little dangerous. He would outline his quite reasonable apprehensions on hearing the news of Nestore's death, make it absolutely clear that the secret of Operation Medusa would remain forever sacrosanct, and demand further details of who had murdered Soldani and what was being done to bring them to justice and protect the two remaining members of the Verona cell.

He would enclose his mobile phone number with a date and time for Alberto to call, allowing him a week to formulate an appropriate and satisfactory response. The letter would be posted from one of the larger local towns that he could reach easily by train from the unmanned station at which he had arrived, Crema perhaps. When the time came for Alberto to call, he would make a return trip in the other direction, to Mantua, taking the call on the train. They would never be able to trace his whereabouts, and at the very least he would know exactly where he stood. One thing he had learned from his time in the army was that while imaginary fears exhausted and paralysed him, real and present danger left him cool and collected. It was time to confront the enemy, whoever they might be, to force them to come forward and reveal themselves. Whatever the outcome, it could not be worse than living in a state of perpetual uncertainty and inchoate terror.

VII

As soon as Zen entered the bar just off Via Nazionale, the broad paved ditch between the Viminale and Quirinale hills, he felt an intruder. The political centre of the country might lie further down the hillside, at Palazzo de Montecitorio and Palazzo Madama in the *centro storico*, but this was where those entrusted with the dirty work of implementing any decisions made by the Chamber of Deputies and the Senate gathered. Like its counterpart in the business world, which was also heavily represented, this society was rigidly hierarchical, and the resulting distinctions extended far beyond the workplace. You would no more think of frequenting your superior's bar or restaurant than you would of moving into his office. It would be inappropriate and embarrassing for all concerned.

Zen could not determine the exact status of the clientele in this establishment, discreetly hidden away on a side street near the opera house, but it was definitely a cut above his own; senior rather than middle management. The woman enthroned at the cashier's dais looked as though she had put in a few decades being chased around the desk by most of the men in the bar before taking early retirement in her current position. While paying for his coffee, Zen slid his Ministry identification card on to the counter between them. The woman glanced at it and at him, then reached down into some cubby-hole inviolate from the common gaze, and handed over a blank white envelope.

Without wasting thanks or a smile on her, Zen proceeded to the bar, where despite the tip he had laid down with his receipt he had to wait until several other men, who had arrived after him and had not troubled themselves to prepay the cashier, were served with due ceremony and attention. This was a club you couldn't buy your way into. You had to belong.

The coffee, when it finally arrived, was one of the best Zen had ever had in Rome, where standards were notoriously variable. He turned away from the bar, savouring the velvety essence, and tore open the envelope. Inside was a piece of paper bearing the handwritten message: 'Gardens of the Villa Aldobrandini, 15.00. Destroy this immediately.' Zen shredded the note and distributed the fragments between two of the metal canisters serving as ashtrays and rubbish bins, but it was with a heavy heart that he walked out into the cold streets. There were messages that were in themselves messages, and in this case the news did not sound good.

The sun had come out by the time he reached the hanging gardens of the Villa Aldobrandini near the foot of Via Nazionale, and, hanging low in the sky at this time of year, its light was blinding. He climbed up the marble steps past the exposed brickwork of some Imperial Roman structure which, stripped of its marble finishing, looked much like the remains of a late-nineteenth-century factory.

The gardens themselves, some ten metres above street level, consisted of a maze of gravel paths curving between islands of lawn edged with stone verges and punctuated by headless antique statues and the bare trunks of ancient chestnuts, cypresses, palms and pines. There were sufficient evergreens to provide a verdant background, but in general the trees were oppressively overgrown for the setting, and much of the shrubbery had a faded, moth-eaten air about it.

In addition to the usual contingent of insomniac deadbeats and feral cats, the gardens were populated by a few local people walking their dogs and an alfresco ladies' hairdressing salon. Here and there amongst the trees, about a dozen middle-aged women who knew exactly how much they were worth, down to the last lira, sat perched on folding plastic chairs being made reasonably presentable for a reasonable fee by much younger women who had brought all they needed for the job in bags and boxes. No licence, no rent or rates to pay; a no-frills service at a no-frills price.

Although the gardens were quite small, their intricate layout made them seem deceptively large, and it was some time before Zen made out the figure of his superior standing by the wall at the far end, looking out at the view over Piazza Venezia and the Capitoline to the Gianicolo and the line of hills on the north bank of the Tiber. Brugnoli looked smaller than Zen had remembered him from their one previous meeting. He was wearing a navy-blue cashmere coat worn open over a suit which managed to suggest by various almost imperceptible details of cut and fabric that it was not a mere garment but rather an ironic statement about such garments, but so expertly and expensively executed that most people would never notice the difference, still less that the joke – whose punch-line was of course the price tag – was on them. In short, this was not a business suit, but a 'business suit'.

'Good to see you,' Brugnoli exclaimed as they shook hands. 'So glad you could make it.'

He made it sound as though Zen had done him a personal favour by showing up. Unsure how to respond to this unfamiliar rhetoric, Zen opted for silence.

'How are things going?' Brugnoli continued, steering his subordinate down a side path well away from the nearest hairstylist and her client. 'I trust your new position is satisfactory?'

'Perfectly, thank you.'

'And your private life? I hear you've moved to Lucca.'

'Yes.'

'Charming place. Couldn't live there myself. Too quiet. But it suits you?'

'It does.'

'Good, good.'

He paused and looked round, then buttoned up his coat. They were in the shade of the great trees now.

'I understand that you've been looking into this business about the body they found in that military tunnel.'

Zen nodded.

'With what results?'

'Well, I inspected the scene of the discovery with one of the Austrian cavers who found the body, and then talked briefly to a junior doctor at the hospital in Bolzano who had been present at the autopsy.'

'What about the *carabinieri*? It's their case, after all.'

'I spoke to a Colonel Miccoli by telephone, and he expressed a willingness to meet me. When I went to the *carabinieri* headquarters in Bolzano, however, I was informed that he was unavailable.'

'What about his colleagues? Were they cooperative?'

Zen hesitated.

'They were correct,' he said at last.

'But not cordial?'

'Not exactly.'

'Nor particularly forthcoming.'

'No.'

'No,' Brugnoli repeated. 'No, I don't suppose they were.'

They walked in silence for some time.

'We're having a bit of a problem, you see,' Brugnoli said at last, pausing to examine the bark of a giant palm tree.

'A problem?'

'With our friends in the parallel service. They've rather slammed the door in our faces, to be perfectly frank. No fine phrases, no specious evasions. Just bugger off. And this at a very high level. Very high indeed.'

They split up to pass a young mother trying to quiet a fractious child in a pushchair. He should be walking, thought Zen. These gardens must seem like the Brazilian rainforests to him. He wants to explore and conquer, subdue the native tribes and discover the lost treasure of El Dorado. But his mother is afraid he'll fall over the parapet and dash his brains out on the pavement beneath. We no longer trust our children, and then wonder why they grow up untrustworthy.

'Did they give a reason?' he asked Brugnoli once they were out of earshot.

'Oh yes. They weren't polite, still less cordial, but to use your own telling phrase, they were correct. They gave a reason. They also enjoined on us in no uncertain terms not to divulge this reason to anyone below ministerial level. Nevertheless, I'm now going to tell you.'

'Wait a moment,' Zen interrupted. 'I'm not sure that it would be appropriate for you to confide in me. I mean . . .'

Brugnoli laughed and moved on again, steering them away from an elderly man walking a dog and an alcoholic, passed out in the shrubbery.

'What you mean is that you don't want my confidences, *dottore*. Fair enough, but I'm afraid you don't have a choice. I'll only give you the outline. That's almost all they told us, for that matter. Briefly, they claim that the corpse which was found was that of a soldier who was accidentally killed during a military exercise.'

Brugnoli paused, but Zen made no comment.

'The need for secrecy, according to *la Difesa*, is because the victim was a member of an elite special force drawn from within the army on a volunteer basis and modelled on the British SAS and the American Delta Force. Its very existence is officially denied, and no comments are ever made about its personnel, training or operations. Still less about any fatalities that result. The next of kin are of course informed, but even they are not always told the truth about what happened.'

Zen's mobile started chirping. He checked the caller's number and then switched the phone off with an apology to his superior.

'At any rate,' Brugnoli continued, 'our sources – and I stress that they are at the very highest level – claim that the First World War tunnel where the body was found is regularly used as a training site for this unit. Tradition, esprit de corps, our glorious forefathers and all that. They further claim that due to an unfortunate set of circumstances the young man was killed. For obvious reasons, they don't wish any of this to come to light, and have therefore taken the necessary steps to ensure that the matter remains secret.'

'My informant at the hospital in Bolzano told me that the *carabinieri* raided the premises in force last week and took away the corpse, all personal effects, as well as the photographs and tape-recording of the preliminary post-mortem.'

Brugnoli stopped at the edge of the gardens, staring up at a vast bureaucratic *palazzo* constructed strictly according to Mussolini's preferred architectural techniques, avoiding the use of imported steel. A man was looking down at them from a third-floor window, or perhaps just admiring the view of the gardens in the late autumn sunshine.

'Also, according to my source, the victim's clothing was civilian and had had all the identifying marks removed,' Zen remarked.

Brugnoli puffed sardonically.

'The Defence people will say that that was perfectly normal. These men belonged to a unit trained to work undercover or behind enemy lines. They don't wear traditional uniforms.'

'Not even shoes?'

'Shoes?'

'The corpse was barefoot.'

Brugnoli thought about this for a moment, then gave a dismissive shrug.

'They'll say that he was wearing army issue boots which had to be removed to prevent a positive identification. They've got every angle covered, Zen.'

He turned away and started to stroll down one of the side paths.

'When did this supposed incident happen?' asked Zen.

'They declined to be specific on that point. "For reasons of operational security".'

Zen stopped and fussed over lighting a cigarette to cover his growing feelings of alarm. Both literally and figuratively, Brugnoli was leading him down the garden path, and into what was potentially very dangerous territory indeed.

'You're probably wondering why they left the corpse in situ,' his superior went on. 'Well, they claim that the fatal accident involved a test with some sort of nerve gas, one of those chemical warfare things. Since they could not be sure about the potential risk involved, they decided to seal the site by exploding a charge to block the tunnel. The family was told that their son had been killed in an unfortunate accident which had disfigured him so badly that it was necessary to hold a closed coffin funeral to avoid distressing the mourners.'

'But the tunnel was not blocked. The body was discovered by those Austrian youngsters and then extracted by the *carabinieri*. I crawled in there myself.'

'They suggested that there must have been some subsidence since the event.'

'That's impossible. The rock in those mountains is like iron.'

Brugnoli turned to Zen with a level gaze.

'You don't think for a moment that we believe any of this, I hope?'

'What does it matter whether we believe it or not?' Zen demanded. 'We can't disprove it, because they haven't given us anything to disprove. The identity of the victim is being withheld, along with the date and nature of the alleged incident, access to witnesses and physical evidence, as well as all records of the post-mortem examination. Frankly, they might just as well have said that the case had to be hushed up because the victim was an alien invader from outer space and the public would panic if word got out. And if all this is being relayed to us "at the very highest level", then it is only at such a level that any progress can be made. I therefore fail to see what steps I can effectively be ordered to take in the matter.'

This last phrase was spoken in the coldest and most bureaucratic tone Zen was capable of, and it made its effect. Brugnoli took his arm with a defusing laugh and walked him towards the only exit and entrance to the gardens perched high above the street.

'*Caro dottore*! There's no question of ordering you to do anything at all. This is not the old days! Remember my motto, "Personal choice, personal empowerment, personal responsibility". If you don't feel fully committed to a course of action, you're not going to perform well and achieve the desired results.'

'And just what are the desired results?'

Brugnoli gestured broadly.

'You have rightly objected to being unnecessarily burdened with confidences, so I shall not go into details or name any names, but the fact is that in the current political situation, with a cabinet reshuffle widely rumoured to be imminent, there is a distinct tension between certain high-level players in the Defence Ministry and those on our own team. Potentially there's a very great deal at stake, believe me.'

Both men stopped dead as a haggard figure erupted from the shrubbery on their right, demanding money. One of his arms had been amputated at the elbow, and his skin was the colour of the tree trunks all around. He was dressed only in shorts and an undershirt, and kept talking incessantly and incomprehensibly in a series of loud, stabbing phrases.

Brugnoli ignored the beggar and walked on. Zen dug into his pocket and poured some loose change into the man's remaining hand.

'You shouldn't do that,' Brugnoli remarked when Zen caught up with him. 'It only encourages them.'

'It's my insurance policy.'

'What's that supposed to mean?'

But Zen chose not to answer this question.

'What has the current political situation to do with this specific affair?' he asked instead.

Brugnoli sighed heavily.

'*Dottore*, you surely must have experienced cases where you could not immediately achieve your primary objective, for lack of evidence or cooperative witnesses or whatever, but where you were able to make progress by pursuing a secondary objective where these conditions did not obtain and then using that as a lever to crack open the original problem. Well, it's the same here. It would be counter-productive, and for that matter probably futile, for us to tackle *la Difesa* openly about this matter, which is in any case peripheral to our real interests. But assuming that they are indeed lying through their teeth, then a skilled operative such as yourself might be able to turn up some potentially interesting material which might provide us with the advantage we need to address the larger issues concerned.'

Zen nodded slowly, as though all these long words and abstract concepts had confused him. In reality he was assessing the respective risks involved in accepting or refusing Brugnoli's proposition.

'So what you want . . .' he began ponderously.

'What I want is a huge scandal that will be front-page news for days if not weeks, better yet the head of some eminent name on a plate, and ideally a confession implicating the entire Defence Ministry from the *onorevole* himself down to the night cleaning staff. However, I'll settle for almost anything – just some grit to throw in the machinery and generally foul things up.'

Zen was silent for a long time.

'The Austrian caver gave me some digital photographs his friend had taken of the corpse,' he said eventually. 'They're not very clear, but he suggested that it might be possible to do something called "an enhancement".'

Brugnoli nodded vigorously. 'No problem! One of my first initiatives was to upgrade all such equipment and facilities. Just go to Technical Services on the second . . .'

He broke off.

'What do these photographs show?'

'As I said, the prints aren't very clear, but potentially a marking of some sort on the dead man's arm, possibly a tattoo. It might be of assistance in making a positive identification of the victim.'

Brugnoli pursued his lips judiciously.

'Then you'd better get it done privately.'

'You don't trust our own technicians?'

'I trust them to do good work. I don't trust them not to leave copies of it lying around in some computer file where the opposition might find it. And if it means anything at all to us, it'll mean a lot more to them.'

It took Zen a moment to grasp the point.

'The Ministry of Defence has a spy within the Viminale?' he asked.

'I'd be amazed if they didn't. Almost certainly several, in fact. Not to mention the secret services. Disgruntled operatives who feel they've been wrongfully passed over for promotion, time-servers with a year or two to go until retirement who want to feather their nests while there's still a chance, that sort of thing. Hence the deliberately indirect manner in which this meeting was set up. You're already known to the *carabinieri* in Bolzano, and they will almost certainly have reported your visit there to their masters at the Defence Ministry. If I had simply told you to come to my office this morning, that fact might well have been reported and the obvious conclusion drawn.'

'Perhaps you should use someone else then,' Zen suggested rapidly. 'Someone untainted by previous associations with the case.'

Brugnoli's expression revealed that he had not been deceived by this attempt to wriggle out of the assignment.

'No, no! You're the man for the job, Zen. After all, the fact that you've already begun enquiries makes it all the more natural that you should then follow them up. What must be protected at all costs is any connection between your level and mine. If a lone officer doggedly pursues further evidence in this case, that's one thing. But if our enemies begin to suspect what we're really up to, they will immediately take steps to neutralize the threat.'

And possibly the 'lone officer' concerned, thought Zen.

'The rules of engagement are that you are to report solely to me, and in person,' Brugnoli continued. 'Not by phone, either land-line or mobile, nor by email, fax, letter, postcard, carrier pigeon or any other form of overt communication, unless of course I initiate the contact. Our *modus operandi* must allow for total deniability by all concerned while the operation is in progress. If you need to contact me, write an unsigned note stating a place and time, seal it in a plain envelope and leave it with the cashier at the bar you went to today.'

Zen nodded wonderingly.

'She's that trustworthy?' he asked.

Brugnoli took a luxurious amount of time to answer.

'She used to be my mistress,' he said complacently.

He glanced at his watch decisively, as though to cover this indiscretion.

'Right, well, I must be going. Please remain here for at least ten minutes after I leave. I'm almost certain that we have been unobserved so far, but one can never be too careful.'

'Oh, just one small thing . . .'

Zen was searching in his coat pocket for his note-book and a pen.

'While I was in Bolzano, I ran into a patrolman named Bruno Nanni.'

He wrote the name down, tore out the sheet and handed it to Brugnoli.

'He's doing his hardship time up there, and it seems to have been very hard on him indeed. Basically he's an excellent young officer, very willing and capable, but he's totally out of his depth in the Alto Adige and, I have to say, given to occasional outbursts which in my opinion might reflect negatively on the force's reputation in that sensitive area. I hate to bother a man like you about a trivial matter of this sort, but I was just wondering if . . .'

'Where does he want to go?' asked Brugnoli.

'Bologna.'

The other man nodded.

'I'll send a memo down to Personnel this afternoon.'

'I think it might be best.'

To Zen's surprise, Brugnoli walked over to him and tugged the sleeve of his coat.

'Eh, *dottore!*' he said with a light laugh. 'Don't take all the supposed changes around here too literally. Yes, many things have changed, but the important ones remain the same. That applies to your relationship with me and the people to whom I was alluding earlier. You look after us, and we'll look after you. Do you understand what I'm saying?'

Zen gave a series of rapid nods.

'Yes,' he said. 'Yes, I understand completely.'

VIII

During the period of quarantine that Brugnoli had imposed, Zen phoned the caller whose number had appeared on the screen of his mobile earlier, apologized for being unable to respond at that time – 'I was in a meeting' – and arranged a rendezvous. He then took himself off to a cheap and cheerful bar on Via Nazionale where he ordered a glass of spumante, for no particular reason, and read a series of long, intelligent and densely analytical articles in *La Gazzetta dello Sport* on the burning issue of the moment, namely whether the coach of the national football team should be replaced after the recent series of humiliating results against opponents whose countries in some cases hadn't even existed ten years earlier, and if so by whom.

At one o'clock promptly, he was standing on the pavement of the steep street a bit further down the hill, opposite Palazzo Colonna. He had to wait about twenty minutes before a car drew up at the kerb. It was a dark blue Fiat *macchina di rappresentanza* of the type associated with high-level government officials. The driver stepped out and opened the back door for Zen to enter. He was a young man, short and swarthy even for a southerner, with intensely black eyes and hair, wearing a superannuated suit slightly too tight for his bulky physique, a white shirt and blue tie and an incongruous peaked cap. He looked like a part-time assistant to a cut-price provincial undertaker.

Gilberto acknowledged Zen with a deliberately casual nod, and then added an incomprehensible aside to the driver before closing the glass partition to the front compartment.

'What was that?' asked Zen as the Fiat squealed away.

'Just giving Ahmed directions.'

Zen thought about this for a second, then decided to ignore it.

'Glad you're free for lunch,' he said brightly. 'Where are we going?'

Gilberto pushed a button on the console in the central arm-rest. There was a whirr of machinery as opaque blinds descended over all the windows and the glass partition, cutting them off totally from the outside world.

'What on earth?' exclaimed Zen.

Gilberto laughed and pressed another button, lighting up the sealed interior.

'Hope you don't mind, Aurelio, but the answer to your question about lunch is a bit of a secret, actually. You'll understand once we get there.'

'How did you ever get hold of this beast? I thought they were all reserved for the top dogs.'

'So, what am I, shit?'

'No, but you were up to your neck in it, the last I heard.'

'That was before the revolution. You're not really keeping up with current affairs, are you, Aurelio? Of course for you state employees there's no need. But some things have changed there too, like these cars. Obviously *il Cavaliere* didn't want his people driving around in cars produced by *l'Avvocato*.'

Zen's faint smile acknowledged this reference to the legendary enmity between the Prime Minister and Giovanni Agnelli, the creator of Fiat.

'Besides, there was the whole question of image,' Nieddu went on enthusiastically. 'One of the many aspects of Berlusconi's genius is that he is the first politician since Mussolini to grasp the vital importance of presentation. That's why he was able to defeat his opponents so convincingly last time out. All the little lefties were sitting around discussing real issues, matters of substance and policy, and then of course disagreeing and splitting into factions and insulting each other and telling people at all costs not to vote for the ideological heretics who had failed to grasp the correct course of action at this historically significant moment, etcetera, etcetera. Meanwhile Silvio just sat there, smiling at you from posters, magazines and TV programmes, looking every inch the man of power that he is and never making the mistake of mentioning any concrete proposals or programmes. "Trust me", was the message. And the voters did. He didn't win the election. His opponents lost it.'

'With a little help from the press and TV, most of which he owns.'

'So did the Christian Democrats and the Socialists and Communists back in the old days. That's not the point. People have had enough, Aurelio! That's what it comes down to. Take these cars, for example. They're like those ZIP limos that the Politburo used to drive around in. In the public mind, they're associated with the former regime, with cliques, cabals, corruption and all the endless *misteri d'Italia*. Did Andreotti have Mino Pecorelli and Della Chiesa killed? What really happened to La Malfa? Who planted the bomb in Piazza Fontana? How and why did Roberto Calvi die? The truth is that no one cares about all that stuff any more. Berlusconi knows it, so he dumps the whole fleet, allowing yours truly to pick up this rather toney low-mileage vehicle at a knockdown price. Not only that, but since the association with unquestioned power and prestige still operates at a subliminal level, Ahmed can indulge his distinctive driving style, which was honed at the wheel of a jeep in the Taurus mountains incidentally. He therefore has a natural tendency to ignore the presence of other traffic unless it's very heavily armed and armoured.'

Zen didn't reply. Indeed, he hadn't really been paying attention to Gilberto's rant, but rather to the sounds and feel of the car's progress around corners, piazzas and junctions, over cobblestones, paving blocks and asphalt pitted by tram lines.

'I didn't know there were any good restaurants in Prenestino,' he remarked at length.

Gilberto laughed indulgently.

'Very good, Aurelio! I should have known better than to try and fool you. But in fact we're going a bit further out than Prenestino. It's not exactly a restaurant, either, more the staff canteen. But you'll eat well, and the price is definitely right. Anyway, enough of this. What do you want from me this time?'

'Nothing. I told you.'

'And my mother told me that *la befana* wouldn't bring me any presents at Christmas if I wasn't a good boy. I didn't believe her either. Come on, Aurelio. I really don't mind, but let's just get it over with so that we can both enjoy our lunch in peace.'

Zen slapped his friend on the thigh.

'Gilberto, I swear by all that's holy that when I called you this morning from the train I just wanted to have lunch and catch up on how things are going. But as it happens something did come up subsequently that you might be able to help with. It's a question of some digital photographs that I need to have enhanced. Well, one of them anyway. I've got a compressed file on disk with me. It would need to be unzipped, of course.'

He sat back, feeling slightly smug at his command of this jargon. Gilberto, on the other hand, took not the slightest notice.

'Of course,' he said, opening a cabinet invisibly recessed in the walnut facia before them and taking out a flask of clear liquid and two small glasses. He filled the glasses on the shelf provided by the hatch of the cabinet, then added mineral water from a small plastic bottle. The liquid in the glasses turned a cloudy white. Gilberto passed one to Zen.

'*Salute!*'

Zen sniffed the glass. The odour was overpowering, but it took him a moment to realize what it was. Liquorice was one of those childhood delicacies that he had forgotten about.

'Like it?'

Gilberto had downed his glass and was lighting a cigarette.

'What is it?' Zen asked, taking a sip.

'Damned if I know. A variety of arak, I suppose. They're not supposed to drink at all, of course, but . . .'

'Who are you talking about?'

Nieddu turned to him with a teasing smile.

'You're supposed to be a detective, Aurelio. I've already given you three clues.'

Zen dug out his own cigarettes.

'I'm a police investigator, Gilberto,' he said in a stiff tone that immediately sounded silly to him.

'Ah, right. So what are you investigating at present?'

The car had left the main road and was turning this way and that through a grid of side streets, often slowing or braking sharply.

'You can't expect me to tell you that. Particularly when you won't even tell me where we're going.'

'Fair enough. I just thought it might have something to do with Nestore, you see.'

'Who?'

'Nestore Soldani. A former business associate of mine.'

'Never heard of him.'

Gilberto peered at him with something like disbelief.

'Don't you watch the news? It's been a big story for the last two days. Someone planted about a kilo of weapons-grade explosive under the driving seat of his car.'

'I've been away. Work. Haven't had time to watch TV.'

The car made a left turn on to a deeply potholed surface, then veered sharply right and came to rest. The driver leapt out and opened the door on Gilberto's side. He then ran around to assist Zen, but he had already managed for himself. The car was parked in the yard of what looked like a factory dating from the *abusivo* building boom of the sixties or seventies. Nieddu opened a rusting metal door in the wall, then led the way along a corridor and up a flight of bare concrete steps.

'This way,' he said, opening a door to the left.

The room inside was cramped, stuffy and unattractive. A desk piled with papers and computer equipment stood at one end, a low coffee table and two chairs at the other. A dour-looking elderly woman appeared at a door at the far end of the room and said something incomprehensible. Without glancing at her, Nieddu replied in the same manner.

'What language is that?' asked Zen.

'Kurdish.'

'You speak Kurdish?'

'A few phrases. It's all I need. Give me the file with the photographs.'

Zen handed it over. Nieddu slipped it into the computer and busied himself with the mouse and the keyboard for a few moments.

'OK, here they are,' he said. 'Which one was it you wanted enhanced?'

Zen studied the images on screen, then pointed.

'That one.'

The gallery disappeared and was replaced by a full-size display of the picture he had selected, showing an almost unrecognizably broken body.

'Hmm, very dead,' commented Nieddu.

'A climbing accident,' Zen explained.

'Don't bother lying, Aurelio. It's boring for both of us. Which bit do you want to know more about?'

'Right here, the mark on his arm.'

Gilberto examined the screen more closely for some time, then stood up and looked Zen in the eyes.

'You said you weren't investigating that business,' he said very quietly.

'What are you talking about?'

'I'm talking about Nestore Soldani! You tell me you'd never heard of him, then hand me a disk containing a shocking image of his corpse, hoping that I'll crack, break down and spill the beans. They said in the papers that no traces of the body had been found, but of course that was just another lie. Still the old-style hard-line *commissariato* techniques, eh Aurelio? The country's changed all around you, but you're too busy working to keep track of what's going on, just like Berlusconi's opponents. You've learnt nothing and forgotten nothing.'

Zen gripped his friend's arm tightly.

'For the love of God, Gilberto, calm down! Listen, this friend of yours, this Nestore, what happened to him?'

'You know what happened!'

'I swear to you that I don't.'

'Everyone else in the country does! He was blown up in his car at the entrance to his villa in Campione.'

Zen released Nieddu's arm.

'Then there's no connection. This photograph is of a corpse which was found in a remote area of the mountains east of Bolzano. No villas, no cars.'

Nieddu stabbed at the screen.

'Then what about the tattoo? Nestore had one just like that on his arm.'

Zen shrugged.

'Plenty of men have tattoos. Even women, these days.'

'It's the same, I tell you!'

They were interrupted by the elderly woman barging in with a large tray which she set down on a low table. It was covered with dishes of food of a kind utterly unfamiliar to Zen. Gilberto said something in the guttural language he had used before. The woman bowed to both men and left, closing the door behind her.

'You swear you knew nothing about this?' Gilberto asked Zen solemnly.

'On my mother's grave.'

Nieddu nodded curtly.

'All right, let's eat.'

'What is this stuff?' Zen asked as they sat down at the low table.

Nieddu produced a bottle of white wine and another of mineral water from a small fridge in the corner.

'The local cuisine,' Gilberto replied, pointing. '*Kelemî, niskan, hevîr. U gost*, I think. *Lortek, balcanres, ciz biz, gostê ristî* . . . Not sure about that one, but it's all delicious. The only exception is the beverage they favour, some concoction made from soured milk. One taste I've failed to acquire. Normally I just have one or two of these dishes, but I told Tavora that I was entertaining a guest today so she laid on a feast. In their culture, where famine has always been a threat, it's very important that on a special occasion there should be too much food served. But don't worry, just have what you want. Anything we don't eat will be used up.'

Gingerly at first, then with increasing appetite, Zen began to sample the plates of grilled meats, vegetables, bulgar wheat and rounds of bread like very thin pizza crust. It was indeed all delicious.

'So how did you get involved with these people?' Zen asked.

'Well, they're illegals, of course. Their country, which doesn't exist, has been a war zone since anyone can remember. Historically, the only choice the Kurds have had is whether they want to be oppressed and massacred by the Iranians, the Iraqis or the Turks. So many of them try to leave. A few, like this lot, make it.'

'And where do you fit in?'

'I'm not doing it as a humanitarian gesture, needless to say. They wouldn't accept that anyway. Very proud bunch. Basically what happened was that our needs coincided. These people – they're all part of the same family, incidentally – needed food, lodging and protection from the authorities. I needed a loyal and trustworthy work force. I was introduced to the head of the clan through contacts in the city down in Puglia where their ship landed and we struck a deal. I've kept my side of the bargain and they've kept theirs. And Rosa is delighted, needless to say. If I even thought about making a pass at one of the younger women, they'd get to me before she did. With these people, it's marriage or death.'

'How many of them do you employ?'

'Thirty or forty. It's hard to keep count. Anyway, I leave that sort of thing to their boss. They all live and work here, don't speak Italian, and almost never leave the compound. It's a bit like one of those abandoned farm complexes you see from the motorway in the Po valley . . .'

'*Cascine.*'

'That's right. The landowner housed and fed the sharecroppers who worked for him. It was like a little village. Well, that's what I'm doing here.'

'But what do they do for you?'

'Ah well, that's something I'd rather not go into.'

'So it's illegal.'

Gilberto looked pained.

'Really, Aurelio! Must you use these crude terms? You're completely out of step with the new way of thinking. The Italian people have re-elected as their prime minister a man who is under investigation, amongst nine other charges, for having paid a judge half a million dollars to find in his favour over a take-over battle. His first action on taking office was to ram through changes in the law to prevent the case going to court before the statute of limitations runs out, and he's now trying to pass another one that will give him the right to select the judge of his choice before the case goes to trial. And you're asking *me* if what I'm doing is illegal?'

Zen laughed.

'Anyway, it's not,' Nieddu went on. 'Well, not seriously illegal. Just an import and distribution operation.'

'Drugs, I suppose.'

Unexpectedly, Gilberto also laughed.

'That's right, drugs. And cigarettes, but only for my personal use. A nostalgia thing. In the Third World, the packets don't come with all that stuff about cancer being bad for you. Here, that's about all they do say. Pretty soon they'll pass a law making the health warning bigger than the packet. You'll ask the *tabaccaio*,

"Can I have a health warning, please?", and there'll be a pack of cigarettes stuck to the back of it.'

He clapped his hands loudly. The woman appeared and removed the tray of uneaten food, then returned with a pot of coffee and two cups.

'So where do you want me to send the blow-ups of those photos?' Gilberto demanded.

'You're still willing to do it?'

'Not personally. I don't have the equipment. But I know someone who does, and he's fast and discreet.'

'I thought that after that business about . . .'

'Don't be ridiculous! I said I would do it and I'll do it. That's what I like about these Kurds. As long as you're family, and I'm honorary family, they never break their word.'

'I'm not family,' said Zen.

Gilberto smiled.

'You saved my marriage. That makes you honorary family. Do you have a computer?'

'Gemma does.'

'Nice to hear that you know someone who's living in the twenty-first century. Is she on-line?'

'On which line?'

Gilberto mimed exasperated despair.

'Can her computer talk to other computers?'

'I think so. Yes, it must do, the one at the pharmacy. She places her orders that way.'

Gilberto looked intently.

'She's a pharmacist? Well, well.'

'What do you mean?'

'Never mind. What's the address?'

'I'm not sure. It's in Lucca, Via Fillungo, but I don't know the number.'

Gilberto gave him another crushing look, then produced a business card and handed it to Zen.

'Give this to her and tell her to send me a blank email. As soon as the enhancement is ready, I'll attach it and send it back.'

Zen poured them both more coffee and lit a cigarette.

'Tell me about Nestore Soldani,' he said.

Nieddu took an almost physical distance by his look.

'You told me that he had nothing to do with the case you're investigating.'

'Absolutely not, Gilberto. But you say it's been a lead story for several days. I'll be dropping into the Ministry before meeting Gemma at the station, and I might be able to find out who is working on it, maybe pick up a few details to pass on to you.'

He sat back and shut up. Gilberto Nieddu nursed his coffee and his cigarette for so long that Zen thought the gamble lost, but then he put both down and started to talk in an even, unemotional tone.

'I first met Nestore in the late eighties, through a mutual friend. I'd just left the police and gone into the electronic security and espionage business. Soldani had just left the army and was looking for work. He'd been an officer in the Alpini – a volunteer, if you can believe that. Anyway, he had skills I needed and I used him on a few jobs, but he was too ambitious to stick with me for very long. The next thing I heard, he'd moved to Venezuela and had set up a variety of operations similar to those that I've been involved with over the years.'

'Meaning illegal,' risked Zen.

Gilberto Nieddu modulated one hand in mid-air.

'On the cusp, Aurelio. On the cusp.'

He stubbed out his cigarette and glanced at the clock on the wall.

'Venezuela has rich resources of oil, as you probably know. We have none. Soldani also had contacts, notably a former comrade-in-arms who had even more contacts, some with high management figures in the state petrol firm AGIP. In short, Nestore was able to facilitate a very lucrative and mutually advantageous deal between the respective governments involved, undercutting the price to which Venezuela was officially committed by its agreements with the other OPEC countries. He took an appropriate percentage and then wisely decided to quit while he was ahead and retire to the old country before things turned politically nasty in Caracas, which they did very soon afterwards. But of course he couldn't be sure what his reception would be this end either, so he played it clever. Whilst over there, he changed his name, just to be on the safe side, took out Venezuelan citizenship under his new identity and then moved to Campione d'Italia. He bought a property there, which you have to do in order to become resident, and then got in touch with me out of the blue. I think he may have been a bit lonely. He invited me to come and stay, but I never got around to it. We were never close. As I said, it was a business relationship, while it lasted. But I was still shocked to read about what happened to him.'

Zen nodded and stood up.

'So who do you think did it?'

Gilberto Nieddu shrugged.

'Who knows? Nestore probably had other irons in the fire, stuff he hadn't told me about. He claimed that he'd retired, which he could certainly have afforded to do, but men like that never really retire, any more than you or I ever will. Fine, everything's perfect and life's a bowl of cherries, but how are you going to get through the day? Nestore would have been wheeling and dealing within ten minutes of hitting the runway at Malpensa, and he wasn't one to avoid risk. Rather the contrary, in fact. I can even imagine him courting it, particularly at his age. So I can only suppose that he got entangled with some real nasties, underestimated the threat and got rubbed out.'

Zen nodded neutrally but did not move.

'That tattoo,' he said.

'What about it?'

'You recognized it immediately, even from the un-enhanced print.'

'Back when he was working for me, Nestore used to wear short-sleeved shirts if the weather was warm. Showing off his biceps and chest hair, the macho look. The tattoo was very distinctive. I commented on it.'

'Distinctive in what way?'

'It was quite small and detailed.'

'What did it show?'

'A woman's head.'

'No script?'

'No. Just the head, covered in hair in one of those ethnic styles. You know, sort of dreadlocks.'

'Did you ask him what it signified?'

'I can't remember. No, wait a moment. I think he said it was something he'd had done while he was in the army. Some sort of fraternity for the junior officers. Anyway, I may be mistaken about the resemblance. Once the enhancement's been done we'll know for sure. They can do amazing things now, setting off one fragment against another in contrasting colours and so on. I should be able to send you something in the next couple of days, depending on how busy they are. Meanwhile, Ahmed will drive you wherever you want to go. For both our sakes, please keep the blinds closed until you are well clear of this area. You have your life, Aurelio, and I have mine. In either case, a little knowledge can be a dangerous thing.'

'Is his name really Ahmed?'

'Do you know, I've never asked.'

IX

Claudia called for the car at eleven. The sun had come out, and the air flowing in through the opened windows of the apartment seemed to be starting to warm up. Not actually hot, of course, not at this time of year, but still possible.

The traffic, on the other hand, was impossible, as usual. Where had all these people come from? What were they doing there? Where were they going, and why? There were just too many of them, that was the problem. Other people were like food or drink, or lovers for that matter. What you needed was 'an adequate sufficiency', as her father used to say. Anything more was not only superfluous, but potentially noxious.

When her parents were still alive, there had been no need for cars. They would just walk from their town house to Porta San Giorgio, take the chuffing train that went out into the Valpolicella and on to the shores of Lake Garda, and then alight in the straggly village where the villa stood almost opposite the station. But now the train had gone, like her parents, like the villa itself. Like Leonardo.

Lost in her memories, Claudia was a second or two late noticing that the traffic light had changed. Some sharply-dressed teenage whippersnapper promptly recalled her to her duties as a responsible road user with three aggressive blasts on the horn, and then, while she was still groping for the gear lever, cut in front of her with insolent ease, as if to say 'Time to check into the nursing home, Grandma!' Bastards. It wasn't just that there were so many of them, and the majority so young and contemptuous, but that all sense of decorum had been lost. Everyone was out for what they could get, like a brood of *contadini* snatching the only drinking mug in the house from each other's hands.

It suddenly occurred to her that the reason why she had such happy memories of the villa was that her parents had always seemed happy there. Well, one of the reasons. But perhaps that explained the Leonardo business as well. Like any child, she had desperately wanted her parents to be happy, but she didn't know how to help them and they didn't seem able to help themselves. Adults were supposed to know how to do things, but Claudia had realized very early on that her parents were utterly useless when it came to happiness. They didn't have the first clue. Except at the villa. Which was presumably why, in her mind, it had become a magic place, with limitless and beneficent powers.

The vanished railway had run alongside the road, so once the gridlock of the city fell behind Claudia was able to follow her childhood journeys in her mind, marking the stops that the train had made and the things which had happened there. That was where the terrifying lady had complimented her on her gloves. One wore gloves then, of course. '*La contessa Ardigò*,' her mother had whispered, once the fearful apparition had alighted. And that other time, much later, in her teens, when a young *contadino* had taken something from his trousers and sprayed her with it like a water-pistol. It had smelt alkaline; strong, but not disgusting.

On this occasion her mother had made no comment, since the incident had happened while Claudia was standing alone on the vestibule at the rear of the train, admiring the view, and she hadn't felt it necessary to share the experience with her parents. She was already aware that there were many matters in their own lives that they did not share with her, so she had just been returning the compliment really, proving what a well-brought-up young woman she was, thanks to their constant and 'ruinously expensive' – her father – provisions for her. There were certain things that a lady did not discuss, even with her parents.

Thirty minutes after leaving Verona, Claudia reached the outskirts of the village, now even more straggly than before. She turned right past a garish concrete block of apartments into what was still a country road, then left into the lane behind the former property and parked in the shadow of the high wall whose every stone had seemed to her, as a child, to be formed from the compacted essence of those blessed souls dwelling in paradise of which the priests spoke.

None of the new houses on the other side of the lane – infill from the boom years of the economic miracle that had given the Veneto a higher per capita GPA than Switzerland – showed any sign of life at all. It took her a tremendous effort to acknowledge that they were really there, let alone inhabited. In Claudia's mind, that space would always be a bare upward slope of farmland lined with vines strung on wires.

She got out of the car and walked over to the green wooden door in the wall. All this stuff about her parents! She had made an agreement with herself not to think about that. And especially not about Leonardo or the later consequences. But it hadn't seemed to work. Whatever one was not supposed to think about ended up occupying more brain room than the things you were supposed to think about. It was like a tax that had to be paid on oblivion. Sometimes she wondered if it was worth it.

She unlocked the garden door, went through and locked it behind her. Then, eyes closed, she turned around and leant back against its wooden boards. At least a minute passed before she opened her eyes again. It was all right. Everything was just as it ought to be, just as she had left it. The principal joy of the garden was that she had absolute control over it. So she did theoretically over the apartment in Verona, of course, but people came and went there, even if by invitation only, and left unmistakable traces of their presence behind. The garden was a pristine zone. No one ever came here except her. And Naldino, once. That had been only fair and natural. Here, after all, he had been conceived.

Her destination was to her left, but she didn't glance that way, preferring as always to proceed by indirection. She walked along the gravel path winding beneath the tall sycamores and holm oaks, nodding in a familiar, slightly bored manner to the mould-stained bust on its plinth, as one did to a servant, before moving on towards the pond where obese carp glided past below the screen of water lilies.

Ahead of her now was the line of cypresses that she had planted to prevent the garden being overlooked from the new apartment block beyond. They were ugly beasts, but had grown out fast over the years, just as the nurseryman had promised, shooting up and filling in so as to completely conceal the high wall that she had insisted that the developers build to seal off her remaining parcel of property. Such had been her idea, and it had worked perfectly. The line of trees served its purpose, but in another sense it didn't really exist at all, any more than the backdrop at the theatre that everyone is aware of but which no one looks at. What counted was what lay in front of it, not the painted curtain or the strident barricade of bare concrete behind. Only the stage mattered, and that was set, lit and glowing with atmosphere.

Now it was time to turn back, crossing the grassy sward to reach another path strewn with a thin layer of blackened gravel. The two branches had originally met, further up the property, and had led to the double glass doors of the villa which gave out on to the garden. Her destination was in sight now, but she still didn't look at it, keeping her eyes on the ground before her or the trees above. Every step she took, each move she made, was strictly choreographed, a ritual dance. For this was sacred ground. The usual rules were suspended here, supplanted by a much more rigid set.

Once she had passed the huge elm tree that dominated this corner of the garden, it was permissible to look up and take in the miniature house with its green door and shutters. One rationale for this ritual was that she was always irrationally convinced that the house wouldn't be there. The villa had gone, as had so many other things, and all of the people concerned. Why shouldn't this, in many ways the most unreal of all, prove to have been just another of the false memories that her imagination was throwing up with increasing frequency these days, in its vain attempts to explain the inexplicable?

She got the key out of her pocket with her right hand, then transferred it to her left. This too was part of the ritual, for when the little house had magically appeared, on her seventh birthday, she had been *mancina*. It had taken a lot of time, and much pain, for her parents and teachers to cure her of her perverse left-handedness, with its implication of being one of the sinister, of having been touched by the Adversary.

But her parents had also given her this house, perhaps in part as recompense. Many of her memories might have been falsified, but not those of that birthday. The work had been done secretly, over the winter, and her parents had played their part to the hilt. When the day came, they had tied a length of muslin across her eyes and then led her down the garden of the villa amid a banter of jokes and teasing phrases, before placing her just right and then removing the blindfold. And she literally had not been able to believe her eyes. Nothing in the rest of her life – not even Leonardo – had been as magical and as sweet as that moment.

As the front door creaked open, the odours leapt up and assailed her. She stooped to pass under the lintel, then straightened up as much as she could, her hair brushing against the ceiling. The first time she had taken him there, Leonardo had immediately banged his head on a beam and fallen against her, perhaps in surprise. They were wearing only their swimming costumes, and both had laughed excessively at this bizarre accident befalling two adults in a house made for a child. A light sprinkle of plaster dust had coated Claudia's bare shoulders and the upper slopes of her breasts. Leonardo had solicitously brushed it away, with many apologies for his clumsiness.

Against the wall to her left, between the windows, hung a blank banner of black satin. Her mother had not permitted mirrors in the family apartment in Verona, except in the bathroom, claiming in her some-times slightly creepy *Südtirolisch* way that they stole your soul. But in the case of Claudia's playhouse her father had prevailed, arguing that it would make the main room seem lighter and bigger. After Leonardo's death, she had not been able to bring herself to remove or destroy this mirror which had witnessed so much, but neither could she bear to meet its implacable gaze, so she had covered it over with a layer of cloth.

Below it stood a tiny dresser, a perfectly propor-tioned miniature replica of the one in the living room of the apartment, and indeed by the same manufac-turer. She opened the cupboard and retrieved one of the bottles of Cinzano Rosso she kept stacked there, then took a glass from the shelf above. The sweet red liquid, tinged with bitterness at the edges, flowed down her throat and brought a summery glow to her body. The light glowing through the squat four-paned windows was thin and weak, but with the help of the alcohol it created the right effect. The angle of the sun around the equinox was of course identical at either end of the year, but autumn had all the momentum of summer behind it, while winter's exhaustion held spring back.

Now she moved across the room, past the fireplace, the table and chairs, and the pretend stove on which she had lovingly cooked pretend meals for her dolls. The door at the end led to the bedroom where she had taken a nap after lunch every summer day as a child. The rules had been clear. Nights had to be spent in her room at the villa, but this house was hers during the day. Her parents were not permitted to intrude, although Claudia had contrived to invite some of her school-friends. She had made the most of that privacy and freedom then, and even more later.

She closed the door behind her and hung her coat on the peg behind it, despite the fact that the lower half trailed on the tiled floor, then lay down in a foetal crouch on the tiny wooden bed. The pillow absorbed her head and released its own hoarded scents in return. This bedding had never been washed since the first time that she and Leonardo had lain there. She could still smell the hair lotion he had used, and more, the very scent of *him*. Curiously, her own she could not distinguish, although it must profusely have been there.

But how had it all begun?

Her glib memories, when she consulted them, tended to unreel the affair like a film or a play, where every action and phrase is foreknown and inevitable, but they were false. It hadn't been like that. It couldn't have been. On the contrary, not the least of the thrills involved had been that they were both finding their way all the time, each of them anticipating an excruciatingly embarrassing rebuff at any moment.

The very fact that Leonardo had come out from his barracks in Verona to the villa, one weekend when he must have known that Gaetano was away at a NATO conference in Brussels, 'in order to return some books on military history that Colonel Comai was kind enough to lend me', incurred a slight risk in itself.

Claudia had received him on the patio behind the villa. She had been swimming in the small pool that had now been buried beneath the concrete parking lot of the new apartment block, and was wearing her bikini with a towelling robe over it. It was an August afternoon, a still, massy heat that threatened thunder.

He had apologized profusely for disturbing her and kept rather distractedly insisting that he should leave at once. Claudia had invited him to stay for tea, and had succeeded in making him feel that it would be impolite to refuse. She had then removed the towelling robe, with the excuse that it felt clammy, and clad only in the bikini had basked in the sun for some time, prompting the tongue-tied young lieutenant with a series of questions about his family, background and aspirations. She had not looked at him, but had felt very strongly his eyes upon her. When tea was brought, she had slipped back up to her room in the villa and returned wearing a silk wrap that she allowed to fall open from time to time, particularly when she leaned forward to pour the tea. When he finally left, she had told him that he was most welcome to return at any suitable time.

'You don't need to invent excuses,' she'd told him. 'I get quite lonely and bored here when Gaetano's away. I would welcome some company.'

No, that couldn't be right. She would never have been so forward, so *obvious*. Not the first time, anyway. And even if she had, he would never have taken her up on it, fearing some disgrace that could ruin his career for ever. So how had it all begun?

Of one thing she was sure. Their initial meeting, outwardly unexceptionable, had been at the regiment's annual dinner and ball, an occasion that could hardly have been more public. The colonel had naturally introduced some of his 'stable', as he called them, to his much younger wife, and then encouraged them – under the circumstances, practically ordered them – to dance with her. His legs were already giving him hell, the merest intimations of the torment to come later, when they'd had to have the chair lift installed at the villa. At that stage Gaetano could still stand, walk and, when required, march without undue difficulty, but he couldn't have danced with any pleasure, even if he'd wanted to. As it happened he didn't, but neither did he want Claudia to be left seated with him, a sad wallflower, while the other wives tripped the light fantastic and engaged in a bit of mild and utterly harmless flirtation.

Lieutenant Ferrero had taken up his duties with an alacrity which Claudia had initially ascribed to the young man's desire to ingratiate himself with his commanding officer. They had performed a polka, a gavotte and a foxtrot together before Leonardo relinquished her to one of his fellow officers. She had wanted him immediately, of course, and equally immediately dismissed the thought. Quite apart from anything else, she was well aware of being about ten years his senior. As a military city of long standing, Verona had more than its share of 'barracks blowflies', as they were known. Lieutenant Ferrero would have had no difficulty in getting his needs attended to quickly, safely and cheaply.

But at the end of the evening he had returned, and in a subtly different manner requested Claudia's company for the last dance, a slow waltz. She had been wearing a silk shawl, but the hall was so hot and stuffy now that she removed it, making the full effect of her very low-cut dress visible for the first time.

As soon as the music started, she became aware that something was wrong. Earlier, Leonardo had been an exemplary partner, moving gracefully, always dead on the beat, never leading aggressively nor hanging behind. Now he seemed to have turned slightly spastic. His body was bent at an odd angle, and his movements seemed gauche and inhibited. He might almost have been Gaetano, on the few occasions when she had managed to tempt him on to the dance floor.

When she tightened her arm on her partner's back, pulling him towards her, trying to straighten him up, the reason for his awkwardness became apparent: a massive erection that even his military-issue underpants were barely able to restrain. Their eyes met and locked. *Das Blick*, her mother had told her once. That was where love began. All it took was that unfakeable, petrifying look, and you were lost.

Nevertheless, as yet nothing had in fact been lost. They remained the only people present who were aware of what had happened. At the conclusion of the dance, Leonardo, now making no attempt to conceal his predicament from her, had very correctly returned her to her husband's side without a word spoken, bidden them both goodnight and left with his fellow officers. Then, ten days later, he had appeared uninvited at the villa, supposedly to return some books. Nothing illicit had occurred at that meeting either. Gaetano had been abroad, but the servants were very much in evidence and Claudia was expecting a woman friend for dinner that evening.

So how had the affair itself begun? Another meeting at the villa had been arranged, that much was certain. And it must have been done in person, face to face, before Leonardo caught the train back to Verona that first time. There were no mobile phones in those days. All calls to the barracks went through the switchboard, and as desperate as she had been, Claudia would never have risked putting anything in writing. The most insistent of the versions that presented themselves to her now had it that she had invited him – on the front step of the villa, completely out of the blue, dismayed by the imminent prospect of his physical absence – to return the following Wednesday. She might have told him that she was having some friends over for the day, an interesting and influential couple who might well prove helpful to his career. She had certainly known that her husband would be attending a two-day meeting at the Defence Ministry in Rome to report on the NATO conference.

She had given the servants those two days off, explaining that in her husband's absence she would be returning to Verona. There was still the risk of snooping neighbours, of chance encounters in the village, even of Gaetano's unannounced return due to illness or a cancellation. In short, she had gone slightly mad, deranged not so much by the sexual prospects in store, although that was a powerful drug, as by an irresistible sensation that the contingent chaos of everyday life was finally cohering into a meaningful narrative that she had to follow, no matter where it might lead.

Yes, but how had it all begun?

However the invitation had been phrased, Leonardo had come, and to the tradesmen's entrance at the side of the villa, which Claudia had left open. She explained this by saying that it was the servants' day off and that she would be entertaining her guests by the pool in the garden and might not hear the doorbell. In reality it had been to minimize the possibility of his being seen by prying eyes.

She had been swimming topless in the pool when he arrived, and for a moment she thought she had been too brazen and ruined everything. Confused by her nudity and the absence of any other people, Leonardo looked as though he was about to bolt at any moment. When she picked up the towel she had left at the edge of the pool, wrapped it around her torso and climbed out, he had accepted with a brief nod her story about how the other couple had cancelled at the last moment for family reasons. She had calmed him down by putting her top back on and then producing a man's swimsuit from the wicker chest where the towels were kept and insisting that he go into the house and put it on. She kept a variety of spare suits for visitors, she said, in case they had neglected to bring their own. In reality, the suit was Gaetano's.

Leonardo had obeyed her instructions, like the polite young man he was. When he emerged from the villa, Claudia had to fight very hard against her instinct to stare shamelessly at the swimsuit, so very much more interesting did it appear than when worn by her husband. They both went into the water and swam energetically for some time, pretending to each other and to themselves that this was the point of the exercise. Then they emerged, rubbed themselves roughly dry, and lay down side by side on the large beach towels spread out in the sun.

After a while, Claudia had sat up and started applying Ambre Solaire to all the bits of her that she could reach, chattering on the whole time about the extreme sensitivity of her skin and the potentially disastrous effects of the August sun. She had then turned over and asked Leonardo to spread some of the fragrant bronze oil on her back, please. Oh, and just undo the strap of my top, would you, so as not to leave a white strip on the tan. She might even have told him to rub her harder to make sure that the oil penetrated the skin deeply, or some such nonsense. It had been like revisiting her adolescence, but with all the knowledge and authority of her current position. Which she had used quite mercilessly. She wouldn't have put anything past her.

He'd complied with her instructions without a word, but stopped when he came to her buttocks, but she'd asked him to keep going, yes, and her thighs as well please, all the way up to the costume, because the skin was so sensitive there and even a minor burn could be agonizingly painful. He knelt close above her to do this work, straddling one of her legs with his, and from time to time their bodies had touched.

Once it was over, he lay down beside her again. They didn't speak – the heat permitted that – but she knew that he was looking at her and lifted herself up on her elbows to reach for her cigarettes, her breasts just clearing the reclining bikini top so that her nipples showed a few centimetres from his fingers. But still he made no move.

When he finally announced, in his oh-so-well-brought-up voice, that he really should be getting back, thank you so much for inviting me, it's been a great pleasure, she thought that she'd lost. And if she lost that day, she would have lost everything. Her pride would not have permitted her to make a similar demonstration again without an appropriate response from him.

Then she'd had her great insight, her stroke of genius.

'Very well,' she'd said, getting to her feet, 'but before you go you must come and look at the little house down at the bottom of the garden. My parents had it built for me when I turned seven and I've kept everything just the way it was. It's a quite extraordinary place, like something in a fairy tale. In fact I think it must be unique. You feel as though you've left the real world behind from the moment you cross the threshold.'

He had of course agreed, like the polite young man he was, and pronounced himself duly impressed with the exterior, which she told him had been faced by real craftsmen, the kind you couldn't find any longer, using the best stone from the quarries at San Giorgio di Valpolicella. They went inside, giggling and joking about the diminutive size of the entrance, and Claudia closed the door.

Straightening up instinctively, Leonardo had knocked his head on the ceiling, sprinkling her with plaster which he apologetically brushed off. But the movements of his fingers continued long after the last traces of white dust had vanished, becoming slower and slower even as his breathing became ever more rapid. Their eyes met, exactly as they had that first time. Only now they could do something about it. Claudia placed one hand on his back, just where it had been during the waltz, and pulled him urgently towards her, her other hand at the nape of his neck, dragging his open mouth down on hers. And then . . .

That was how she remembered it, most of the time at least. But she also knew that memories change a little each time you revisit them, and she had revisited these memories just about every day and night of her life since Leonardo died. By now she had no clear idea how much was original and how much a replica, more strongly engineered in order to support the weight of the significance the whole event now had for her. Perhaps the literal truth had been erased by the version that had now supplanted it. Perhaps it had been too humdrum and confused, a documentary patched together from faded photographs and old newsreels where everyone walks too fast, rather than a Hollywood movie with glamorous stars, perfectly realized production values and a sense of knowing exactly where it is going.

She rose from the bed, brushing off her clothes. The play-house was filthy, but she couldn't bring herself to clean anything here. The only real evidence was the fading prints they had taken later with the new instant camera that Paloroid had brought out at about that time. She eyed the drawer in the chest beside the bed where she kept The Book, but left it closed. The last time she had looked at the photographs she had been sickened. She looked puffy and unhappy, Leonardo gawky and awkward, and everything was so matter of fact. No, there was nothing to be gained from that. The material had to be lovingly preserved but it didn't need to be viewed, any more than one would wish to view the remains of some dear departed beneath his immaculately tended grave.

This was the house of memory, the house of remembrance, sealed off from the ravages of time. Gaetano had set foot in it just once, immediately after Claudia had inherited the villa on her mother's death, only to declare that it should be demolished and replaced by a vegetable garden. But Claudia, as custodian, had prevailed, pointing out that the expense of demolishing such a substantial structure would be far more than the resulting plot was worth, and also discreetly suggesting that their children could play there just as she once had. She had wanted that, she had wanted them. She had not known that there would be no children with Gaetano, that his sperm was no good.

Gaetano had never raised the matter again, and Claudia had curated the little house with loving care for over a quarter of a century, even renouncing a sizeable sum of money to retain it when she had sold the rest of the property to the development company that had demolished the villa to build that block of condominiums. It had often occurred to her that she must have been mad so to do, so pointless could it seem on her bad days, but now she was vindicated. It all made sense!

She had of course never thought that Leonardo would ever die, let alone before her. And even if he had, his parents would have been given the body, had there been one. But according to Danilo that beloved body had miraculously resurfaced somewhere, somehow, in conditions of the greatest secrecy. Perhaps Leonardo's parents did not know. As far as they were concerned, their son had died in that plane crash. For that matter, they might well be dead themselves by now. The outcome was clear: the body must be brought back here. This was where it belonged, not in some alien cemetery.

She poured herself one more glass of Cinzano Rosso before replacing the bottle. But what about the Ferrero family? The parents might be dead, but hadn't he had siblings? Two sisters, she seemed to recall. And even if they made no legal claim to the remains, how could she possibly do so? It would mean disclosing everything, and that might well prove fatal. The law didn't care about love, but it cared very much about murder. It would be sheer insanity for her to take any kind of initiative in the matter.

She finished her drink and went back outside, locking the door of the miniature house behind her. What a beautiful dream, though, to be able to scatter Leonardo's ashes amongst these trees! That would close the circle, and ease the pain that had gnawed at her ever since his death. It would be a very private ceremony, just her and her lover, on a day like this at the end of summer, with all nature stooping for renewal beneath the burden of its own weariness.

And Naldino, of course. She'd have to invite him, although with any luck he wouldn't bother coming all the way up from his foodie cooperative just to show some respect to a father he had never met. Even his mother got little enough these days. Still, if he refused, that was his business. At least she would have given him the opportunity.

It was only once she reached the garden door, having duly followed the long winding circular path through the grounds, that the solution to all her problems struck her. The insight was so overwhelmingly powerful that she gasped very much as she must have done that day thirty years ago when the man in Leonardo finally overcame the boy, and he took her.

Naldino! The authorities might refuse to let her have the body, but they couldn't refuse him.

X

Zen walked slowly back along the street to the house, a satisfied smile on his lips. The day was cool and grey, with a scent of rain in the offing, but his spirits were not overcast. Among the various things that had become clear since he had moved in with Gemma, on a temporary basis which seemed to have become *de facto* permanent, was that he was the earlier riser of the two, and she had a sweet tooth and – without being in the least boring or demanding about it – quite liked to be pampered. The result was this expedition, which had become a tradition whenever he was at home.

Zen had discovered, in the course of the sort of casual enquiries and undirected researches that were part of his personality, that the bakery which supplied the most renowned café in Lucca was located a relatively short distance from their house. The café itself did not open until seven, but the pastries for which it was famous were ready long before that. It had only remained for him to make a private arrangement with the *pasticciere*, and he was able to combine the healthy and pleasant effects of an early-morning walk through the twisty, awakening back-streets of the town with the pleasure of seeing the delighted smile of a greedy child on Gemma's face when he awoke her with some sumptuous confection and a freshly-made cup of milky coffee.

Their relationship, which Zen had characteristically assumed was going to be difficult if not doomed from the start, was proving on the contrary to be the easiest and most pleasant that he had ever known. It had a quality of lightness he had never come across before, an almost total absence of stress and effort, of painful compromise and problematic negotiation. It was as if they had both done all that, put in their time and paid their dues, and now wanted simply to relax and enjoy themselves. Not in any grand extravagant style, but in everyday details such as this daily breakfast ritual. Mild satisfaction and a total absence of fuss seemed to be their common, unspoken goal, to which each contributed as if by instinct.

When he entered the apartment this morning, however, he was surprised and slightly irritated to find Gemma in the kitchen, already showered and dressed, making coffee and listening to the news.

'You're supposed to be in bed,' he told her grumpily.

She switched off the radio and kissed him.

'Not today, darling.'

'What's so special about today?'

'It's my birthday.'

He set the parcel of pastries down on the counter, feeling obscurely aggrieved.

'You should have told me. I could have got you a present.'

'I don't need anything. But you can take me to lunch, if you want.'

'There are no decent restaurants here.'

'Not in the town, no. The locals are too stingy to support anything worthwhile.'

She put on an exaggerated version of the local accent, which Zen could just about recognize but still not replicate. ' "Why waste a lot of money going out when we can eat perfectly well here at home for a quarter of the price?" '

'Venetians are the same.'

'But there's a good place up in the Serchio valley. At least, I like it. Simple and unpretentious, but the food's genuine and the place is very pretty. Unfortunately today's also the day I have to meet a sales rep from Bayer about their line of new products, as well as filing a mound of overdue paperwork with the regional authorities. That's why I'm making such an early start. I was going to do it all while you were away, but those people from the gas company came round and just tore the place apart. I couldn't leave them here unsupervised, of course, but it was impossible to work with them hammering and banging away.'

She poured coffee for them both.

'There's a problem with the gas?' Zen asked.

'Well, I didn't have one. But they said they'd had a complaint from someone else in the building, so they sent some workmen around to check that the system was functioning normally.'

'And?'

'Well, they installed a new meter and replaced some of the piping. Apparently it's fine now.'

Zen savoured a few bites of a brioche still meltingly warm from the oven.

'When was this?' he asked.

'While you were in Bolzano.'

He nodded.

'Dangerous stuff, gas. One takes it for granted, but it's potentially lethal. We don't want to be asphyxiated or blown up. Particularly on your birthday.'

Gemma looked at him oddly.

'You checked their identification, I suppose?' Zen continued.

'Whose?'

'The men who came about the gas. Sometimes petty criminals use a ruse like that to get into someone's apartment, then tie up the occupant and clean the place out.'

'Nothing like that happened. They had valid ID, were wearing uniformed overalls and obviously knew what they were doing.'

173

'I'm glad to hear it.'

Gemma rose.

'Well, I'd better get over to the pharmacy.'

She went to get her coat, briefcase and bag. Zen finished the remaining coffee, staring out of the window at the blank plastered wall opposite. When Gemma reappeared, he followed her out of the apartment on to the landing.

'When the Ministry called here to arrange that appointment in Rome, was Brugnoli's name mentioned?' he asked in an unusually quiet voice.

'How else would I have known it? It may even have been he who phoned, I don't know. The caller just told me that he wished to see you the next day in Rome. I told you all this when I met you off the train in Florence.'

'Sorry, I was rather distracted that morning.'

'You certainly were.'

'It was that case I was working on. Creepy business. But that's all over now. Now, when do we go to lunch?'

'I'll be back by half past eleven. I'll make a reservation from the shop, but we should aim to leave by twelve at the latest. *Ciao!*'

'*A presto, cara.*'

Gemma hurried down the stone steps and disappeared round the corner, the sound of her suede boots echoing back up the stairwell, while Zen made his way thoughtfully back to their apartment.

There was a lot to think about. He walked through to the kitchen, where he disassembled the *caffettiera* and rinsed it out, then stacked the breakfast plates and cups in the dishwasher with the load from last night, added detergent powder and switched it on. What a wonderful invention dishwashers were! You just piled all the dirty stuff in, listened to the machine making its soothing swooshy sound for an hour or so, then opened it up and everything was sparkling clean. If only there were a similar appliance for the other problems of life.

Having run out of tasks to take his mind off his worries, he lit a cigarette and reluctantly attempted to confront them. Until proven otherwise, he had to proceed on the assumption that the supposed visit from the gas company had in fact been a pre-emptive surveillance operation mounted by Brugnoli's enemies at the Defence Ministry, or possibly even the secret services. If the ID and uniforms were fake, this indicated a high level of professionalism and resources.

The object of the exercise would presumably have been to tap the phone line and install area microphones linked to micro-transmitters. The only way to be certain would be to return to Rome, contact Brugnoli through the agreed cut-out and have him order in an electronic security team to sweep the apartment. But that would merely serve to confirm the opposition's suspicions about Zen's involvement. Better to leave the bugs in place and use them to convey disinformation.

A distant shrilling recalled him to the present. It was his mobile phone, which he had left in the pocket of his overcoat. He walked through to the hallway, retrieved the shiny slab, stepped back out on to the landing and closed the door behind him before answering the call.

'*Pronto!*'

'Dottor Aurelio Zen?'

'Speaking.'

'Here is Werner Haberl, the doctor you spoke to in Bolzano the other day.'

'Ah, yes. How are you, doctor?'

'Very well, thank you. I apologize for calling so early, but you asked me to get in touch if there were any further developments regarding the matter we discussed.'

'Absolutely, but may I call you back? I'm on another call at the moment.'

'No problem, I'm here all morning. I give you the number of my direct line.'

Zen noted it down and then folded up the phone with a mental note to use it with extreme caution in the future. If they had gone to all the trouble of bugging the apartment he shared with Gemma, they would almost certainly be monitoring his mobile.

Five minutes later, he was walking down Via del Fosso. It had started raining lightly, and there seemed to be no one about. At the corner he turned left towards the church of San Francesco, stopping at the tobacconist's to buy a carton of Nazionali and a phone card. At the payphone opposite the church he inserted the card and dialled the number that Werner Haberl had given him in Bolzano. He checked the street while it rang. There was nothing unusual to be seen.

'*Hallo.*'

'*Herr Doktor Haberl, bitte.*'

'*Am Apparat.*'

'It's Aurelio Zen, doctor. My apologies for the delay. Now then, what were you saying about our friend in the tunnel?'

'Yes. So, I have just heard from a colleague that a man named Naldo Ferrero has phoned the hospital yesterday. He claimed that he was legally entitled to take possession of the body and wished to know how he should go about it. When my colleague told him that the cadaver was no longer in our custody, he became quite agitated and threatened to make a formal *denuncia* to the police. It was then explained to him that the police themselves had removed the body.'

'On what grounds did he lay claim to the corpse?'

'Well, that's why I thought you might be interested. This Ferrero said he is the dead man's son.'

Zen was silent for a moment.

'Did he leave a contact number?'

'Yes, yes, we have all his details. We do that as a matter of routine, at the beginning of a call. Do you have a pen and paper?'

Zen wrote down the claimant's address and phone number and thanked Werner Haberl profusely for his cooperation. Then he depressed the receiver rest and inspected the street again. As before, everything seemed normal. He dialled again. The phone rang over a dozen times before a weary-sounding woman answered.

'La Stalla.'

'May I speak to Naldo Ferrero, please?'

'Just a moment.'

She set down the receiver and Zen heard her call 'Naldo!' distantly. The amount of credit left on the phone card had roughly halved in value before a man finally came on the line.

'Yes?'

'Good morning, Signor Ferrero. I'm phoning about your late father.'

He paused, but there was no reply.

'I'm from an insurance company,' Zen went on. 'It seems that there is some dispute about the manner and date of your father's decease. I was hoping that you might be prepared to let me have half an hour or so of your time with a view to clarifying these and other issues arising. There's a good deal of money involved.'

More silence, then a contemptuous grunt.

'Insurance company, my arse,' said Ferrero. 'My father died thirty years ago. His body was not recovered, but the fact of his death was not in dispute. Any outstanding insurance claims would therefore have been settled at that time. So who the hell are you?'

'Someone who might be able to help you recover your late father's remains after all these years.'

'I'm perfectly capable of doing that myself. And if, as I suspect, you're from the police, then it may interest you to know that I am in the course of preparing a formal appeal to the judiciary in Bolzano denouncing the illegal intervention that took place at the hospital there, resulting in the removal of my father's corpse and the conspiracy of silence regarding its present whereabouts. And that's all I have to say on the matter!'

The phone slammed down.

Zen's final call was to the customer service desk at the local office of the gas company. He gave a false address in Via del Fosso and explained that he had heard that there had recently been an emergency call-out to another house in the street because of a reported leak. Could the company please confirm that this had been taken care of, and that there was no possible risk to nearby homes? After a computer search, the service representative told him that he must have been misinformed. There had been no gas leaks reported anywhere in Lucca within the previous month.

He left the cabin and walked back the way he had come. The only person he saw was a derelict with a broken nose and shaven hair nursing a bottle of wine on a bench next to the channelled river that flowed down the centre of the street.

When Gemma returned shortly before eleven-thirty, Zen was in the bedroom putting the finishing touches to his packing. He closed up the battered suitcase and carried it into the living room.

'Bad news, I'm afraid,' he told her.

'You can't cancel lunch! Not on my birthday.'

'No, it's not that. But I have to go away for a few days again.'

'What now?'

'I just had a call from the family lawyer in Venice. Had to take the call outside on the stairs, incidentally. Couldn't get a clear signal here in the apartment, and then the damn thing died on me completely.'

This for the benefit of anyone listening in on the installed bugging devices.

'Anyway, there's apparently been some sort of snag over my mother's will. Nothing serious, he says, but I'll need to pop up there to sort it all out and sign some papers. And when I called the Ministry to request leave, just as a formality, they told me I could take advantage of being in the area to check progress in some murder case in Padua. It sounds unutterably boring, but I couldn't very well say no. But I should be back in a few days, with any luck.'

'You seem to have an awful lot of work all of a sudden.'

'That's the way this job always is. It comes in waves.'

'Actually, that works out quite nicely. My son has apparently met someone who he thinks might turn out to be "quite serious" and wants me to vet her. This will give me a chance to spend a couple of days away. Now then, let's get going.'

'Perhaps you could drop me at the station afterwards,' Zen said very distinctly. 'There's a train to Florence around five that connects with the Eurostar to Venice. That way I can see the lawyer first thing in the morning and get it over with as quickly as possible.'

Gemma put her briefcase down on the table, then clicked her fingers, opened the flap and extracted a number of sheets of paper.

'I almost forgot. That friend of yours in Rome you asked me to exchange email addresses with sent you these pictures. He says that . . .'

Zen cut her off hurriedly.

'I'll look at them in the restaurant. Come on, let's go out and celebrate your birthday!'

Under the pretext of being concerned about the off-side rear tyre of Gemma's vehicle, Zen inspected the street carefully before they set off, and then again as they drove through the back streets. There was no obvious sign of a tail.

Like Zen's native Venice, Lucca was a real *civitas*, though bounded not by water but its massive encircling walls. When you passed through one of the tunnel-like portals, you knew that you had left the city; when you passed in again, there was no doubt that you were back. He found this both relaxing and reassuring. They drove through the modest post-war suburban fringes of the town and up into the pleasant, winding valley of the Serchio. The rain was more intense here, but it suited the landscape, as intensely rural as Lucca was urban: unoppressively pretty and unspectacularly wild, unassuming, unspoilt and almost unvisited.

The restaurant was homely but attractive, with a smouldering wood fire that perfumed the entire room, and the food as good as Gemma had promised. They shared a bowl of home-made *pappardelle* with a sauce of wild porcini mushrooms, followed by a *fritto misto* of rabbit, lamb and chicken with astringent steamed greens. The wine was drinkable, the almond tart just right and only the coffee a bit of a disappointment, but at that point who cared?

Over cigarettes and a glass of the inevitable local *amaro* liqueur, whose digestive properties were extolled at some length by the proprietor, Gemma brought out the prints she had made from Gilberto Nieddu's email attachment of the enhanced digital photograph.

'What was it he said?' Zen asked as he glanced through them.

'There was a very brief cover note that I didn't bother to print up. He just said to tell you that the mark on his arm is the same.'

Zen nodded. The prints presented the tattoo in various shades of distinction, as well as its original black on the ochre background of the shrivelled arm. It showed the head of a young woman enclosed in a thick square frame. Her hair was knotted, her eyes blank, her expression unfathomable.

Zen passed the pages to Gemma.

'What do you make of these?'

'It's Medusa,' she replied immediately.

'Medusa?'

'Well, one of the Gorgons. Medusa's the best known, because of that legend involving Perseus. She turned whoever beheld her to stone, but he reflected her face in his shield, nullifying her power, and then cut off her head. One of those Greek myths. I read somewhere that it's a classic symbol of male fears about women's sexuality.'

'I'm not afraid of your sexuality, am I?'

Gemma smiled and kissed him.

'Not at all. In fact you seem to quite like it.'

Zen took the papers back, folded them up and tucked them into his inside pocket.

'Thank you for lunch,' said Gemma as they drove back down the wooded valley.

'I'll bring you a real present when I come back from this trip.'

'I don't need anything, Aurelio. I told you so.'

'All right, but don't you want anything?'

'I want you to be happy.'

At the station in Lucca, Gemma accompanied Zen into the booking hall, where he ordered a single ticket to Florence in a very loud voice, repeating the name of his destination several times, as though the clerk were deaf or stupid or both.

'There's our gas-man,' Gemma remarked once this laborious transaction had been completed.

'What?'

Zen was still putting his ticket and money away.

'One of the men who came to sort out that problem with the gas. Over there, standing in the corner.'

He glanced over quickly. It was a slightly more respectable version of the drunk he had seen that morning on a bench in Via del Fosso.

'Well, well. Small world.'

Gemma gave him one of her charming deprecatory grins.

'Small town, you mean,' she said, kissing him on the cheek.

Zen boarded the train when it arrived from the coast, but in the event he did not travel to Florence. Smoking was prohibited on inter-regional trains, so when they reached Pistoia it was perfectly natural that he should go and stand just inside the automatic doors and enjoy a much-needed cigarette, bringing his bag with him for safety. When the alarm signalled that the doors were about to close, he waited until the last minute and then jumped through the gap down to the platform.

Once the diesel unit had pulled out, he bought another ticket, this time to Pesaro via Bologna, and then retired to a café opposite the station until it was time to board the last train of the day on the branch line north, one of the first ever constructed through the Apennine barrier and now hardly used for passenger traffic.

XI

The weight-and-pendulum clock in its tall, coffin-shaped case at the far end of the cavernous space marked the time as seventeen minutes past ten. The taxi driver had made it very clear that he would remain on call no later than eleven.

No lights were to be seen through the miserly windows, and those inside consisted of low-wattage bulbs as yellow as old newsprint. The room was so cold that the breath of both men was visible. A bone-chilling north-easterly outside alternately scuttered and slashed at the building, raising weird moans and wails punctuated by the death-watch beetle sounds of the clock. Zen leaned forward across the bare refectory table, his fingers interlaced.

'I repeat, Signor Ferrero, the only real chance you have of finding out what happened to your father is through me.'

'Which father?'

In other circumstances, Zen might have suspected an attempted joke, but he had already established beyond a shadow of a doubt that the other man had absolutely no sense of humour.

'The one whose name you bear and of whose remains you are presently attempting to claim custody. I am prepared to assist you in that attempt, to the limits of my ability, in return for your full cooperation.'

Naldo Ferrero stared at him with open hostility.

'What business is that of yours?'

Zen did not reply. Having had his ear talked off for the best part of an hour about the evils of globalization, the birth of the 'Slow Food' movement, and the need for a new rural economy based on sustainable organic farming practices, he was pretty sure that Naldo wouldn't be able to tolerate silence for very long.

'I don't need to do any deals with the police,' Ferrero retorted. 'My judicial application is perfectly in order, and my claim can be proven by DNA testing. Besides, since when have you people been so caring?'

Zen made the mistake of smiling ironically.

'It's all part of the reforms of the new administration. We're here to serve the public.'

The other man's face became even tighter and darker.

'So! You permit yourself to joke about it now, do you? On balance, I think I preferred the old naked face of power to this new mask, Dottor Zen.'

'Me too, but for some reason they didn't see fit to consult us. Now then, do you want to play cards or do you want to piss around?'

'I beg your pardon?'

'A Venetian saying. God is getting beaten at a game of *scopa* with Saint Peter, so He performs a quick miracle that changes the cards so that Peter is left holding a losing hand. My question to you was the apostle's response.'

Ferrero gazed blankly back at him. The poor man had no idea how to deal with either silence or humour. An earnest garrulousness was his only means of confronting the world.

'I've already told you everything I know,' he declared stolidly.

'All right, let's try and separate the wheat from the chaff and summarize what you have told me, omitting any reference to agriculture, foodstuffs and grass-roots movements dedicated to putting the "commune" back into "Communist".'

Zen consulted the notebook lying open on the table between them.

'You learned of the discovery of an unidentified body in a system of abandoned military tunnels from the television news. Your mother, Claudia Comai, resident in Verona, had already informed you, following the death of her husband Gaetano, that your biological father had in fact been one Leonardo Ferrero, who had died before your birth in a plane crash over the Adriatic. She now phones to say that the body that has turned up in the Dolomites is his and instructs you to make a formal application to take possession of it.'

'Those are the facts.'

'Very well, but let's try and put a little flesh on them, shall we? And may I remind you once more that you are not under oath and will not be required to sign a written statement on this occasion. That will of course change if I suspect that you are attempting to conceal anything or to protect anyone.'

A particularly violent gust of wind hacked at the house like an axe. The still, stale air inside seemed to vibrate under its assault.

'I have nothing to hide,' Naldo Ferrero stated truculently.

'That's as may be. But your mother certainly does.'

'Leave my mother out of this!'

'I'm afraid that's not possible, assuming that she told you the truth. Did you believe her?'

'Why would she make up a story like that?'

'Well, it would be easy to suggest a number of reasons. Let's assume that she'd had an affair with this Ferrero, had been genuinely in love with him, and that he'd broken off with her and then died. She might have tried to convince herself that you were his son so that something of him would remain.'

'My mother's not crazy!'

'All right, let's assume that her version of events is true. We know that Leonardo Ferrero died in a plane crash. How sane is it, after all these years, for her to tell you to make a claim for an unidentified body discovered deep underground on the basis that it is his?'

Ferrero got to his feet.

'Do you think I give a damn either way?' he shouted. 'I never even met the man.'

'You changed your name from Comai to Ferrero,' Zen reminded him.

'That was to please my mother! Everything I've ever done has been to please her. She asked me to contact the authorities in Bolzano and I did so. When I told her the result, she asked me to make a judicial application, and that's what I'm in the process of doing. She's my mother and I love her. This business obviously means a lot to her for one reason or another, so I'm playing my part and doing as she wishes. Personally, I couldn't give a damn who my father is.'

He strode away and disappeared round the corner of the bar. Zen lit a cigarette and looked around. Il Ristorante La Stalla was closed for the season, but even at the height of summer it was hard to imagine such an isolated venue packed out with the boisterous crowd of noisily relaxed hedonists that would be needed to make sense of what looked like, and almost certainly was, a converted barn.

Indeed, the whole establishment had an indefinable air of failure about it, of having been bypassed by more recent developments to which it had been either unable or unwilling to adapt. Naldo had explained that it had been set up back in the eighties on communal lines, with money from a trendy left-wing film director who had installed his son here and set him up as a chef in an attempt to wean him off heroin. The cure had apparently worked only too well, for the son had subsequently left and opened a restaurant down on the coast near Ancona, a move which had been regarded as rank betrayal by the rest of the collective. To abandon their idealistic project up here in a remote location of the Apennine foothills – only accessible by a long unpaved track off a very minor road near a village that hadn't been marked on the map consulted by Zen's taxi driver – and then set up his own non-non-profit business in a hideous glass and stainless steel box right at the heart of the shameless consumerist hell down by the beach. And making a fortune at it too! Five months' work a year and then off to Mauritius or Thailand for the winter. It was sickening, just sickening.

There had apparently been some other defections at about the same time, possibly connected to the fact that the film director's subsidy also abruptly dried up, so when Naldo appeared he had been warmly welcomed. The ethos of the commune dictated that all work on the farm and in the restaurant must be done 'authentically', meaning either by hand or with the most primitive and basic equipment such as would have been used by the share-cropping family who had once lived there. It must have been easy for the remaining pioneers to see the point of having an extra set of keen, youthful muscles about the place.

But the sense of failure ran deeper than that. There was a generalized reek of frustration, even despair, as unmistakable as mould. *Things hadn't worked out the way they were supposed to.* The members of the commune had worked their fingers to the bone, followed the idealistic principles of the movement to the letter, but they'd been let down by events. And not just here! The whole country, it had turned out, was ideologically rotten to the core. After all the valiant and tireless struggles against entrenched corruption, blatant scandals, extreme right-wing terrorism, attempted military coups and a host of secret organizations aimed at keeping the powerful in power and everyone else in subjection, those responsible had finally been ousted, only to be replaced by Silvio Berlusconi and his opportunistic pals. It had turned out that the majority of Italians did indeed want *un paese normale*, only not as the left had intended that slogan, meaning a 'Scandinavian' model of probity and socialism with a human face, but in the most literal sense of the phrase: a country much like any other; no better, no worse.

That's what they'd voted for and that's what they'd got, leaving the *sinistrini* to weep into their pasta and bean soup prepared from ingredients grown according to the highest principles of biological agriculture, and to squabble self-destructively about whose fault it was that everything had gone wrong. Not for the first time, Zen reflected on the irony of the fact that those who had explicitly declared History to be the final court of appeal should be so reluctant to accept its judgements.

The dry strokes of the long-case clock combined in a syncopated pattern with two sets of footsteps. Marta, the short, anxious-looking woman who had greeted Zen upon his arrival, went behind the bar and started sorting glasses. Naldo, wearing his usual sullen grimace, headed back to the table. Zen suddenly felt an overwhelming desire to get out of there, and fast. When it came to interrogations, his rule of thumb was simple: if you can discover the thing that a man despises about himself, which may of course be very different from what others despise about him, then he's yours. But despite his best efforts, he had failed to find this crucial key to Naldo Ferrero, and there was nothing more for him here. He stood up, crushing his cigarette out on the floor.

'I shall need to speak to your mother, Signor Ferrero.'

'You can't.'

Zen sighed. How he would have loved to take the little squirt down to the police station in Pesaro and make him sweat blood!

'I can get her details from my colleagues in Verona, of course, but I thought you might have wished to save me the time and effort. Never mind. The net result will be the same.'

'Your time and effort will be wasted. My mother has gone to Switzerland.'

Zen was genuinely surprised.

'Leaving the country at this juncture casts considerable doubt on your account of her role in this affair, to say the least,' he remarked coldly.

'It's got nothing whatever to do with that! She always goes to Lugano at this time of year. The next time she calls, I'm going to tell her to stay there until further notice. Whether or not she had an affair with someone thirty years ago is of no relevance to the identity and manner of death of this body that's turned up. She knows nothing about that and I'm not going to let you terrorize her as you've tried to terrorize me!'

He stood there, swaying slightly on the balls of his feet, as if expecting to be punched and quite prepared to hit back. Ignoring him, Zen took out his mobile and called the taxi driver, who had driven on to a neighbouring town after dropping him at the restaurant. The man said he would be there in fifteen minutes. Zen put his phone away and started towards the door.

'Would you like a drink or something while you wait?' the woman behind the bar asked as he passed. She was small-bodied but large-breasted, with an amiable air of blowsy sensuality that must have absolutely devastated the ranks of some small-town PCI *sezione* a decade earlier. Now she looked wiser and sadder and worn-out in some way that went beyond mere physical or mental exhaustion.

'The espresso machine is turned off during the week, and it takes ages to heat up, but we have beer or . . .'

Zen sensed that she was trying to compensate for Naldo's aggressive manner earlier, out of both politeness and concern about the possible consequences.

'Do you have any grappa?' Zen asked.

The woman raised her eyes to his for the first time.

'We have a local one, hand-made in limited batches using small copper stills . . .'

'I'd be delighted to try it,' Zen replied with a warm smile. 'But only on condition that you join me.'

The woman looked anxious again.

'Well, I don't know. There's so much to do.'

'Like what?'

'Well, there are the pigs to feed. I meant to do it earlier, but then the water pump broke down and . . .'

'Signor Ferrero will take care of all that. In view of its impeccable credentials in other respects, this establishment must surely be an equal-opportunity employer.'

He turned to Naldo, who was still standing on the same spot, seemingly lost in whatever long irresolvable internal tussle occupied his time and energies.

'This is your opportunity to experience at first hand the rewards of plumbing and pig husbandry,' Zen told him. 'I'm sure we can count on you not to throw away a chance for personal enrichment which may never come again.'

Naldo turned furiously to the woman.

'Are you going to let him talk to me like that, Marta?'

'It was only a joke!'

Zen sensed that this was a line that had been used so many times that it was by now worn out. He also belatedly realized what it was that Naldo despised about himself: his dependency, his lack of decisive virility, his *mammismo*.

'And besides,' she went on, 'it wouldn't do you any harm to get a little exercise. I've told you over and over again that physical work activates the endorphins and helps with your depression.'

Naldo scowled his way out to the back of the premises, leaving Zen with an odd feeling that he'd just scored a point of some kind, even though he hadn't been playing to win. Marta poured a shot of a clear spirit and a glass of wine and set them both on the counter in an unhurried way.

'*Saluti*,' she said. 'I don't drink spirits myself, but I've been told that this one's good.'

Zen sniffed the glass, then took a long sip. It was indeed a very good try for an area with no tradition of producing grappa, although lacking the last degree of refinement which producers in his native Veneto could achieve.

'Excellent,' he said, producing his cigarettes and offering one to Marta, who shook her head.

'So why are the police after Naldo?' she asked.

'We're not after him. I'm trying to help him locate and identify his father's body, that's all.'

He glanced at her.

'Has he ever talked about that aspect of his life to you?'

When she did not reply immediately, he threw up his hands.

'Sorry! You offer me a drink and the next thing you know I'm grilling you.'

'It's not that. I'm just not sure what you want to know, or what it would be proper for me to tell you without consulting Naldo.'

Zen nodded his understanding of the situation.

'Let me tell you what he told me,' he said. 'Basically, he said that his mother claims to have had an affair thirty years ago with a man called Leonardo Ferrero. The man died shortly after she had become pregnant. Claudia passed the baby off to her husband as his. He apparently never suspected the truth. Later, after his death, she revealed all this to her son, who started using the lover's surname as his own at his mother's request. And she now claims that this unidentified body that's turned up is that of her lover.'

Marta nodded.

'That's about all he told me, except that this Leonardo was in the army. That's all he knows.'

She finished her wine and poured them both a second measure.

'But you know more,' said Zen, studying her intently.

Marta took her time about answering, but it was a silence with which she was at ease, unhurriedly working out what she wanted to say.

'Growing up as I did, it's difficult to trust the police. There was so much brutality and deceit . . . But I will trust you anyway. You have a very positive aura.'

Aurelio Zen had had his share of compliments in his time, but this was a new one. Did it have something to do with one of those sample bottles of new lines in aftershave that Gemma brought home after her meetings with the sales representatives?

'I heard about it from one of the founders of this project, one of the original Turin activists,' Marta said.

'Later he decided that our work here was counter-revolutionary and went off to Mexico to try and organize the Indian rebels. Anyway, at the meeting we convened to discuss Naldo's joining the collective, Piero was very much against it. Naldo was already calling himself Ferrero then, and he mentioned to someone that his father's name was Leonardo. This got back to Piero, who immediately became suspicious. According to him, Leonardo Ferrero had been involved in a Fascist military plot to overthrow the government. He had revealed details of this to a journalist and was killed shortly afterwards in a mid-air explosion that was never properly investigated. Piero claimed that the whole affair was bogus. The revelations that Ferrero made to the journalist contained no substantive information, while he himself was not on the plane that blew up. The leaked hints about the conspiracy would serve to either confuse or provoke the left, while Ferrero's presumed fate would terrify any real potential traitors in the organization.'

'But what did all that have to do with Naldo? He doesn't strike me as anyone's idea of a very competent conspirator.'

Marta laughed.

'That's what the rest of us thought, and Piero was overruled. I think that's when he started distancing himself from the project here, to be honest. He was used to getting his own way in a highly disciplined and hierarchical party apparatus. We still used the language and went through the motions, but the place was basically a hippie commune. He thought we were a bunch of amateurs.'

A car drew up outside, its headlights glaring in through the windows. A horn blared three times.

'Who was the journalist that Leonardo Ferrero allegedly spoke to?' asked Zen, stubbing out his cigarette.

'I forget. But he was apparently a big name back in the seventies. Widely respected on the left and widely hated on the right. He used to do a lot of work for *L'Unità*, Piero said. Brandoni? Brandini? Piero had known him, of course. Everyone knew everyone in those days. It was a party in both senses of the word. That was half the appeal of it, the thing that everyone tends to forget now.'

'Did anyone ever mention this to Naldo?'

'Of course not! The only question was whether his joining us would cause trouble in one way or another. Once a collective decision had been reached that it would not, the matter was dropped.'

'And he never raised the issue himself?'

'I very much doubt whether he even knows about it.'

Zen nodded.

'Or cares. He certainly didn't seem very interested in cooperating with me.'

'*Naldo è quello che è*. It may not be possible to help him, though I'd love to be able to. But some people would refuse a lifebelt you threw them. They would rather drown than be beholden to anybody.'

The horn sounded again. Zen went to the window and waved.

'I've been here ever since he moved in,' Marta went on in the same calm voice. 'We even had a little fling at one point. But I don't really know anything about him. I don't think he does himself. Children who grow up without the parent of their own sex are often like that, I think. You have to be known in order to know, and if you don't know yourself then it's hard for others to know you. Does that make any sense?'

Zen wrapped his coat around him.

'Well, thank you very much, *signora*. How much do I owe you for the grappa?'

Marta shrugged dismissively and walked him to the door.

'I'm glad you enjoyed it. You must come back some time when the restaurant is open. It can get quite lively in season.'

Her tone of voice belied her words.

'I'll try to do that,' Zen lied.

Once clear of the front door, the force of the wind almost swept him off his feet. He climbed into the waiting taxi, which immediately swung round in a circle and started down the dirt track. Looking back, Zen saw Marta still standing in the open doorway.

'Good dinner?' the driver asked.

'They were closed.'

'I'm not surprised. Who in his right mind would drive all the way up here? But you can't talk sense to these yuppies from the north. They come down here looking for the simple life and authentic values. I could tell them a thing or two about that! My father used to farm around here. Not as a sharecropper – we owned the land. Of course, all the kids had to do their bit too, but as soon as he died we sold up. *Un lavoro massacrante, dottore.* Back-breaking labour, hour after hour, day after day. These incomers are pleasant enough people in their way, but frankly they don't have the brains that God gave hens. *Finti contadini* is what they are. It's all make-believe. The real country people couldn't wait to quit, any who had the chance. Some of my friends even volunteered for the *carabinieri* or the army, just to get out. When we were in our teens, we used to go down to the sea on a Saturday night in summer, looking for some fun. All the girls used to laugh at us with our peasant tans that stopped at the biceps, the nape of the neck and the knees. But we were out in the sun all day working! Mind you, that was back before they put cancer in the sunlight.'

He broke off briefly as they approached the junction with the paved road.

'Have you booked a hotel, *dottore*?'

'No, I . . .'

'I can recommend a very good one. Modern, clean, quiet and very good value, right by the . . .'

'Do any night trains stop at Pesaro?'

A brief pause. The man obviously didn't know, but equally obviously wasn't going to admit it.

'Well, yes. A few. Are you heading north or south?'

'North.'

'Milan?'

'Switzerland.'

A much longer pause.

'Ah, well, in that case you want to take the plane from Bologna. Too late now of course, but you can get a good night's sleep at this hotel I was talking about, run by a friend of mine as it happens, so there won't be any problems about you arriving so late, and then get off bright and early tomorrow morning.'

'No, I think I'll look into the trains.'

'But it'll take hours, *dottore*! Maybe even days!'

'That's fine. I need some time to think.'

XII

'Il Paradiso è all'Ombra delle Spade.' Yes, he thought. 'Paradise lies in the Shadow of the Swords.' He must have passed the First World War memorial at the heart of this part of Rome, the district he called his 'village', at least twice a day for over twenty years, but the concluding phrase of its simple, poignant inscription never failed to move him.

The sun had already slid down below the line of rooftops to the west, casting shadows that reached across the broad boulevard. Alberto moved like a tank through the groups of afternoon shoppers shuffling about as aimlessly as the windblown dead leaves of the lindens that lined the kerb.

All'Ombra delle Spade. He had lived there all his life, but what did they know of such things, these infantile adults in their quilted acrylic jackets and two-tone designer sports shoes? He tried not to despise them, although he knew that they would despise him. They were rather to be pitied. Yes, get the latest-style clothing, the latest mobile phone, the most powerful motorbike, the most fashionable pedigree dog. Get it all, if you can! It won't make you happy, but it may eventually bring you what you least desire but most need: the knowledge that happiness is an illusion.

Almost half a million Italians had passed over into those paradisiacal shadows during the Great War, with another million crippled for life, but the country had quickly recovered. Now, though, the Italians were dying out. The birth rate was amongst the lowest in the world, with the population predicted to decline by a third in the next fifty years. That meant the end of the extended family that had held the nation together for centuries. And when you looked at the coddled brats who were the end result of this genetic experiment in self-immolation, it was hard to argue that this was a case of *pochi ma buoni*. It was as if the Italians had collectively lost the will to live. The only reason that the population rate had remained roughly stable until now was the continual influx of illegal immigrants, who of course spawned like sardines. Italy had suffered countless invasions in the course of her long and chequered history, but never before had the nation's very survival been dependent on the fecundity of the invaders. The ultimate invasion, the ultimate defeat.

But all that was still decades away, when he would be dead and buried. In the meantime, he was at peace with himself. He had done his duty, and that was all that anyone could do. There were even a few pleasures left in life, such as lunch. Alberto's tongue explored his hefty rear molars, worrying away at a tuft of pork that had got jammed into a crevice. One ate well at Da Dante. Solid, rich Roman food, in a solid, rich Roman establishment on Via dei Gracchi, in the heart of solid, rich Roman Prati. Nice crowd, too, the right sort, even though these days most of them wouldn't know who the Gracchi were. They could recite the names of a hundred characters from the latest movies and TV shows, but they wouldn't have a clue about the Gracchi, particularly the kids. Half of them couldn't remember 1975, let alone 175 BC. Some old dead guys, who cares? The arrogance of the young.

He knew who the Gracchi had been. Servants of the Latin people, and upholders of their rights against the corrupt and indolent landowners who had enriched themselves with war booty while leaving the soldiers who had fought those wars too poor to support their families. True, the Gracchi had broken the law, but only to defend a higher law and a nobler concept of the historic good of their city and country. They had will-ingly sacrificed their own interests, and indeed their lives, for the greater interest of the community and the nation as a whole. Which was all he had ever striven to do. To act for the greater long-term good of the people. Nothing for himself. No one could ever reproach him for that. And where laws had been broken, it had always and only been to keep a more important law intact.

One of his three mobiles rang. The encrypted line.

'*Pronto.*'

'It's Cazzola, *capo.*'

'Hold.'

Alberto walked to the end of the block, then turned right into a quiet side street.

'Well?'

'I'm afraid we seem to have lost contact.'

'You what?'

'The target told his girlfriend yesterday that he had to go to Venice to sort out some problems with the family lawyer regarding his mother's will.'

'That sounds plausible. His family's from Venice and his mother died recently.'

'But he also told her that the police were sending him to Padua to report on the status of an on-going murder investigation. I checked with our friends in Padua. There are no murder cases underway there.'

Alberto heaved a rhetorical sigh.

'Wonderful. So he's realized that the apartment has been bugged and is using the equipment to feed us a pack of lies.'

'Unless it's a cover story he was feeding the girlfriend so that he can go off and visit his mistress somewhere.'

'He doesn't have a mistress.'

'Oh.'

'Congratulations, Cazzola. This is a major set-back. Not only are the bugs and phone tap now useless, but he now has confirmation of the importance of the operation.'

'It's not my fault, *capo*! I swear I did everything by the book.'

'All right, all right. No point in worrying about that now. You've lost him. When and how?'

'Well, it was the girlfriend's birthday and they went out for lunch at a restaurant in the country. Before they left, he told her to drop him at the station in Lucca when they got back, so I waited there.'

'Instead of which she drove him to an unknown destination.'

'No, no, they came to the station, and I overheard him buying a ticket to Florence. I'd already monitored him telling the girlfriend that he was going to change there to the Eurostar for Venice . . .'

'Get to the point, Cazzola! I've got an important appointment in fifteen minutes.'

'Well, I followed, of course, taking a seat in the next carriage so as to prevent subsequent recognition, but with a good view of the target through the connecting door. All by the book.'

A pause.

'Only when the train arrived at Santa Maria Novella, he wasn't on it,' Alberto commented wearily.

'No. He got up to have a smoke while the train stopped at Pistoia and didn't return to his original seat. I assumed that he'd taken another one, in the part of the carriage I couldn't see from where I was sitting. I caught the next train back to Pistoia, but there was no sign of him there either.'

Alberto glanced at his watch. There was no time to get angry, and no point.

'Don't worry about it, Cazzola. He'll show up sooner or later. Meanwhile, get on with the other items we discussed. Go and visit Passarini's sister first. The usual procedure. Who knows, you might even run into our missing target. I have a feeling that our paths are converging. In which case, just make sure you get there first.'

He slammed the phone shut, returning to the boulevard and starting to walk briskly. That it should come to this, he thought. Here he was, an old man in an increasingly strange land, facing the supreme crisis of his career and at the mercy of a dolt who wouldn't be worth wasting a bullet on when the time came. But there was no question of using the good people, except for information gathering and logistical support. For the dirty work, he had only himself and the faithful but incompetent Cazzola to depend on.

Too bad he couldn't have this Aurelio Zen on his side. He'd checked him out on the database as soon as that *carabinieri* colonel in Bolzano had reported Zen's involvement with the case. He sounded like a good man. A bit younger than him, but essentially the same generation, the sort who understood. They'd stopped making them after '68. Had a reputation for going his own way and using irregular methods, but there was nothing wrong with that as long as the cause was just. No reported political affiliations. There had been some sort of fuss when an operative named Lessi had tried to implicate Zen in the death of one of his colleagues down in Sicily, but nothing had come of it. Reportedly Lessi had always been regarded as a bit of a loose cannon on deck and had disappeared from view after being forcibly retired, much to everyone's relief.

Anyway, Zen was of no real importance, Alberto reminded himself. The key to the whole affair remained Gabriele Passarini, the one remaining member of the original Medusa cell besides himself. Once he had been taken care of, the police could sniff and snoop around to their hearts' content. He would then retire to his house here in Prati, close the shutters, ignore the news and relax, conscious of a job well done and a life well spent.

He turned his thoughts to his imminent meeting with some people from the Ministry of Defence that had been requested, in terms that amounted to an order, 'to clarify the situation'. In other words, to ensure that their arses would be covered if anything went wrong. Alberto hadn't felt it appropriate to refuse, but he had cited reasons of security for changing the venue from the Ministry itself to Forte Boccea, the headquarters of the military intelligence service.

They had in turn declined that option, obviously not wanting to give Alberto home advantage any more than he wanted to play away at their ground. The result had been a compromise, in the form of a largely disused barracks and training camp in the heart of Prati, just a few minutes from Alberto's home. The detour from the restaurant where he had eaten lunch had added ten minutes, and Cazzola's call another five, but he would still be just in time.

He had given the meeting a considerable amount of thought, to the point of debating whether or not to wear his uniform. In the end he had decided against it, on the grounds that any overt display of his status and authority would be outweighed by the implication that this was a purely military matter. These men would be either high-level civil servants or up-and-coming politicians. Either way, their goal was to rise in a political hierarchy where military rank counted for nothing. They would wear suits, so he was wearing a suit.

He had also spent much time considering what exactly to tell them. This was almost impossible to decide in advance, since he couldn't be sure how much they already knew and to what extent they might be prepared to give him a free hand, if only to keep their distance from the whole affair. In the end he had formulated a menu of possible options that he hoped would cover most eventualities, but it still remained to choose and execute his responses correctly on the spot and without apparent hesitation. These people might be civilians, but it would be an error to assume that because of this they were necessarily stupid.

The urban villas to his right had given way to a blank stretch of high wall topped with angled barbed wire and signs reading *Zona Militare*. A few minutes later, Alberto reached the gate, showed his identification to the sentry at the gate and warmly acknowledged his respectful salute. Matters had improved beyond all recognition since the government had ended the draft. Now the intake consisted of young men who were personally pre-selected for the military virtues, instead of a gaggle of resentful scum resigned to the bleak prospect of two years' servitude as the cost of keeping the army democratic and the country safe from a possible armed coup.

'Your guests are already here, sir,' the sentry said, pointing to a black limousine drawn up on the other side of the courtyard, where a bored-looking driver in a peaked cap and dark glasses leant against the right front wing, smoking a cigarette and reading a newspaper.

'When did they arrive?'

'About ten minutes ago. Three of them. They were shown up to the former deputy commander's office in B wing.'

Alberto checked his watch. They had arrived early, damn it, trying to score a point before the meeting had even started. Well, if they wanted to play stupid power games, he still had a few tricks up his sleeve.

'Is the colonel back from lunch?' he asked the sentry.

'Not yet, sir.'

'Contact the senior lieutenant on duty and tell him to proceed to the commander's office on the double.'

'Yes, sir.'

Alberto walked straight across the courtyard, through a door in the archway leading to the parade ground, and up two flights of stone steps. He glanced cautiously along the corridor at the top, then turned right and entered the first door he came to.

It was not a grand room, but it felt inhabited and business-like. There were papers and files on the desk, and large maps and framed certificates of military awards on the walls. Best of all, Alberto knew the man in nominal command of this moribund establishment, having dropped in from time to time when he was feeling nostalgic for the old days. He also knew that the colonel's lunch was invariably followed by a two-hour siesta at his private quarters on the other side of the parade ground.

The door behind him opened. It was the duty lieutenant. Alberto gave him his instructions and then went behind the desk. The chair was an old-fashioned swivelling affair in very dark oak. He adjusted the height of the seat until his shoes barely touched the ground, took a pen and a piece of paper from the stationery tray and began to write at random as the door opened again.

'Ah, there you are!' Alberto remarked urbanely as the three men walked in escorted by the young officer. 'I was beginning to wonder what had become of you. Please, take a seat. Lieutenant, fetch another chair.'

'There's no need for that,' snapped one of the Ministry officials. 'I prefer to stand. I've been sitting for almost fifteen minutes in the office next door as it is!'

Alberto looked duly concerned.

'Really? I do apologize. You must have been shown to the wrong room.'

The three newcomers looked uncertainly at each other as the lieutenant saluted and left. The one who had spoken waved the other two impatiently into the chairs on their side of the huge desk. He was in his mid-thirties, prickly and pushy, and made no attempt to conceal his distaste at the manner of the reception that he and his aides had been accorded.

'I am Francesco Belardinelli, principal private secretary to the deputy Minister,' he told Alberto. 'You know what we're here to discuss. There seems to be some considerable degree of divergence about the precise facts involved. Please be good enough to give us the whole story in your own words. Keep it brief, though. I can only spare an hour, and thanks to this mistake we have already wasted a quarter of it.'

The younger of the two aides switched on a small tape recorder and placed it on the desk, then took out a notebook and poised a pen over it. His older colleague sat tight, looking up at the ceiling like a builder checking for signs of damp. The secretary and the spin doctor, thought Alberto. He felt like a schoolboy hauled up before the headmaster to explain how the window of the old lady's house on the corner came to be broken. Fortunately he had his answer ready.

'I'm afraid I can't comply with your wishes,' he said.

Francesco Belardinelli eyed him with incandescent frigidity.

'What is that supposed to mean?'

'This matter involves national security issues of the very highest sensitivity,' Alberto replied evenly. 'Under the terms of my remit, I am only empowered to reveal the full facts directly to the Minister.'

'I am a representative of the Minister,' Belardinelli rapped back.

'So is the driver who brought you here.'

'How dare you?' the other man shouted, now openly furious.

Alberto spread out his hands in a conciliatory gesture.

'It's a question of security clearance, *dottore*. The first thing I did when this meeting was arranged was to check yours. I regret that it is not of a sufficiently high classification to permit me to divulge the full facts involved. I am however quite prepared to address any questions you may have, as long as the answer would not conflict with the limitations I have already mentioned.'

'This is sheer insolence, Guerrazzi! You SISMI people are required to report to the Ministry.'

'I am only required to report to my immediate superiors, to the Minister of Defence in person, and of course to the Prime Minister and to the President of the Republic should they so desire. Not to principal private secretaries with a B3 security clearance.'

Belardinelli hammered his right fist into his left palm.

'Right! So this meeting is a complete farce and a total waste of time.'

He turned to the other two.

'We're leaving.'

Alberto got to his feet.

'Wait a moment, *dottore*! I'm sure we can work out a compromise solution that will satisfy your needs while ensuring that security remains intact. To get us started, may I ask why this affair is of such interest to the Ministry in the first place? It's really just a dirty little secret dating back thirty years, of no contemporary relevance whatsoever except in so far as its revelation would cause severe embarrassment to the armed forces, resulting in destructive criticism and loss of morale. Steps are being taken to ensure that this does not happen, and I have no doubt that the whole thing will be forgotten in a week or two. Frankly, you would do much better to leave the matter to the professionals and avoid any involvement.'

Belardinelli eyed him across the room.

'I appreciate how difficult it must be for you to understand the wider issues involved, *colonnello*, locked as you are into your little secret society of codebooks, classified files and security clearances, but even you may be aware that a cabinet reshuffle is imminent. If it goes wrong, one or more of the coalition parties might withdraw, bringing down the government. Our rivals at the Ministry of the Interior have already launched their own investigation . . .'

Alberto nodded. 'An officer named Aurelio Zen.'

'*Bravo*. I'm glad to hear that you are at least efficient. Nevertheless, there is clearly a secret to be discovered here. You have refused to reveal its precise nature, but you admit that it exists. If this Zen manages to unravel it, and this cock-and-bull story about a training accident involving nerve gas which we have been disseminating is revealed to be a lie, then the people at Interior will have scored a major coup. They will naturally make the most of it, and the outcome might well determine the fate of the present government. Is that clear enough, or would you like me to draw you a cartoon version?'

Alberto decided to let him have that one. He nodded submissively and sat down again.

'I completely understand and share your concern, *dottore*, but may I remind you that what you rightly term the cock-and-bull story about nerve gas did not originate from SISMI, but from certain elements within the army who were desperate to explain the fact that the victim found in that alpine tunnel had been reported killed following an explosion on board a military flight over the Adriatic.'

'So they knew who he was?' Belardinelli shot back.

'They knew who he was.'

'Despite the fact that the *carabinieri* had listed the body as unidentified.'

'I was able to help them.'

'And how did you know?'

Alberto sighed regretfully.

'The answer to that question would involve one of the breaches of security that I alluded to earlier. Let us just say that through various channels and resources available to my department, I was provisionally able to identify the body as being that of one Lieutenant Leonardo Ferrero.'

'But instead of communicating this information to the *carabinieri* in Bolzano, you invoked the national security emergency clause and ordered them to seize the body and effects from the hospital and transfer them to Rome.'

Alberto shrugged.

'It was perhaps a little precipitate, but it seemed the best course of action at that juncture.'

Belardinelli shook his head incredulously.

'Very well,' he said. 'So the body is that of an army lieutenant named Ferrero. Which regiment?'

'The *Alpini*.'

'And how did he die?'

This was the moment that Alberto had been building up to. He stood up and glanced around the room, as though worried about being overheard.

'It was indeed the result of a misadventure, although not at the time nor in the manner of the version retailed to you by sources in the armed forces. The actual facts are very different. You must realize, first of all, that military mores were very different at the epoch of which we are speaking than is the case now. For example . . .'

'We haven't time for a lecture on military history, *colonnello*. Kindly restrict yourself to the facts.'

'Very good. It appears that Lieutenant Ferrero and a number of his fellow junior officers were participating in a form of initiation ritual that was quite usual at the time. Those concerned spent a weekend or even longer on furlough in the military battlegrounds where so many members of their regiment had given their lives during the Great War. As you have reminded me that time is short, I shall not describe in detail the various ordeals which they were required to undergo in order to become "blood brothers" of our glorious dead. Suffice it to say that they were extremely arduous and painful. Unfortunately Lieutenant Ferrero must have suffered from some undiagnosed physical condition which rendered the initiation rites fatal.'

'Why did those with him not simply report what had happened and have the body recovered then and there?'

'The others naturally reported the tragedy to the colonel in charge of the detachment of the regiment in Verona on their return. Rightly or wrongly, he decided against disclosing the truth about Ferrero's death, since that would have meant revealing the nature of the activities involved. Given the unstable political situation at the time, he feared that this would be seized upon by left-wing propagandists in an attempt to further discredit the armed forces. His initial idea was to recover the body and say that Ferrero had died during a training accident, but a few days later a military flight from Verona to Trieste happened to go down with all hands over the Adriatic. The colonel arranged for Lieutenant Ferrero's name to be included on the list of those missing.'

Belardinelli caught the eye of the older aide, who was now checking the walls for cracks.

'He's good, isn't he?'

'Very,' the other man responded.

It was impossible to tell whether this was intended as a compliment.

'What about Ferrero's family?' Belardinelli asked Alberto.

'His father is now dead. His mother is suffering from advanced Alzheimer's and is in a nursing home. There are two sisters, but of course they believe that their brother died in that plane crash thirty years ago.'

'And where is the corpse at present?'

'In the morgue of a military hospital here in Rome.'

Alberto gestured deferentially.

'I didn't feel it appropriate to take any further action until we had spoken, *dottore*.'

Belardinelli strode over to the desk, switched off the tape recorder and gestured to his two aides to get moving.

'Have it cremated,' he told Alberto. 'At once. Under a false name. Dispose of the ashes yourself.'

At the door, he turned again.

'This man from the Viminale.'

'Zen?'

'Yes. If you get a chance, bury him too. Do you understand?'

Alberto nodded complaisantly. 'Of course, *dottore*. Of course.'

XIII

Well, thought Claudia, this is different. Difference was of course why one came here in the first place, but still.

'Certainly,' she said. 'I'd be delighted.'

The man smiled in a gracious, deferential way, but there was a look in his eye . . . A good ten years younger than me, she thought as he walked off towards the stairs. Just like Leonardo. Ten years meant a lot more back then, of course. But still.

Claudia turned back and tried to apply herself to her game. Venetian, he'd said, when she queried the name. *'Venessiani gran signori.'* He certainly seemed to have all the qualities of a gentleman, but the interesting kind who knows exactly when to stop behaving like one. *'Veronesi tuti mati,'* the dialect rhyme concluded. People from Verona had the reputation of being a bit crazy, and Claudia felt in the mood to do something crazy.

But that was another reason why one went abroad. Campione wasn't strictly speaking abroad, of course, but its ambiguous status made it still more fascinating. The place was an exception to every rule, a case apart.

And afterwards one took the ferry back to Lugano, just around the peninsula and across the lake, and alighted at the stop a few steps from the Grand Hotel Lugubre Magnifique, as she always thought of it, so reassuringly Swiss, sedate and safe.

She and Gaetano had come here at least once a year back in the early days, and always, as now, in the off-season. She would never forget the sense of excitement and occasion, and above all the way Gaetano changed when they were there, becoming even more ardent and edgy, as though he were one of the serious gamblers the casino had attracted then, men who thought nothing of hazarding a million lire – a lifetime's wages for many people in those days – on a night's play.

In reality, though, Gaetano had spent little time at the tables.

'Why do you bother coming if you're not going to play?' she'd asked once.

'I'm visiting my bankers,' he'd replied with an oblique smile.

He'd been at Campione before and during the war, when, according to him, it had been a notorious base for espionage, money laundering and shady unaccredited diplomats on various inadmissible missions.

But as long as she and her husband made a few token appearances together in the *sala dei giocatori*, it had been perfectly in order for her to return there without him, and her presence was accepted without the slightest comment by the staff and the other players. In a way it was like going to church. There were certain forms that had to be observed, but the only thing that really mattered was that they all worshipped the same god. In this case, money.

But the money had never been important to Claudia. Any more than God, for that matter. It was the freedom she loved, the sexy air of sweat and risk and tension. She had always set herself very strict limits on how much to lose, and then stuck by them rigidly, just as she had in her extramarital affairs. There were rules not to be broken, although she had broken the fundamental one with Leonardo: never to get involved with someone whom you and your husband knew socially. But Leonardo too had been a case apart.

A rattle of coins recalled her attention to the game she had been playing mechanically all along. One hundred francs, the maximum jackpot! A good omen, she thought, slipping another coin into the slot. Still, the nerve of that Zen, plonking himself down at her machine while she'd slipped out for a moment to attend to an urgent personal need. And then apologizing so charmingly and inviting her to have coffee with him later that afternoon.

It was humiliating, being reduced to playing the slot machines, but it would have been even more humiliating to come alone in the evening to play in the quiet, spacious rooms upstairs reserved for the *giochi francesi*, where the serious gamblers foregathered from ten or eleven o'clock on. Besides, the old villa which had housed the casino in those days had been demolished in favour of this fadedly glitzy monstrosity, shortly to be replaced in its turn by the state-of-the-art Las Vegas fantasy structure they were building just a step up the steep hillside behind. Everything changed. The important thing was to try not to care too much.

Twenty francs down now. She lined up the symbols, punched hold on a couple of columns, and then turned the wheels loose. What *had* Gaetano been doing all those times they'd come here so many years ago? Even then, as a scatterbrained newly-wed, she noticed that he had always brought a couple of empty suitcases that were no longer empty when they returned across the border at Chiasso. That was before they'd built the motorway, of course, and she remembered all too well the sometimes interminable delays at the border.

Gaetano had been tense then, his body stiff with stress in the back seat beside her, his mood withdrawn and almost angry. But the staff car, its passengers and uniformed driver had always been waved through customs control without questions, still less a search. Often Nestore was at the wheel. She'd always liked Nestore, in an innocently flirty sort of way. He'd always liked Campione, too. 'If I ever get rich, this is where I want to live!' he'd joked.

Looking back, it seemed odd that Nestore or one of the other young officers in her husband's 'stable' had always been invited along to act as chauffeur. In fact, going there at all had been a bit odd, come to think of it. Gaetano had never taken her to any of the places she really wanted to visit, such as Paris, Vienna or London. Only and always to Campione, a dull little lakeside town dedicated to gambling. And this despite the fact that Gaetano didn't gamble. But she hadn't remarked on this at the time. Young wives don't. Just so long as he's happy. Just so long as he doesn't blame me for his unhappiness. Just so long as he's not interested in someone else.

It occurred to her now that one could very easily have imagined a scenario in which her husband *had* been interested in someone else, and had parked his wife at the casino in Campione, with an underling to keep an eye on her, in order to give him an opportunity to meet his mistress, perhaps in the very room to which she would be returning tonight, and which they had always shared on those earlier visits. But it wasn't convincing. Gaetano had been twenty years older than her, and after they had married, he had very soon ceased to be seriously interested in sex.

On the other hand he had been extremely interested in the contents of the battered leather suitcases he brought back from those yearly trips with his beautiful young wife, one of which had spilled open when he stumbled and let it fall on the staircase of their villa – very much as he himself was to fall later – disclosing an astonishing quantity of one-hundred-thousand-lire notes bundled thickly together with rubber bands. When she'd asked where the money came from, he'd told her in a crisp, harsh tone he'd never used before that this was a professional matter, and then made her swear never to mention the incident to anyone. As if she would! She had been disloyal to Gaetano, but not in that way.

But she didn't want to think about the past. It was just that there wasn't much else to think about these days. So this Zen loomed rather larger than he otherwise might have done. That and a sense that he wanted something. Claudia had toyed briefly with the idea that he simply wanted her, but she had enough common sense to know that the days when strange men would approach her on that basis were almost certainly over, even here in the casino at Campione.

So on what basis? If not for that, then what? She'd never been wanted for anything much else, except for money, in her son's case, and a good word in Gaetano's ear from some of the junior officers. She'd originally suspected that that might be why Leonardo was coming on to her, and had been quite sharp with him on one occasion, a detail she had conveniently forgotten during her reverie at their trysting house the other day. That had set the whole thing back at least a month, when they'd had so little time to begin with. So little time.

Enough. Signor Zen. Yes, there was something of the favour seeker about him, some hint that she had something he needed and that he was prepared to pay assiduous attentions to her in order to get it. But what on earth could it be? It had of course crossed her mind that the man was an adventurer, one of those charming, unscrupulous con men who hung around casinos looking for a suitable target. And despite the fact that she had been playing the slots when he approached her – and he had deliberately approached her, she now felt sure – her manner, clothing and, alas, her age would have marked her down as just such. He certainly wanted something, that much was clear, but what was it?

The only remotely similar thing she could remember had been Danilo in the weeks immediately following Gaetano's death, when he had started being so creepily solicitous. At first she had thought that was just his faggish way of demonstrating sympathy for the bereaved wife, but after a while his constant questions, always delivered as though he was a grief counsellor helping her to come to terms with the reality of what had happened, had begun to seem just a little too pointed and insistent.

What exactly had she been doing when Gaetano fell? Which room had she been in? Hadn't she heard anything? When did she realize what had happened? What had she done then? And so on. And on and on and on, until one day she had finally turned on him and said, quite coolly, 'You think I killed him, don't you?'

And he had. It had been written on his face as he tried desperately to backtrack, to work up enough honest indignation to treat her question with the contempt it should have deserved. Only he couldn't quite do it. Claudia had dismissed him, and when they started to see each other again, a year or so later, the matter was never discussed. Thereafter she had kept Danilo at arm's length until she decided that she had either been mistaken or that he had changed his mind. Either way, it was over. Or so she'd thought, until the veiled insinuations he'd made while breaking the news about the discovery of Leonardo's body.

Speaking of which, she had better call Naldino soon and find out what was happening with the judicial application. Claudia had no illusions about her son. He was well-meaning but indecisive, just like his father, and needed constant prodding in order to achieve anything. Come to think of it, a spell in the army wouldn't have done him any harm. Some people could only achieve their full potential when they were ordered around. An unfashionable truth, like so many others.

At four o'clock, punctual to the minute, her admirer came to escort her out of the main door of the casino, down the curving slope to the main piazza of the little village and into the Bar Rouge et Noir on the corner. This was where the croupiers and bouncers came later in the evening to loosen up before their shift began, the nearest thing that Campione had to a neighbour-hood bar. Claudia was initially surprised that Zen had chosen it rather than one of the more fashionable tourist establishments a little further along the leafy promenade overlooking the lake, but perhaps he liked something a little rougher and edgier. So had Leonardo, once he'd got over his initial inhibitions and grown masterful. And so, to be honest, did she.

She ordered a cappuccino, Zen a beer.

'Do you come here often?' he asked.

It was such a classically lame pick-up line that Claudia almost laughed. Under the circumstances, however, she decided to treat it literally.

'For decades.'

'Really?'

'Oh yes! I used to visit Campione regularly with my late husband.'

Just to let him know that she was unattached.

'You had good fortune at the tables, then?'

'I always broke even.'

'And your husband?'

Claudia was starting to feel relaxed in this man's company. She decided to paint a romantic, glamorous and slightly mysterious picture of her marriage, even though the reality had been rather different. Intrigue him.

'Oh, he was much more successful than me. He used to bring back suitcases full of money.'

'Did he have a system? I've always wanted to hear of a really good one.'

'No, no. He wasn't a gambler. He came here to see his bankers.'

'There are no banks in Campione.'

'Well, that's what he told me.'

Zen nodded. 'So perhaps he was a gambler after all, but at games they don't play in the casino.'

Claudia was confused by this response, but Zen immediately changed the subject and proceeded to ask her a series of 'questions expecting the answer Yes'. This was a phrase she remembered from school, and a technique she remembered from a rather more recent era. Get them used to saying yes and they'll find it harder to say no when the time comes. But what did this Zen want her to say yes to? Dinner here or back in Lugano? Followed by a nocturnal visit to the rooms upstairs at the casino dedicated to roulette, chemin de fer, vingt-et-un and other *giochi francesi*? Followed by what? *Giochi francesi*?

In the end, it all proved to be rather different from what she had imagined.

'Perhaps I'd better lay my cards on the table,' Zen told her, producing a plastic rectangle from his wallet. 'Or rather my card.'

Polizia di Stato, she read.

So she had been conned, after all. And he would take her for everything she was worth, she knew that. He would destroy her. Despite her efforts to forget, some part of her had been expecting this moment for the past fifteen years. Now it had come, but she was no readier to cope with it.

'How did you find me?' she asked, stalling for time.

Zen was obviously still trying the charm, because he smiled.

'I went to see your son, *signora*. Naldo Ferrero. I visited him last night at that rustic restaurant in the Marche. He told me that you were staying in Lugano. I enquired at various hotels until I found the one at which you are registered. The desk clerk told me that you had gone to Campione for the day. One of the staff at the casino then identified you.'

Despite the fact that the money and the number plates were Swiss, Campione was part of Italy, she reminded herself. This man could arrest her here, but on the other side of the lake he would have no such power. She furtively consulted her watch. The next ferry was due in less than ten minutes.

'It's about the circumstances surrounding the death,' Zen continued. 'And, of course, the identity of Naldo's father.'

The time to move had not yet come. Absolute stillness was demanded now.

'I made my statement to the police at the time,' she replied, as though he were an impertinent journalist and she a star caught in an indiscretion. 'They questioned me on several occasions and I said everything I have to say then, while it was all fresh in my mind. The report must still be on file somewhere. I really don't know what you expect me to add now.'

It was a bold sally, but it apparently worked. This Zen suddenly looked discomfited, ill at ease. She glanced at her watch again, then out of the window at the darkening lake.

'Naldo Ferrero told me that he was your natural son by Leonardo Ferrero, and that you had encouraged him to apply for legal custody of a body recently discovered in the Dolomites on the grounds that it is that of his father.'

For a moment, Claudia herself felt thoroughly confused. Don't try and work out his strategy, she told herself. Boldness had worked once. Maybe it would work again.

'That's absurd!'

She sighed and made a gesture indicating how painful it was for her to admit this.

'The fact is, Naldo is something of a fantasist. He always was as a child, but that's natural enough. Now, though . . . My husband, Gaetano, was a hard man in many ways. The barracks and the home were all one to him. Orders were orders, and the slightest disobedience was punished. Naldino took after my side of the family rather than his, which of course made matters worse for both of them. As Gaetano became more intransigent and repressive, his son grew ever more rebellious. And this was an era when rebellion was in the air, remember. Anyway, after Gaetano died in that unfortunate accident, Naldino somehow convinced himself that he was not his son at all, that his real father had been someone quite different. He even changed his name, as though to try and prove it. It's quite a common psychological phenomenon. I believe there's even a word for it, although it escapes me at the moment.'

Zen nodded sympathetically.

'But how could he have known which name to change his to? Where could he have got the idea that his real father was someone who died before he had been born? Someone he had never met or even heard of?'

This was a more difficult question, and one that she hadn't had to face during her earlier questioning.

'Oh, he'd heard of Leonardo,' she found herself replying.

'How?'

'From friends.'

'Friends of his?'

'No, no. Friends of ours.'

'Of you and Leonardo?'

'Of me and my husband, of course.'

Zen took out a packet of cigarettes and offered them to her. Claudia shook her head.

'May I?' he asked.

She nodded distractedly. When was the ferry? There was something in the man's polite manners, long silences and seemingly ingenuous questions that made her absolutely certain that he already knew all the answers and was merely toying with her to see what more he could get her to admit to before his final lethal pounce. Had he found The Book? She'd been a fool to keep it, but it had never occurred to her that anyone would take any interest in events which now seemed, even to her, like ancient history.

'I'm sorry, *signora*, I don't quite understand. Your son was born in 1974, correct?'

'Yes.'

'While your husband died in 1987?'

She nodded.

'So Naldo was thirteen at the time of his death.'

236

Suddenly she saw her way clear.

'Yes. A very delicate age, very difficult. Which is probably why he came to terms with the tragedy by denying that he had ever been his father in the first place.'

Zen's brow remained comically furrowed.

'But, I repeat, why choose as his surrogate father someone who was also dead, and had been from shortly before his own birth?'

Claudia made a large gesture.

'Well, one would have to be some sort of Freudian doctor to explain that! All I know is that he decided at a certain point that his biological father, as they say these days, was a young man who formed part of what we jokingly called the 'stable', the group of junior officers that Gaetano had assembled around him in the regiment, and who all came quite frequently to our house.'

'That group included Leonardo Ferrero?'

'Yes.'

'And Nestore Soldani?'

She looked at him in surprise.

'Yes, him too.'

'Who else?'

'I can't remember all their names. It's so long ago.'

A tiny white speck in the gloaming announced the imminent arrival of the ferry.

'But, I repeat, how could your son possibly have heard of Leonardo Ferrero, who died in an accident involving a military aircraft the year before he was born?'

He glared at her across the table, all charm now stripped away.

'Unless of course Naldo really is your love child by Leonardo Ferrero, as he claims you told him. That would also explain your late husband's animosity to him, assuming, as I think we may under the circumstances, that he had either found out or guessed the truth.'

Claudia scooped up her bag and got to her feet, saying something about needing to visit the washroom for a moment. She rounded the table, pushing against Zen's back. A moment later she was through the door and running as fast as she could towards the ferry dock about thirty metres away. The boat was already alongside, the lines secure. She waved frantically, praying that the deckhand would see her and hold the gangplank long enough for her to board.

He did. She clomped breathlessly down the short flight of steps into the forward saloon and sank into one of the plastic upholstered seats. The boat's engines revved up, then settled back into a steady purring rhythm for the ten-minute crossing to Paradiso, the southern district of Lugano where her hotel was located. She'd done it!

But so had he, she realized as a figure appeared at the far end of the empty saloon. For a moment she was terrified that he was going to come at her as Gaetano had when she'd confronted him with the truth about her pregnancy, slapping and punching her face and breasts and screaming '*Puttana!*'

Nothing like that. He just sat down opposite her, quite calmly, another passenger on his way back to Lugano. The deckhand came round and clipped her return, sold Zen a single, and then went back to join his colleague in the wheelhouse, leaving them alone.

'Did he have a tattoo?'

Say nothing.

'The body they found, the one that your son is trying to reclaim, had a tattoo. A woman's face.'

Say nothing.

'So did Nestore Soldani, another of your husband's "stable". I spoke to his widow earlier this afternoon.'

'His widow?'

'Soldani, also known as Nestor Machado Solorzano, was murdered here a few days ago. Blown up in his car as he returned home to Campione after a meeting with a person or persons unknown.'

Claudia stood up. They were a good hundred metres off the eastern coast of the lake now, surely back in Swiss waters. She could finally allow herself to get angry.

'I don't want to listen to any more of this nonsense! I've had enough of all your tricks and teasing, understand? He fell down the stairs! That's what happened and you have no proof to the contrary. He was a cripple by then, for God's sake! He fell down the stairs. That was the conclusion arrived at by the investigating magistrate at the time and it's never once been queried, not once in all these years. How dare you poke your nose in here now, in a foreign country where I'm on holiday, trying to find a little peace and happiness after so much pain, and bring up the whole horrible business again? How dare you? You have no standing here. The Swiss wouldn't let you clean the toilets in their country!'

The ferry was approaching the dock. Claudia went up the staircase and out on deck. Zen followed, catching up with her as the ferry came alongside.

'Signora . . .' he began, but got no further.

'Shut up! Leave me alone! You're just a bully, like all policemen. Well, you don't scare me, do you hear? I've lived my life, and I have nothing to be ashamed of. Go to hell! *Dio boia, Dio can, vaffanculo!* You can't do anything to me!'

The deckhand was watching them with alarm, trying to work out what was going on. It occurred to Claudia that she and Zen might well appear to him to be the two lovers she had fantasized about earlier, having a classic end-of-the-affair row. She strode down the gangplank and off under the trees. Zen made no attempt to follow, but his voice floated after her from the deck of the ferry which was already pushing off for its final run down to the city centre.

'I'm not going to do anything to you.'

The words were reassuring, but there was a disquieting undercurrent to them. It took her a moment to work out what it was. '*Non ti faccio niente, io.*' He'd addressed her in the familiar form used only with family, close friends, inferiors and people you are condescending to. What a nerve! The emphatic personal pronoun at the end added another dimension to her unease. '*I'm* not going to do anything to you.' So who was? Was he going to try and enlist the aid of the local police chief? The idea was ridiculous. The Swiss were fiercely independent and notoriously bureaucratic. This Zen would need every legal document under the sun, translated into three languages, before they'd even begin to consider arresting a foreign tourist happily spending her money and causing no disturbance whatsoever on their territory.

The clerk at the desk handed her her key with that exquisitely diffident yet friendly courtesy which all the staff seemed to possess as a birthright. Claudia was of course a regular, and a generous tipper. She could afford it. The extent of her fortune, once Gaetano's will was read, had quite bewildered her. Where had all this money come from? Not from his salary as an army officer, that was for sure. She'd asked Danilo, who had muttered about it being one of those things – and how many there were in this life! – that was better not enquired into too deeply.

In her room, immaculately remade in her absence, she opened the windows and then the shutters on to the balcony overlooking the lake. Then she called room service. A plate of Scottish wild smoked salmon, a green salad and a bottle of champagne. A rich elderly widow's sad supper. Well, so be it. She didn't normally drink alone, despite Danilo's snide comment, but tonight she felt like getting slightly tipsy. She deserved it, after what she'd just been through.

The fumes of the lake rose to meet her as she went out on to the balcony, like the bad smell of a goldfish bowl in urgent need of cleaning. Across the lake, the lights of the casino at Campione were reflected in the torpid water. What had this Zen meant about her husband being a gambler at games they didn't play in the casino? Gaetano had never understood gambling, but she had understood it immediately. It brought meaning to your life, if only for a while and at a potentially high price. But there was no price too high to be paid for meaning, nothing that could replace it, nothing that could compare. What was money besides that infinite gift? And, money aside, it didn't matter whether you won or you lost. Something had happened, your life had been structured for a few hours, you wept or you exulted. It was like sex. Yes, that was the only thing that could compare.

There was a discreet knock at the door and a waiter entered with a wheeled trolley bearing her meal. She tipped him lavishly and then, the moment he had left, tore into the salmon and open-throated the wine almost with desperation, like Leonardo making love shortly before he grew cold and dropped her, eager to get it over with before his appetite failed him.

When hers was sated, she surveyed the wreckage of the dinner tray. It had all been so clean and perfectly arranged, and she'd turned it into this mess. Still, it was another meal, she thought with a slight burp. And more meals tomorrow and the day after, and more burps. But no more gambling. No more illusions of meaning, however fleeting. She stepped back out on to the balcony with her glass and the bottle of champagne. Far below, the fan-shaped pattern of the paving stones seemed to beat gently, like wings. She was a little drunk, she realized. And she'd never had a head for heights. Unless that was precisely what she had had, and to excess.

From a room close by, the strains of a solo violin rose above the miasma of the lake, probably the soundtrack

243

to a movie or TV programme that someone was watching. The encounter with that policeman seemed as distant as her childhood. She found herself muttering the German lullaby rhyme which her mother had used to send her to sleep. Her parents had met in the Alto Adige shortly before the war. Her mother spoke almost perfect Italian, but her native tongue was German. Claudia's father, however, had forbidden the language to be spoken in the house. It had remained a secret between mother and daughter, and seemed all the more powerful and precious for that.

How did the rhyme go? Her mother had later claimed it was a poem by a famous writer, but she had always had intellectual pretensions, and the verses were too natural and artless ever to have been written down. Despite the innumerable times her mother had recited it to her, she could only now remember scattered phrases, and realized that she had no precise idea what they meant. *'Nun der Tag mich müd gemacht . . . wie ein müdes Kind . . . Stirn, vergiss du alles Denken . . .'* Something about children feeling tired at the close of day, and it being time to stop doing and thinking, time to let go.

If only she could! But she knew what Zen's appearance portended. He thought he had been so clever, apparently talking about Leonardo and Naldino and Nestore, but she had seen right through him. The discovery of Leonardo's body had clearly triggered a reinvestigation of all the circumstances surrounding Gaetano's death. A new man had come along, insusceptible to the pressures that had been brought to bear on Inspector Boito, and much better informed about the affair with Leonardo, and he had instantly realized the truth. It was all very well to say that he was powerless while she remained in Switzerland, but she couldn't stay at the hotel for ever. And the moment she returned home, he would be watching and waiting, biding his time. They might even arrest her at the frontier. What would she get? Twenty-five years? A life sentence. She would die in prison.

From the room below the music drifted up again, the same theme, but this time taken up by the whole orchestra. Below, the splayed paving stones of the courtyard glowed up at her. '*Und die Seele unbewacht will in freien Flügen schweben . . .*' She'd understood that *die Seele* meant *l'anima*, the soul, and then there was something about flying, but she'd never understood *unbewacht*. And when she'd asked her mother, she had started to weep and then said, 'It means unwatched, unsupervised, without anyone to tell you what to do or say or feel or how to behave or anything else. It means to be at perfect liberty, free at last.'

At the time, this outburst had just made the idea more problematic, not to mention threatening in some sense, as though a taboo had been broken. Nor had she really understood what *die Seele* meant, except as an ideal version of herself, with better hair and none of the acne and period pains and the fat which had been quite a big problem at the time, although it had turned out all right later on. And she certainly hadn't understood *unbewacht*. Watched over was exactly what she had so desperately wanted to be, and particularly when she was asleep, except that her parents weren't up to the job. Her mother's tears had been the final proof of that.

It occurred to her for the first time that in her marriage to Gaetano, and even perhaps her affair with Leonardo, she had merely been replaying the hand of cards that her parents had been dealt, as if to prove to them posthumously that it could after all have been a winner.

She leant over the balcony, gazing down at the paving stones spread out like interlocking angels' wings. *Unbewacht.* She understood the word now all right, and she understood *Seele* and she understood her mother. She also understood, and it was perhaps her supreme moment, that this understanding had come too late, not as an epiphany but an epitaph.

XIV

The door was opened by a bearded man who ignored Aurelio Zen's identification card and waved him into a large room insulated from the harsh external environment of the Milan suburbs both by a hovering layer of stringed music and by shelves of books stacked from floor to ceiling on every wall, leaving only a minimal escape hatch in the form of the door through which Zen had entered.

'Quite a change from the last time the police called on me,' said Luca Brandelli. 'That was back in the terrorist years. For some reason they'd got it into their heads that I knew where Toni Negri and the Red Brigades leaders were hiding out, so they went through the place with a bulldozer. A good third of my research files disappeared for ever.'

'They weren't returned?'

'The files were. Shame about the contents. Still, one can't have everything.'

Brandelli was a stocky, powerful man of medium height, with a full head of loose white curls and a beard to match. He shuffled about the apartment in faded jeans, a baggy sweater and moccasins, as if to proclaim in advance that wherever he was taking his stand, it wasn't on his appearance. No, he'd given up the journalism, he told Zen while he prepared a pot of Chinese green tea in the minuscule kitchen.

'I can get by on my pension, more or less, so I've decided to devote my remaining years to writing a book.'

'What about?'

'A definitive account, explanation and analysis of all the *misteri d'Italia*.'

'A slim volume, then,' commented Zen.

'Virtually invisible.'

They returned to the living room, temporarily bonded by this shared moment of irony. Brandelli walked over and turned off the radio.

'No,' he said. 'Schubert after Mozart won't do. That's when everything started to go wrong. For all his facile melodic gush, Schubert was a neurotic. Even Beethoven, although eminently sane, couldn't escape self-consciousness. Whereas Mozart had no self at all, in his music I mean. Nor should we forget that Karl Marx was born in 1818, and in Trier, a stagnating little provincial town on the Moselle with a glorious past as a Roman colony, a staid present at least thirty years behind the times, and no future to speak of. Some people argue that he rebelled against that very childhood, or at least forgot it. I disagree. You may forget your childhood, but your childhood does not forget you. To all intents and purposes Marx grew up in the 1780s, a child of the Enlightenment, a pre-Romantic. It was only when he went to Paris in his mid-twenties that he formulated his doctrine of "merciless criticism of everything existing".'

The two men sat down, Zen on a spongy sofa, his host on a creaky wicker chair opposite.

'Marx always looked back to earlier eras of production – and hence of course social organization and personal psychology – with a great sense of warmth and nostalgia, just as I look back to the struggles of the working class in Genoa and Turin in the 1950s. Whatever those people were doing, and whatever mistakes they may have made in retrospect, they weren't doing it for themselves. They were as selfless in their work as was Mozart, just as Marx's vision of a socialist future was based on the sense of community, however wrongly organized, that still lingered in the Trier of his youth, but had since been obliterated by Romantic egotism. In Paris, it was all "Me, me, me! My feelings, my needs!". He recognized the danger, and tried to avert it by his overt hostility to the most fashionable contemporary revolutionary movements, and above all by his lifelong labour to formulate a broad, dialectic solution which would transcend the individual in order to remake him. It was a noble attempt, but in the end it failed. The neurotic ego won. Schubert banished Mozart, and we're still living with the consequences two hundred years later.'

Aurelio Zen sipped his tea and said nothing. The room was very warm, almost suffocating. He wished that he had removed his coat, but to do so now might seem pointed. Luca Brandelli cleared his throat stagily.

'But I think that I'm in danger of making my diagnosis appear a symptom of the disease,' he said. 'Enough from me, let's talk about me. In what specific manner may I be of service to the authorities on this occasion?'

Zen took his time about answering and sipped his tea, considering the best way forward.

'I may be able to contribute a chapter to the book you're working on,' he said at last. 'Or perhaps an episode, an anecdote. At worst, a footnote.'

'Concerning what?'

'Something that happened thirty years ago.'

'Well, as I said, my records of that period are incomplete, and my memory is not what it used to be.'

Zen nodded sympathetically.

'Does the name Ferrero mean anything to you?' he asked.

Now it was Brandelli's turn to take refuge in the tea ceremony.

'Leonardo Ferrero,' added Zen.

'Possibly.'

'Possibly meaning yes, or possibly meaning no?'

They exchanged a glance.

'Possibly meaning I'd like to know a bit more about the nature of your interest in this affair before committing myself to an answer. As a good citizen, one naturally wishes to cooperate with the authorities, even though I note that in this instance they haven't presented themselves with the necessary documentation to command an answer. Nevertheless, I still have a somewhat tattered and faded sense of journalistic honour and responsibility. So before going any further, and in the absence of the aforesaid official documentation, I would like to know a little more about the circumstances before replying.'

Talkative, but a bit of a bore, thought Zen. But the man was obviously intelligent, and the combination of his articulate, professorial delivery and cuddly teddy-bear physique made it easy to understand the popularity he had once enjoyed in leftwing circles.

'Let me outline the basic facts. A body has been discovered. It is as yet officially unidentified, but an individual has come forward and asserted that the dead man is one Leonardo Ferrero. I have been assigned to make preliminary enquiries. In the course of these, your name emerged as someone who had known this Ferrero.'

He had actually been on the phone to the editorial offices of *L'Unità* and to the Questura in Milan for the best part of an hour from his hotel room in Lugano before identifying the correct name and full address of the journalist that Marta had remembered as either Brandoni or Brandini. A call to the Ministry would have cut the time to a few minutes, but the risk of his whereabouts being traced and reported was too great.

Luca Brandelli looked at Zen in some wonderment.

'Leonardo Ferrero, eh? Now there's name I never expected to hear again.'

'You knew him, then?'

Brandelli made a qualifying gesture.

'We met. Once. Long ago.'

'Under what circumstances?'

'One moment. Are you asking me to identify the body?'

Zen paused a moment, then shrugged.

'Why not? It can't hurt.'

He took an envelope from his coat pocket and passed over the photographs taken by the Austrian caver who had descended into the blast pit. Brandelli looked through them and frowned.

'Where are these?'

'Photographs of the body in situ at the place where it was found. They're not terribly clear, I'm afraid, and the face is not visible. Not that there was much left of it, according to the hospital in Bolzano.'

'Bolzano?'

'Where the corpse was taken. It was discovered in an abandoned military tunnel in the Dolomites. You may have heard about it on the news, although the story seems to have died now. Or been killed.'

Brandelli handed the photographs back.

'This makes no sense whatever,' he said with finality. 'To the best of my knowledge, Lieutenant Leonardo Ferrero died when a military plane carrying him to Trieste exploded over the Adriatic.'

Zen nodded.

'According to the official records, Ferrero indeed died in a plane accident.'

'Well, I don't necessarily believe that it was an accident, but that's another matter.'

'Nevertheless, an individual with a purely personal interest in the matter and no political axe to grind has asserted that the body recently discovered under the circumstances I mentioned is that of Lieutenant Ferrero. The Dolomites are a long way from the Adriatic, and the body was discovered about two hundred metres underground.'

'So, he's wrong. Or crazy. An attention seeker. What proof does he offer?'

'He says that he's a blood relative of Ferrero and that DNA tests would validate his claims.'

'Then do them.'

Zen replaced his cup on its saucer and leaned back into the sofa, which immediately tried to swallow him. He pulled himself out of its maw and perched on the edge.

'Unfortunately that's not possible. About a week ago, the *carabinieri* raided the hospital in Bolzano at four in the morning and removed the corpse and all records of the preliminary post-mortem examination to an unknown destination. The Ministry of Defence is saying that the victim was a soldier who died in the course of an exercise testing a new nerve gas and that for safety reasons the cadaver was abandoned and the site sealed with explosives. Only it wasn't sealed. Some cavers found their way in there, and I returned with one of them and inspected the area for myself. In short, this business has all the air of being a cover-up for yet another of our little Italian mysteries. I was wondering whether you could shed any light on it.'

Zen rearranged himself on the edge of the sofa in an attempt to find a more comfortable position. There was an ashtray on the glass-and-steel coffee table. He took out his cigarettes and made an interrogative gesture. His host's right hand eloquently indicated that there had been no need to ask.

'Well, it was all a long time ago . . .'

'That's what everyone keeps telling me.'

Brandelli got to his feet.

'I was about to add, so I'd better go and retrieve my dossier on the subject.'

He was back in less than a minute, holding a very slim buff-coloured file.

'The police raid I mentioned earlier did not come as a complete surprise,' he said, sitting down again. 'I had therefore taken the precaution of moving some of the most sensitive material to a bank safety-deposit box.'

Zen finished his cigarette and stubbed it out while Brandelli quickly skimmed the contents of the file.

'Right!' the journalist said. 'My mind is duly refreshed and I will give you a brief guided tour of the salient facts. Off the record, of course, bearing in mind the lack of a search warrant.'

'That's fine. I'm operating off the record myself.'

'Interesting. I've known the police do that on numerous occasions, needless to say, but they've never tried to enlist my help before. In fact they invariably treated me as an enemy.'

Zen nodded. 'Times change,' he said. 'In this case, it's quite possible that our interests may ultimately coincide.'

Brandelli poured them both more tea.

'You astonish me, *dottore*. And at my age it's very unusual to be astonished. Anyway, here we go. The year was 1973. I then worked for *L'Unità* and had already developed something of a reputation for investigative journalism thanks to various pieces which had won me the highest award in the profession, namely a number of death threats. One day I received yet another anonymous phone message. This time the caller claimed to have information to pass on regarding an affair of the highest national importance and wanted to arrange a suitable place and time for us to meet. It had to be in Verona, at the weekend and in the evening. He was very insistent about that.'

'And you assumed that this was the set-up for an actual assassination, as opposed to the usual string of vague menaces and veiled threats.'

'Precisely. Verona was a notorious hotbed of neo-Fascism at the time, and indeed since, so my only surprise was that the hit-man or his employers hadn't realized this. Nevertheless, I couldn't risk turning the caller down out of hand and possibly losing a scoop, so I set up an assignation at a pizzeria in Piazza Bra. I did not of course go there myself, but I enlisted the help of some of the Veronese *compagni* to keep an eye on the venue and let me know what happened. They reported that a young man had duly shown up at the agreed time. He had looked extremely nervous and preoccupied, had waited for about half an hour, looking up whenever anyone entered. When he left, a team of them followed discreetly. His destination turned out to be a local army barracks.'

Zen put down his tea cup and lit another cigarette.

'At which point you were no doubt reminded of the method they use to catch man-killing tigers in India,' he said. 'They tether a goat to a stake, and then when the tiger comes to eat the goat, the hunters emerge from the undergrowth and shoot it.'

Brandelli beamed.

'Our minds obviously work along similar lines, Dottor Zen. My contact was the goat, I was the tiger, and since I had not taken the bait that evening the hunters had not shown themselves. But a few days later the man called again. I apologized for having missed our first appointment and we made another. It was a matter of the greatest urgency, he said, a vital and shocking disclosure that would horrify the public.'

Brandelli shrugged.

'There was still a risk, of course, but the man's tone of voice convinced me that he was either a trained actor or telling the truth. Besides, risk is part and parcel of the trade that I had chosen. At any event, we met. And the first thing he said, once we had exchanged the agreed code words, was that he was an army officer acting under orders.'

Zen looked up sharply.

'And you believed him?'

'I believed him. His manner was that of a dutiful subordinate carrying out a task without regard for his personal feelings or opinions. He displayed no discernible political animus or involvement whatsoever. On the contrary, he remained completely detached throughout. His role was simply that of the go-between, the messenger, executing the orders that he had been given.'

Zen raised his eyebrows.

'He then proceeded to reveal the existence within the armed forces of a parallel entity consisting of selected officers organized into four-man groups. Only one man in each group had access to the next level of command, and none of them to any other groups.'

'The classic cell structure, in other words.'

'Indeed. An invention of the Bolsheviks. My informant claimed that the superior officer who had sent him was a member of one of these cells, but had lately grown disillusioned and now felt that it was his duty to bring the true purpose of the conspiracy to the attention of the public before it could be put into effect. Since he was closely watched at all times, he was doing so through an intermediary.'

'And the purpose was?'

'Nothing less than the overthrow of the elected government and the imposition of a military dictatorship.'

Zen laughed.

'You must have thought you'd won the lottery!'

'It's easy to laugh now,' Brandelli retorted testily. 'For that matter, it seemed pretty far-fetched to me even at the time. But there was so much we didn't know about back then. We didn't know about the CIA-funded stay-behind Gladio terrorist operation, for example, to be activated in the event of the Communists coming to power. Nor about Licio Gelli's P2 organization, specifically intended to provide support and personnel in the event of a right-wing coup. And in which, lest we forget, the *onorevole* Silvio Berlusconi was enrolled with the membership number 1168.'

Zen gave a chastened nod.

'You're right. I apologize.'

'We didn't know about any of that at the time, but what we did know was that the governance of this country was teetering on the brink during that whole decade. It seemed then, and continues to seem now, perfectly credible that certain people should have put in place a plan for bypassing the democratic process and seizing power in the name of "normalization" and "stability". According to my informant, such a plan existed. Its code-name was Operation Medusa.'

At that moment Aurelio Zen did something that anyone familiar with him would have regarded as very uncharacteristic. Whatever his faults, Zen was not physically clumsy, yet now he kicked the low table in front of him hard enough to overturn the tea pot.

Luca Brandelli went out to the kitchenette, returning with a sponge to wipe up the spillage and brushing aside Zen's apologies.

'So what follow-up action did you decide on?' Zen asked when order had been restored.

Brandelli sighed.

'I was still not completely convinced that it wasn't a set-up,' he said at length. 'Not to murder me, but to plant information which could later be shown to be false, thereby discrediting myself, the paper I wrote for, and by extension the entire progressive movement of that period. In short, anyone who tried thereafter to expose any conspiracy of the extreme right – and there were plenty of them, as we now know – would be laughed off stage and told to pull the other one. Nevertheless, I couldn't be entirely sure. I therefore displayed a cautious interest and arranged another meeting a few weeks later, with the excuse that I had to go to Cuba to research a lengthy article on political organization under Castro. That happened to be true, but my real reason for not cancelling the trip was to give the other side, whoever they were, a cooling-off period to reconsider the situation. If they were genuine, I reasoned, then they would re-engage on my return. If it was a put-up job, they might well think that they had been rumbled and drop the whole thing.'

'And what happened?'

'On my return from Cuba, I learned of the plane crash over the Adriatic. The papers published photographs of the two victims, the pilot and the only passenger. The latter was identified as Lieutenant Leonardo Ferrero of the Alpine Regiment, attached to a unit stationed in Verona. I instantly recognized him as my informant in the Medusa affair.'

'Which presumably convinced you of its reality.'

'It certainly swung the balance of probability that way.'

There was a long silence.

'I did what I could,' Brandelli remarked with yet another sigh. 'Through some of the PCI conscripts at the barracks where Ferrero had been stationed, I elicited the names of some men he had allegedly been close to. I wrote to them both, under the pretext of researching a general background article about "The Army Today". Neither replied.'

'What about the senior officer on whose orders Ferrero claimed to be acting?'

Brandelli threw up his hands.

'It could have been anyone! Ferrero was a junior lieutenant. There were plenty of officers superior to him in the hierarchy. I assumed that if the person concerned still wanted to contact me, then he would do so. But I heard nothing.'

'You mentioned that you were not convinced that Ferrero's death was an accident. Perhaps his superior reached the same conclusion and decided to learn from an example.'

'Exactly what I told myself at the time. So I left it at that, while keeping the file open in case I heard any other whispers about this Operation Medusa. That never happened, and of course I had more urgent and pressing matters to attend to.'

'So assuming that this organization existed, the people concerned were either rank amateurs . . .'

'Or consummate professionals. Yes.'

Zen nodded slowly, as if mulling all this over.

'What about the two friends of Ferrero?'

'What about them?'

'They must have retired by now. Have you made any attempt to contact them? Perhaps they might be able to help close that file. And provide some material for your book.'

Luca Brandelli shrugged.

'One was a man named Gabriele Passarini. He runs a second-hand bookshop here in Milan now. I met him for the first time as a result, perhaps five years ago. I was walking around through the centre of town when my eye was caught by a title that I'd been searching for in vain for ages. I went and bought it and the owner gave me his card. I recognized the name and asked him if he'd once been in the *Alpini*. He said he had. I then asked if he'd known someone called Leonardo Ferrero.'

'And?'

Brandelli smiled.

'He almost threw me out of the shop. No, he almost threw himself out. He was in a total panic. Amateurs,

I thought, not professionals. But he wouldn't tell me anything. I don't believe that even you, *dottore*, with the full panoply of the law behind you, could have got anything out of him.'

'He was that tough?'

'Not tough. Terrified.'

Zen digested this for a moment.

'Do you recall the name and address of the bookshop?'

Brandelli produced a business card from the file on his knees and handed it to Zen.

'You can keep that. I don't think I would be a welcome customer again.'

'And what about the other friend of Ferrero's? Have you tried to get in touch with him?'

Luca Brandelli smiled even more broadly.

'I didn't think it worth the trouble, not to mention the trouble it might cause. His name is Alberto Guerrazzi, and he is now a full colonel and divisional commander with the military secret intelligence service.'

Zen looked suitably impressed.

'Which might seem to make them professionals rather than amateurs,' he remarked.

Brandelli clapped his hands together.

'Exactly! Everything contradicts itself. Frankly, I've given up any hope of ever finding out the truth in this matter.'

Zen rose stiffly from his perch at the edge of the sofa.

'Have you really given up journalism entirely?' he asked.

'What do you mean?'

'Well, supposing that I uncovered further information tending to confirm the existence of the Medusa conspiracy, would you be interested in writing a piece about it?'

Brandelli made a non-committal gesture.

'That would depend entirely on the nature and the authenticity of the information.'

'Of course. But in principle?'

'In principle, yes.'

'And could you get it published?'

Brandelli now looked distinctly dubious.

'Why would you want me to do that? You're a policeman.'

'As I said earlier, I'm operating off the record. Anyway, that's no concern of yours. Any material I bring you will be genuine. What I need to know is whether you could get it published.'

Brandelli drew himself up with a certain hauteur.

'My name may not be a household word these days, but I still have my contacts and a certain reputation in some quarters. If there is a story here, I will certainly write it up. I could certainly get it published in *Il Manifesto*. I might even be able to get it into *La Repubblica*. Subject to there being a documented story in the first place. But do you really think there is one?'

'Do you?'

Brandelli made a tired, defeated grimace.

'I would love there to be, of course. But no, I don't really believe it. It's all too long ago. Anyone who knew what really happened, assuming anything did, is either dead or covering their tracks. They're not going to talk. And now that the new regime has successfully cowed the judiciary into a comatose state of inertia, there's no one in a position to make them do so. So to be honest I don't think there's any chance that we'll ever find out what happened to Leonardo Ferrero, or whether there really was a right-wing military conspiracy to take over the country back in the seventies. Anyway, that's all history. And no one will care even if we do. Nowadays people think that history is what was on TV last night.'

Zen buttoned his coat against the chilly streets.

'This is not just a question of setting the historical record straight. Certain high-ranking people in the government have taken a public line on this affair. If it turns out to be false, and you can arrange for the truth to be published, then the whole affair will be on TV not just tonight but tomorrow night and every night for the foreseeable future. Wouldn't people be interested then? And wouldn't you?'

Brandelli considered this.

'Of course I would,' he replied finally. 'And maybe so would they.'

'Never underestimate the power of the people,' was Zen's parting shot.

XV

Of the various transport choices available from Luca Brandelli's fog-bound apartment building, Zen opted for the M3 underground line, the political kickbacks from whose construction had brought down the Socialist government of the city in the early nineties. It turned out to be efficient, cheap and clean, an irony which he did not fail to appreciate.

In the centre, the fog was dense and pervasive. The lines of jammed traffic seemed as permanent a fixture as the rows of five-storey buildings to either side. On the pavements, visibility varied from a few metres to zero. Zen had to trust to luck, intuition and a few directions from passers-by, one of whom sent him totally out of his way. It was only when he stopped to light a cigarette outside a shuttered shop, trying to work out whether he had been going round in circles, that he realized the he had reached his goal. *Chiuso per Lutto*, read a rather faded handwritten sign on the window behind a lattice of steel barriers designed to foil thieves while allowing potential customers to view a selection of the books that would be available for purchase when the proprietor returned to work after coming to terms with his grief.

Some distance down the street, a nimbus of diffused light glowed through the surrounding gloom. On closer investigation, it turned out to be a bar. Most of the customers were ordering coffee stiffened with a shot of grappa or sweet liqueur. Zen followed their example. The café was a dingy, noisy place, but it felt warm and comforting after the streets. The clientele was seemingly a mix of tradesmen, clerks, shop assistants and low-grade functionaries postponing as long as possible the horrors of their journey home.

Zen slipped a banknote across the counter to attract the barman's attention.

'Do you have a hammer I could borrow for five minutes?' he asked.

'A hammer?'

'I've got a flat tyre on my car, but the hubcap is dented and I can't prise it off with my bare hands. And of course there's no chance of calling out a tow-truck in this fog . . .'

The man nodded sympathetically.

'There should be one out the back somewhere.'

He led the way into the rear of the premises, a wasteland full of spare furniture, mineral-water crates and assorted junk apparently being stored on the you-never-know-when-it-might-come-in-handy basis.

There was also a payphone, now a historical relic from the days before the mobile revolution, and a framed aerial photograph showing one of the small towns of the Valpadana, presumably the one in which the proprietor of the bar had grown up: a little circular urban patch surrounded by a vast expanse of arable land dotted with the huge *cascine* farm complexes typical of the region.

'Here you go,' said the barman, returning from some inner sanctum with a hammer. 'I'll need it back, mind.'

'Five minutes.'

Zen pocketed the hammer and proceeded back through the clammy murk to the bookshop. The front door and main window were too distant to reach, but the remaining panes angled out to either side, ending within arm's length. A potential thief still wouldn't have been able to grab the books on display, but Zen wasn't interested in them. There was no sound of footsteps or cars in the street. Taking the hammer from his pocket, he thrust his arm as far as it would go through one of the rectangular gaps in the shuttering, and then struck the window repeatedly. The glass first crazed, then cracked spectacularly. At the same moment, a yellow light flashed above and a piercing siren began to wail. Zen made his way back to the bar and returned the hammer.

'Thanks very much, that sorted it out. Now I'll go and change the tyre.'

'What's all that racket down the street?' the barman asked with a worried expression.

'No idea. Probably a faulty burglar alarm. Those things are always going wrong. More trouble than they're worth.'

Before long, a different siren sounded in the streets, but what with the fog and the blocked traffic it was another ten minutes before the patrol car finally arrived at the bookshop. Zen showed his identification card to the crew, whose attitude instantly changed from truculent suspicion to awed respect.

'I saw everything,' Zen told them. 'Pure chance. I was passing by on the other side of the street. I heard the noise of the glass smashing and went to investigate. The burglar ran off before he could steal anything. I gave chase, but he slipped away in the fog.'

At this point, a man named Fulvio intervened. He was the janitor of the building. No, the owner was away and couldn't be contacted. A family tragedy. Long business. One of those. But he, Fulvio, could be trusted to have the window repaired and to board up the shop in the meantime. Other members of the family? Just for the record, to keep things regular and official. Well, he believed that there was a sister. Paola Passarini. Lived just off the motorway to Varese, in Busto Arsizio, out near Malpensa airport. He didn't know the address.

The police computer did, however. The patrolmen offered to give Zen a lift, but advised that with driving conditions what they were he would be better off taking the train. Besides, the address was strictly speaking out of their territory, being just inside the Provincia di Varese.

They dropped him off at the nearby station of Porta Garibaldi, and Zen completed the journey by train and then taxi through a grim swathe of 'industrialized countryside'. Busto Arsizio had once been a small market town on the fringes of the flood plain of the Ticino river, but the rural surroundings that had once given it a modest sense of identity had now been swallowed up by the ever-encroaching suburban sprawl of Milan.

The apartment was on the top floor of a neo-Stalinist slab at the intersection of two streets whose ridged and pitted surface suggested that the tarmac had been poured directly over a lightly-rolled ploughed field. Zen rode up in a lift bristling with cryptic graffiti, rang the bell and presented his identification.

'Is it about Gabriele?' the woman demanded.

'That's right.'

She started to shut the door.

'I've already told you everything I know.'

'We've never met before, *signora*.'

'I mean your people. The police.'

'Ah, they've been in touch already, have they?' Zen continued smoothly.

'Someone from the *carabinieri*. I told him I couldn't help him.'

'When was this?'

'Yesterday.'

Zen nodded reassuringly.

'Yes, of course. Those were the preliminary enquiries, at local level. I'm come from Rome to follow up. If you could just spare a few moments, it would be most helpful.'

Paola Passarini reluctantly opened the door again, and Zen followed her into the open-plan living area. She was in her late forties, with a childlike elfin face attached to a bottom-heavy body whose exact proportions were obscured by a loose ankle-length dress. Her general appearance suggested that at a certain point she had decided to let herself go and the hell with it. But then there couldn't be much worth keeping up appearances for in Busto Arsizio.

'Would you like a coffee, some tea . . .?'

Her voice trailed away.

'No, thank you.'

'Do sit down. So you think that Gabriele's been kidnapped.'

'Kidnapped?'

'That's what the other man said.'

Zen forced a smile.

'Ah, yes, my colleague from the *carabinieri*. He was a low-level operative and was not fully briefed. I regret the error, *signora*. No, there's been nothing that would point to a kidnapping. Nevertheless, we do have reason to believe that your brother's life may be in danger. One of the men he served with in the army, many years ago, was recently killed in Campione d'Italia. A man named Nestore Soldani. A bomb was placed in his car. You may have seen the story on the news.'

Paola Passarini gestured vaguely.

'But what has this Soldani got to do with Gabriele? I've never heard him mention the name.'

'The hunt for the killers has led to the discovery of certain facts that I cannot disclose at this point, as the investigation is still in progress. Broadly speaking, evidence has emerged that your brother may unwittingly have been a party to the affair behind Soldani's killing. I must stress that there is no suggestion that Signor Passarini was involved in any way in the murder. On the contrary, we fear that he may become the next victim. The fact that he disappeared from his home and place of work on the day following Soldani's death tends to substantiate this theory. It is therefore of the utmost importance that we locate him as soon as possible.'

A mechanical series of bone-jarring bass chords shook the apartment.

'Turn it down, Siro!' Paola shouted.

The aural assault continued unabated. She got to her feet and waddled off towards a hallway at the other end of the living area, opened a door and disappeared. A moment later, tranquillity was restored. Paola Passarini came back and sat down again without comment.

'Have you heard from your brother since his disappearance?' Zen asked her.

'No, I told you. I mean the other man. Nothing at all.'

'Isn't that unusual?'

'Not at all. We've never been close. Months go by without me hearing a word from him. Gabriele is only interested in his books. He's always lived in his own head.'

'Yet he volunteered for the army.'

'That was just to try and get Papa's approval. When we were young, Primo was always the star of the family. Good at atheletics, a soccer star early on, big and physical and full of energy. My father adored him, and ignored us two. That wasn't such a problem for me, as I related more closely to my mother, but Gabriele was very hurt and retreated into himself.'

'Yet he signed up for the army,' Zen insisted.

'After Primo died. A car crash. My father had been something of a hero in the war and had always wanted

Primo to join the forces. He had always refused. Now he was gone, Gabriele tried to usurp his place by following my father's wishes.'

'Are your parents still alive? They might know where your brother is.'

'My father died of a stroke twelve years ago and my mother then moved to Australia. She lives with our uncle on a cattle ranch. They are evidently much closer than my brother and I. Mind you, my father's will didn't help. It left half the estate to my mother and the bulk of the remainder to Gabriele. His idea was that a married daughter should be provided for by her husband. That explains how my brother was able to afford to set up that elegant little antiquarian book boutique of his, not to mention a very nice bijou apartment quite close to the centre.'

Zen mimed sympathy.

'That must have been painful for you.'

'It certainly was. A stab in the back from beyond the grave. Perhaps now you understand why Gabriele and I very rarely see each other.'

A young man walked in through the open door at the end of the room.

'Paracetamol,' he said.

'Are you ill, darling?' Paola Passarini responded in a tone of alarm, rising to her feet.

'Just a hangover. But it's bugging me.'

'The bottle is on the second shelf of the closet behind the door in the bathroom. Do you want me to find it for you?'

'No.'

'Remember to drink a glass of milk with the tablets. Those drugs are all acidic. They'll eat into your stomach lining if you don't have some milk with them.'

'Stop fussing.'

The man turned away irritably.

'So you have no idea where your brother might be?' asked Zen, feeling vaguely embarrassed by his presence at this scene.

'None whatever. He might be abroad. He often travels to Paris or London or Amsterdam or wherever to search for new stock for the shop.'

'Might he have gone to visit your mother in Australia?'

Paola Passarini shook her head decisively.

'I would have heard about it if he had. "Why didn't you come too? It's at least a year since I've seen you!" Etcetera, etcetera.'

The phone rang but was answered before Paola Passarini could reach it. She hovered in the arch to the next section of the room, listening intently. The young man could be heard talking in a deliberately low voice.

'And I'm afraid that's all I can tell you,' she said to Zen, coming back again.

Zen nodded and stood up.

'What about your husband?' he asked.

Paola Passarini looked startled.

'My husband? What does he have to do with it?'

'I thought that perhaps he might have some idea where your brother is.'

'Well, by all means feel free to ask him.'

Her look was by now so intense that he finally understood.

'I'm sorry, I meant . . .'

He gestured with his head towards the sound of the low voice mumbling away.

'That's my son, Siro,' was the reply.

'I see.'

'He writes code.'

'Code?'

'For computers. He submits all his work online, so there's no need to go in to the office every day. And he helps me out with the housekeeping bills. This arrangement makes sense for both of us.'

There was an aggressive quality to her declaration that merely served to undermine it. She'd married young, Zen guessed, quite possibly following a pregnancy intended, like her brother's volunteering for the army, to make a point. But the marriage had been a failure and now she was holding on desperately to the one remaining man in her life, lest she be left all alone. He felt sorry for Paola Passarini, but there was also something unwholesome about her, like fruit picked green that rots before it ripens.

'Thank you for your time, *signora*, and please excuse the disturbance.'

A door slammed and the young man strode back into the living area.

'I'm going out for a while with Costanzo, Mamma.'

'When will you be back?'

'Don't know. I may spend the night at his place.'

'Well, be sure to phone and tell me. You know how I worry otherwise.'

In the end, the two men left the apartment almost at the same time, with the result that they found themselves waiting for the lift together. The resulting awkward silence was broken by Siro.

'I think I know where my uncle might be.'

Zen, whose only thoughts had been about where he was going to spend the night, looked at him in astonishment, but Siro didn't volunteer anything more.

Outside, the fog was thicker than ever. To Zen, it came as a merciful pall blanking out the horrors of the neighbourhood. Having grown up in Venice, it was hard for him to adjust to most other urban landscapes, let alone this psychotic collage of concrete brutalities unmitigated by any sense of order, never mind beauty. The young man pointed up the street, where a neon light blossomed in the plump miasma.

'That's where I'm meeting my friend. Come along and I'll tell you my idea.'

They walked the twenty metres or so to a bleak café set back in the facia of the apartment block. It was empty, and the barman looked as though he had been about to close. A game show blared from the television suspended from a pivot above the bar. Zen ordered a coffee, Siro a Coke.

'It was after the other guy left that it came to me,' he said.

'The *carabinieri* officer who came yesterday?'

'If that's what he was.'

'How do you mean?'

'Mamma was in the bathroom when the doorbell rang, so I answered it. He introduced himself as being from the *carabinieri*. I asked to see his ID and he had a card to back him up. But in the window on the opposite side of his wallet was another card identifying him, under a different name, as a member of the military secret service. I read it upside down.'

Zen looked into the young man's eyes for a very long time.

'You don't miss much,' he said at last.

Siro shrugged.

'Maybe that's why I ended up writing computer programs. It's all a matter of detail. I'm good at that, it seems.'

He shot Zen an incisive glance.

'You didn't know that the secret police were hunting for my uncle?'

'I certainly hadn't been informed,' Zen replied evenly. 'And SISMI is not noted for collaborating with other agencies. But there are often parallel investigations in progress. The right hand frequently doesn't know what the left is doing.'

Siro seemed tempted for a moment to make a witty remark, perhaps of a political nature, but thought better of it.

'What did he look like?' asked Zen.

Siro shrugged.

'A thug, basically. Broken nose, shaven head, workout shoulders. Gave me the creeps, to be honest. He kept asking Mamma about some "place in the country". She told him that Gabriele doesn't own any property other than his apartment in Milan. But that started me thinking. It was only when you showed up that I realized I had known the answer to his question all along.'

Zen finished his coffee and ordered them both another round.

'It appears that your uncle may be a crucial witness in a very complex case that we are investigating,' he said. 'We naturally want to interview him as soon as possible, but to be frank we are also concerned about his safety.'

'You think he may be in danger?'

'I'm convinced of it.'

'And the secret service? Are they part of the protection or part of the threat?'

Zen stared at the floor without answering for a very long time.

'I don't know the answer to that,' he said at last.

Siro nodded.

'It's just that I wouldn't want anything bad to happen to Uncle Gabriele. I don't see much of him these days, but he was always very kind to me when I was young. And my idea may be nonsense. But I don't want to betray him if he doesn't want to be found.'

Zen grasped the young man's arm urgently.

'If the *servizi* are after him, he will be found whether he wants it or not. So that's no longer an issue. The only question is who gets there first. Would you rather it was them or me?'

Siro gulped down some more Coke.

'In the past, Mamma's family were landowners,' he said. 'It all started about a hundred and fifty years ago, when they got wealthy from a brickworks they owned here in Milan. They bought an agricultural estate in the country with the profits, and added to it over the years. And a century later, when Gabriele was a boy, that's where the family used to spend the summer months. My grandfather finally sold the property in the late sixties. It had been operating at a loss for some time. The *contadini* were all moving here and finding jobs in construction or factories, and the ones that were left were demanding higher wages and better conditions. That era was over. So he sold up, but the buildings remained. They were of no use for modern mechanized farming, but would have been far too expensive to demolish.'

'You see them all over the Po valley,' Zen commented, 'but I've never been inside one.'

'I have. My uncle took me there on a day trip from Milan. I must have been eight or nine at the time. To be honest, I couldn't understand why he'd bothered. Just this huge expanse of fields, flat as a pancake, and drainage ditches and irrigation canals and rows of trees, and then the *cascina* itself, which was already falling into ruin. All I understood at the time was that this was tremendously important to him, and because I wanted to please him I pretended to be interested as he showed me around the stables and the byre, the hayloft, the threshing floor and all the rest of it. The light, he kept saying, that pearly quality you only get here in the Valpadana. And then he showed me the little room he'd used when he was a child, up in the old dovecote above the family house, with all his books and a view for miles. "That was the only time in my life when I've been truly happy," he told me. And I believed him, even though to me it was just a broken-down stinking ruin.'

A man dressed in jeans and a leather jacket opened the door.

'*Ciao*, Siro!' he called over. 'Sorry about the delay, but this fog . . .'

Siro gestured to Costanzo to wait.

'You think he's there now?' Zen asked.

'He might be. He would feel safe there, I know that.'

'And where is it?'

'Ah, that I can't tell you. We arrived at some small local railway station, I've forgotten the name, then cycled along these flat country roads for what seemed like hours. Somewhere north of Cremona, I think. And now I must go.'

The two young men left. The barman reached for the remote control to turn off the television.

'Wait!' Zen told him.

The television game show had given way to the news while he and Siro had been talking. The presenter was now running through the minor items at the end of the bulletin, the sweepings from the day's events. It was the video of the hotel that had attracted Zen's attention. An expressionless voice-over explained that a female Italian tourist had fallen to her death from the balcony of her room in Lugano. The Swiss police were treating it as an accident. Her name had been given as Claudia Giovanna Comai, a former resident of Verona.

'Call me a taxi,' Zen told the barman abruptly.

'Where to?'

'The station.'

The barman shrugged.

'Frankly, with the weather like this it would be quicker to walk.'

Zen did exactly that. From Porta Garibaldi he took the *metropolitana* to the Central Station, where he caught the last train to Verona with twenty minutes to spare.

XVI

The worst part was having to take the underground. There was something aggressively demotic about this system of transportation that never failed to remind Alberto of everything that was wrong with the country. From the security point of view, however, it had the virtue of near-total anonymity.

Lepanto, his local station was called, after the street where the station was situated. Below ground, next to the tracks, the walls were plastered with huge advertisements in French informing the hordes of blacks pouring in from North Africa how they could telegraph the money they made illegally in Italy back to their starving broods in the desert, so that they too could hire a *scafista* to smuggle them in to pillage the wealth of Europe.

The platforms were packed with jostling, raucous, over-excited students from the high school on Viale delle Milizie. How many of them had the slightest clue what Lepanto signified? The seventh of October 1571. The decisive naval victory of Christianity over Islam, settling that matter for another four centuries. News as up-to-date as today's headlines, but where were the Sebastiano Veniers and the Augustino Barbarigos of today? Cervantes had served among the Spanish forces during that encounter, and had sustained injuries that had permanently maimed his left hand, but he counted Lepanto ever afterwards as the most glorious day in his life, beside which the composition of *Don Quixote* was a mere bagatelle.

The letter from Gabriele had arrived two days earlier. Alberto had at once forwarded the envelope, though not of course the contents, to the service's *Scientifica* unit. Their forensic experts had found minute traces of corn, fertilizer, mould and birdshit. An agricultural location was evidently indicated, but that and the Crema postmark was all there was to go on. However a little discreet research in the provincial land registry office had revealed that the Passarini family once owned an agricultural estate in the Valpadana. Cazzola, who had already interviewed Gabriele's sister Paola without result, had been dispatched there on Friday to do some preliminary investigation. His call had arrived that morning.

'I've visited the property, *capo*. I took some photographs and I've got a full description, but in accordance with your orders I didn't investigate further.'

'Very good. How soon can you get back to Rome?'

'In a few hours. By this afternoon at the latest.'

'We need to meet in person so that I can fully debrief you. Location seven, time D.'

'*D'accordo, capo.*'

The orange train finally disgorged itself from the tunnel, almost unrecognizable beneath the graffiti that obliterated even the windows, huge curvy garish crazed capital letters spelling God knew what, but certainly nothing sane or good. As if that wasn't enough, at the Spagna stop the carriage was invaded by a mob of Veronese football hooligans who packed the space, drinking *limoncello* out of a communal bottle, smoking in open defiance of the law, and screaming '*Roma, Roma, vaffanculo!*' in an obscene, pagan chant. Alberto was dearly tempted to take out one of his numerous false IDs and arrest the lot of them on the spot, but of course that was impossible under the rules of engagement.

In the event, the soccer fans got off two stations later at Termini, presumably to catch a train back north. Unfortunately the few ordinary solid Italians who had been aboard also left, to be replaced by a mob of blacks and gypsies and asylum seekers who had been begging, picking pockets and selling counterfeit junk outside the main railway station all day, and were now going home to their illegal squatter camps on the fringes of the city. With a slight chill, Alberto suddenly realized that he was the only Italian in the carriage.

Nothing happened. If anything the atmosphere grew warmer and more relaxed as the stations ticked away. All the foreigners were chatting away to each other, laughing and telling stories in their barbaric tongues. Alberto was hesitant to admit it to himself, but what it felt like, to be perfectly honest, was something very similar to the society in which he had grown up back in the fifties. Here too there was that sense of community and of shared experience that had all but vanished from the peninsula during his lifetime. He could of course never feel at home with these people, but they seemed to feel at home with each other, each in his own clan with its own language and traditions. What did the Italy of today have to offer in return? That pack of drunken football yobs, or a bunch of flashy yuppies with one spoilt designer child in tow like a pedigree dog. We've lost something, he thought. We're stronger in lots of small ways, but they're stronger in one big way.

Nevertheless he did not relax his guard. When he left the train at Cinecittà, one stop before the terminus, a group of four Moroccans or Senegalese followed him up the escalator. They were intensely black, all dressed in loose, brightly patterned cotton robes, their skin burnished like some precious metal. As he reached ground level, a gust of cold air blew in through the portal leading to the street. They're going to freeze in that desert gear, he thought with a mixture of admiration and contempt, buttoning up his heavy overcoat and lighting a cigarette.

Suddenly they were all around him, closed in like a pack of wild dogs, one of them demanding something in mangled Italian. Alberto had no idea what he was saying. He knew only that the tone was loud, insistent and menacing, and that he was all alone. He instinctively pulled his knife and stabbed out at the nearest of the four, but the man was no longer there. Alberto whirled around, carving the air to left and right, until an inexorable grip stilled his wrist, immobilizing the knife. Two brown eyes, infinitely wide and deep, looked into his.

'What sort of animal are you?' said one of the men.

And then it was over and they were gone, striding away like gods, laughing and talking amongst themselves, not bothering to glance back and see if he was coming after them. They'd even left him the knife, because for them he didn't count. He was just a sad old man who had panicked because some strangers had asked him for a light at the entrance to an underground station.

'*Ma che razza di animale sei?*' Well, he'd soon show them the answer to that. Not those illegal immigrants, who would never dream of bringing the incident to the attention of the authorities, thank God, but the only two people who still mattered. They'd soon find out exactly what sort of animal he was! He checked his watch, but there was no need to worry. 'Time D' was still a good twenty minutes off, and it would take him no more than half that to reach the spot. He had timed the route carefully, as he always did, although he had never used 'Location seven' before. It was somewhere he had been saving for a long time as a 'one-time-only' venue, in much the same way that he had nurtured Cazzola along for many years as a potential one-time-only resource, should the need arise.

He had spotted Cazzola shortly after taking up his post as a divisional commander at SISMI's head-quarters. He had already formed a clear impression of the kind of man he was looking for – young, insecure, ambitious, diligent, malleable but not too bright – and Cazzola fitted this identikit portrait to perfection. Alberto had taken him under his wing, flattered and encouraged him, and arranged for him to be promoted into a meaningless but fine-sounding role as his personal aide-de-camp. Within a year, he owned Cazzola. 'You're like a father to me,' the young man had once blurted out.

Once Alberto's authority had been established beyond question, he had tested out his protégé on a few minor but strictly illegal missions of no real importance in themselves. The object had been to ensure that Cazzola was prepared to perform any and all tasks under Alberto's personal direction and authorization, reporting only to him, and to keep quiet about them at the time and afterwards. He had passed these tests with flying colours.

So when the long-dreaded eventuality finally came to pass, Alberto had the instruments he needed to hand. Over the years, he had used the resources of the *servizi* to keep track of the other two former members of his cell. Nestore's move to Venezuela, and the change of name and citizenship that followed, had thrown him off the scent until Soldani had solved the problem himself by enlisting Alberto's help in setting up various illicit but lucrative deals involving petroleum and guns. With an antiquarian bookshop licensed with the city of Milan under his own name, Gabriele had posed no such problem. In both cases, Alberto's approach had been oblique and tacit. Each year on the anniversary of Leonardo's death, he had sent them both a blank post-card of the Cellini bronze depicting Perseus holding the severed head of Medusa, as a reminder both of the event that would link them for the rest of their lives and also of the fact that he knew where they lived.

As soon as the storm broke, however, he had moved on to the offensive, using the considerable powers which his position afforded him for information gathering and logistical support, and then calling in Cazzola to execute his orders. Nestor Machado Solorzano, as Nestore now styled himself, had been his first target. Cazzola had kept him under surveillance, reporting on the target's helpfully regular life and then breaking into his wife's car and identifying the type of *telecomando* that the couple used to open the automatic gates of their villa. After that it was just a question of requisitioning some Semtex and a radio-controlled detonator from stores for a fictional anti-terrorist operation and then putting Cazzola's bomb-making training to work, linking the two together in an unobtrusive package and retuning the detonator to the wavelength of the remote control transmitter.

While he and Nestore were having their meaningless discussion at the remote station halfway up Monte Generoso, Cazzola had put yet more of his technical skills to work in the mainline car park down by the lake. His tutor, a former professional car thief whose sentence had been halved thanks to the intervention of one of Alberto's contacts, boasted that he could open any car in less than twenty seconds without attracting attention or setting off the alarm. Cazzola had proved an excellent pupil, and the bomb had been planted under the driving seat of Nestore's BMW Mini Cooper S even before its owner had boarded the train back down the mountain.

One down, one to go. The second operation was always going to be more difficult, since the target would have been alerted to the danger by the first. Hence Alberto's decision to tackle Gabriele after Nestore, on the basis that he had always seemed duller-witted, more timid and altogether less of an apparent challenge. Alberto had formed this opinion when they were junior officers thirty years earlier, and had seen no reason to revise it now. What he hadn't counted on was Gabriele simply disappearing.

But disappear he had, and if he hadn't made the stupid mistake – so typical of a weak, frightened man – of sending Alberto that letter full of bluff and bluster, he might never have been found until Gabriele eventually emerged and returned, as he must have done sooner or later, to his normal life. Alberto had been prepared to wait if necessary, but he hadn't been at all happy about it. The situation was too unstable and unpredictable and there was just too much at stake. For Alberto personally, of course, but also for the nation and above all the honour and reputation of the forces pledged to defend it. Still, it had all worked out for the best in the end. Once he had attended to this little chore, he would travel north in person and remove the last remaining threat to the pristine secrecy that had always surrounded Operation Medusa.

He unbuttoned his coat and transferred the knife from it to his right-hand trouser pocket. The street along which he had been walking was bounded to his left by a high wall. There were no cars about, and it was too cold for pedestrians to venture outside. Alberto opened the unmarked metal door, stepped inside and closed the door, leaving it unlocked.

The key had come into his possession almost ten years previously, after he had met one of the managing directors of Cinecittà at a reception. The next day he had phoned the man and mentioned that a friend of a friend was trying to seduce a married woman, so far without success, and had had the crazy idea of taking her to the famous open-air lots of the film studio one sultry August night and trying his luck there. For obvious reasons they could not enter through the main gate. The friend once removed in question was a leading political figure, whilst the woman's husband was none other than . . . Was there by any chance a way of entering the complex unobserved? It would only be a matter of an hour or two, and the persons concerned could naturally be counted upon to be discreet, not to mention grateful.

A key to one of the service doors to the complex had duly been provided, and returned shortly afterwards along with a lengthy and salacious account of how the imaginary tryst had gone, but not before Alberto had made a copy. He had then filed this away in a safe place where he stored many other potentially useful artefacts until the managing director in question retired and his own involvement in the matter had been entirely forgotten. Alberto was not one to rush his plans, nor to leave anything to chance.

At thirteen minutes past ten precisely, the 'Time D' referred to on their mutual schedule, the door in the wall opened and Cazzola walked in. Alberto, obscure in the gloom lit only by the faint radiance of a distant street lamp, waved to him. His subordinate approached and handed over a manilla envelope.

'It's all in here, *capo*. The exact location, photographs, a map and a full written report.'

'Any sign of anyone living there?'

'None that I could see. The property is set well back from the road. It's really only a paved lane anyway. The land is dead flat and there's almost no cover. It looked as though there were fresh bicycle tracks leading up the driveway to the place, but if I'd tried to stake it out and do a proper surveillance I might have been spotted. I'll be only too glad to go back and break in if you want. It's an old abandoned *cascina* out in the middle of nowhere. If our man is there, I can easily get in and take care of him.'

Alberto put the envelope in his coat pocket and patted the other on the arm.

'No, no. No need for that.'

He had started walking along a track between the enormous blind walls supported by scaffolding. A building site, one might have thought.

'Are you sure that you weren't observed?' Alberto murmured.

'Well, the sister saw me of course, but she's already forgotten I exist. Apart from that it was strictly by the book every step of the way. False identities, no personal contact, no paper trail. I came and went like a wraith.'

'Good for you, Cazzola.'

They had reached a clearing between the structures on either side. To their left was one of the piazzas in Assisi. Medieval buildings in the warm pink stone from Monte Subasio framed the façade of a large church with a circular rose window above the western portal. To their right stood one of the Imperial forums, its pillared basilicas and monumental arches entirely undilapidated and restored to their austere if slightly vulgar glory. Alberto held out one hand to either side.

'Which way?' he asked.

Cazzola stared at him confusedly but did not speak.

'Since we're here, we might as well take full advantage of the facilities,' Alberto remarked jocularly, leading the way into the Roman forum.

'This is one of the sets they used for all those epics they churned out back in the fifties,' he explained. 'Before your time, of course, but they brought in a lot of foreign money at a time when we desperately needed it.'

He took off his overcoat and laid it over a section of low wall that resounded hollowly as his foot struck it. Next to come off was his jacket.

'What are you doing, *capo*?' asked Cazzola with a slight edge of anxiety.

'I want to show you something.'

Alberto rolled up the right sleeve of his shirt. He turned his arm towards the other man, pointing out a small black tattoo with the forefinger of his left hand. Cazzola advanced awkwardly, as if too great a physical proximity might seem disrespectful.

'What is it?' he asked in a low voice.

'The head of Medusa. One of the Gorgons. Mythical monsters.'

He rolled his sleeve back down and fastened the cuff.

'I wanted you to see it, Cazzola, because that's what this whole business has been about. A clandestine military operation of the nineteen-seventies, code-named Medusa. It was to be activated in the event that the revolutionaries and anarchists who were running around rampant at that period ever managed to come to power. Those of us in the organization pledged ourselves ready to take whatever steps might prove to be necessary to restore law and order. Do you understand?'

Cazzola nodded dumbly.

'Good,' said Alberto. 'Only I had to be sure, do you see?'

'Sure of what?'

'That you'd understood.'

He bent his head suddenly.

'Damn!'

'What's the matter, *capo*?'

'One of my contact lenses has fallen out. See if you can find it, like a good lad. I'm half blind without it . . .'

But Cazzola was already down on his hands and knees, searching the fibreglass paving stones minutely. Alberto moved round to stand behind him, reaching into his trouser pocket.

'Who's that?' he gasped.

As Cazzola raised his head to look around, Alberto grasped his chin from behind, tugged it sharply up and slit his throat.

So much blood, he thought. But none on his clothing, although the coat would have covered any stains. He wiped his fingers off on a length of toilet paper, then put his jacket and coat back on and dropped the knife, gloves and the wad of paper into the self-sealing plastic bag he had brought along for the purpose. Back at home, he would wash and dry the knife carefully. It had served him well in the past, and might well do so again in the future.

So much blood. About twenty thousand Turks had been killed at Lepanto, together with half that number of Christians. The human body contains almost six litres of blood. Say one hundred and eighty thousand litres in all. The scuppers of the galleys must have been awash in it, the Gulf of Patras turned to a new Red Sea.

Once the initial pressurized gush had subsided, Alberto carefully searched the body, but Cazzola had indeed been doing everything strictly by the book, and there was nothing that could have identified him. Even if there had been, enquiries would not get very far. Like every other agent of SISMI, Alberto himself included, all records of his existence had been removed from the hands of the civil authorities and destroyed. To all intents and purposes, Cazzola had never existed.

Like a wraith, Alberto thought with satisfaction as he closed and locked the metal door behind him.

XVII

Zen's train was due to arrive at Verona shortly after two in the morning, but delays due to the fog prevalent throughout the region lengthened the journey time considerably. He dozed off immediately after the departure from Milan, but woke once they reached Brescia, knowing that he wouldn't be able to sleep again. In many cases he had worked on, there had been a moment like this when events took on a rhythm of their own, imposing themselves like a dance partner who has suddenly decided to lead. But never had he felt this change with such urgency as now.

From the station he caught one of the two remaining cabs in the rank to the Questura on the east bank of the Adige, showed his identification to the desk sergeant and asked for the duty officer and a double espresso. The former turned out to be a gangly, dopey-looking youth who was probably in his mid-twenties but looked like a teenager to Zen. He had apparently been awakened from a deep sleep, but his manner turned rapidly from resentment to alarm as this nocturnal intruder displayed his credentials and explained the reason for his visit.

'A local resident, one Claudia Giovanna Comai, died some thirty-six hours ago as a result of a fall from her hotel room in Lugano. The Swiss are treating it as an accident, but my superiors at Criminalpol have reason to suppose that this is not in fact the case. They have therefore dispatched me here to search the archives for various documents which might tend to prove or disprove this hypothesis. It is a matter of the greatest urgency, as the time of my arrival, so inconvenient for both of us, should amply demonstrate.'

While the young officer was still groggy from this blow, Zen followed up by demanding the use of a secure internal landline to call Rome and report progress. He was shown into an office on the ground floor and left there while his guide went off to look for the key to the archives. Zen called the operator at the Ministry of the Interior and directed her to put him through to the police authorities at the provincial capital in Cremona.

His reception there, coming from the source it did, was far more cordial than the one he had been accorded personally in Verona. Zen outlined the sketchy information he had acquired from Paola Passarini's son regarding the property previously owned by the family and sold by them in the late sixties, and requested that full details be obtained from the local *comune* the moment they opened. He would ring back later in the day to learn the outcome.

As soon as the duty officer unlocked the door leading to the vast storage area in the basement, Zen felt at home. Archives were much the same all over the country, and he had visited most of them at one time or another in his career. To him they were sad but restful places, sheltered graveyards for forgotten intrigues, mysteries and atrocities about which no one cared any more. Above all, they were complete. Italian bureaucrats might have their faults, but like the medieval monks they resembled in so many ways they never threw anything away, although they had of course been known to destroy a document on orders from above, or to let certain well-connected persons remove it while their backs were supposedly turned.

This aspect of official record-keeping had been of some concern to Zen, given the apparent situation. His other worry was the computer screen perched on a desk near the door, but the young officer assured him that although the catalogue was gradually being digitized, this process was slightly behind schedule owing to technical problems and staff shortages and so far covered only those cases dating from 1994. The earlier material was accessed through a series of card index filing cabinets using a system perfectly familiar to Zen. He dismissed his companion with an unsubtle hint about his no doubt needing to get some more sleep, and then set to work. Shortly afterwards the desk sergeant appeared with a plastic mug containing a double shot of espresso. Deep in communion with the files, Zen almost made the mistake of tipping him.

The documents on record in the names of Claudia and Gaetano Comai were not extensive, and apart from the inevitable interlarding of pages regarding purely routine matters they solely concerned the matter of the latter's death. Zen settled down to read them, noting various details from the contemporary reports and also the name of the officer who had conducted the investigation enquiries. When he had everything he needed, he replaced the files and went back upstairs.

The desk sergeant had never heard of any Armando Boito, and very much doubted that his superior would have either.

'We're too young,' he explained in a cringingly apologetic tone of voice that Zen had never before heard used with those particular words. 'The Personnel people keep all the records on former staff on file, of course, but they won't be in until eight.'

Zen walked out under the portico of the Questura for a smoke. A rain as serious and solid as hail was falling. Beyond the other side of the street, the vast bulk of the Adige glided past like the collective unconscious of the sleeping city, a viscous colloid the colour of old blood, laden with muck and garbage, amorphous forms and sodden hulks, shattered hopes and broken dreams. The massed range of the Alps behind had unleashed a storm that would fill the wide channel of the river close to the level of the high embankments by evening. People would shake their heads and exchange fashionable worries about the climate changing, but in truth it had always been like this. There were no land-scapes in Italy. Nature had always been the adversary.

Every instinct was telling Zen to push forward. Short on sleep, but high on adrenalin and caffeine, he felt restless and totally wakeful, but there was nothing he could usefully do until the day staff arrived for work, both here and in Cremona. It then occurred to him that he was going to need to rent a car, and that the places that opened earliest would be at the airport. He went back inside and got the number of the local taxi cooperative from the duty sergeant. At this point, having thrown his weight to such good effect, he could probably have talked his way into getting driven out there in a patrol car, but he already sensed that things were rapidly approaching a point where the fewer official dealings that were involved the better.

When the taxi dropped him off at the airport, the only sign of life in the glistening terminal was a check-in line for some crack-of-dawn cut-price flight to Ibiza. The car rental booths were right down the other end, near the arrivals gate, a walk of what felt like almost a kilometre, and none of them was open. Zen sat down on one of the array of steel benches nearby, fighting the urge to lie down and surrender to sleep by thinking about his interview with Claudia Comai. He realized now that she had understood everything he said *alla rovescia*, inside out. 'I made my statement to the police at the time,' she'd told him. 'They questioned me on several occasions and I said everything I have to say then, while it was all fresh in my mind. The report must still be on file somewhere.'

He tossed restlessly about on the seating, which seemed to have been designed, like certain fast food outlets, with a view to limiting to the absolute minimum the time that anyone would want to use it.

'I've had enough of all your tricks and teasing, understand? He fell down the stairs! That's what happened and you have no proof to the contrary. He was a cripple by then, for God's sake! He fell down the stairs. That was the conclusion arrived at by the investigating magistrate at the time and it's never once been queried, not once in all these years!'

And then those terrible vulgar blasphemies and obscenities that no lady such as Claudia evidently aspired to be should ever have let pass her lips in public. '*Dio boia, Dio can, vaffanculo!*' Zen muttered the phrase aloud now. It was addressed to himself, as she had addressed it at the time, but filled with a very different kind of disgust.

When the car rental people finally arrived, Zen hired a small Fiat with a waiver allowing him to drop it off at any one of the firm's agencies in Italy. Back at the Questura, the usual morning queue of immigrants and asylum seekers in search of residence and work permits had already started to form. In the mood he was in, Zen didn't waste any time on the sensibilities of the clerical staff in Personnel. Within five minutes he had the last recorded address and telephone number of Inspector Armando Boito, who had retired in 1991 and might easily be dead by now.

Zen had parked the Fiat illegally right outside the building, thereby obstructing one lane of what now revealed itself to be a major traffic artery. The first thing he saw when he got in was a white parking ticket fluttering under the windscreen wipers. He got out again, tore it in two and dropped it in the road, thereby adding littering to his local crime record. You had to hand it to the Veronesi, he thought as he pulled away, what they lacked in charm they made up for in efficiency, particularly when *schei* – dosh – was involved.

It took him almost an hour to get out of the city, partly because he was a timid and inexperienced driver and partly because he had no idea where he was going, but mostly because he was trapped in a counter-Adige of nose-to-tail commuters who knew precisely where they were going and had no patience for this bumbling amateur who was fouling up the system. He only escaped in the end because he happened to see a direction sign with the word 'Valpolicella' and immediately veered right across two lanes of traffic in a manner that elicited a number of colourful comments which he was fortunately unable to understand since they were in a form of dialect specific not to the Veneto in general but to the city of Verona in particular.

After that, it was pretty straightforward. He stopped at a petrol station and asked directions, then rang Boito's number from the payphone. The call was answered immediately, and by the man himself. This time Zen wasted no time on a cover story. He told Boito exactly who he was and what he wanted, and got an immediate and positive response.

San Giorgio di Valpolicella was reached by a turning off the main road which wound up into the hills looming mistily above the plain below before twisting to a halt in the entrails of a village that was clearly very much older than anything Zen had seen on the drive there. Boito had said that he would meet him at a bar in the centre of the village, next to the church.

'You can't miss it. It's the only one.'

He was right. Zen parked in the piazza and walked over to their rendezvous, a typical rural watering hole lacking either charm or pretension.

A man in his sixties, with a shock of white hair cropped short and the thickset, four-square, slightly Germanic look of the local population, rose to his feet and greeted him. Zen made token apologies for disturbing Boito so early, which were graciously brushed aside. They both ordered coffees and then the retired inspector told his story.

He remembered the Comai case well, he said, because it was one of those where he was reasonably sure that a crime had been committed, but had not been able to prove it.

'They stick with you, those ones! She got away with it, you think, and I wasn't intelligent or powerful or lucky enough to make her pay. So you end up feeling guilty yourself, almost as if you were the criminal. The whole business leaves a nasty taste in your mouth. Do you understand what I'm talking about?'

'I certainly do.'

'Gaetano Comai, the victim, was in his seventies at the time. His wife Claudia was about twenty years younger. Their son Naldo was in school and it was the housekeeper's day off. Gaetano had retired from the army by then, after a long and distinguished career. He suffered from circulatory problems and could only walk with the aid of a metal frame. At their house in Verona there was a lift, but at the villa here in the Valpolicella they installed a chair lift so that he could get up and down the stairs. Are you familiar with those contraptions? It's basically a platform fitted with a chair and powered by an electric motor, which runs up and down the staircase in a steel track mounted beneath the banisters.'

'I've heard of them.'

'The first we knew was when Signora Comai called the police station in Negrar with an incoherent message about an emergency, please come at once. No specifics. That was a bit odd in itself, don't you think? Your husband is lying critically injured after allegedly falling downstairs, but instead of calling an ambulance you call the police.'

'Did you ask her about that?'

'She claimed to have been in shock. Anyway, the patrolmen arrive and immediately radio for an ambulance, but when it gets there Signor Comai is certified dead. Meanwhile the policemen have taken a statement from his wife about how the accident occurred.'

'Her husband had been upstairs, having an afternoon nap,' Zen recited. 'She was downstairs reading in the main *salone*. She heard the tapping of his walking frame as he came along the gallery, then the whine of the chair lift in operation, a sharp cry and a series of heavy thuds. She ran to investigate and found his crumpled body at the foot of the stairs and the lift still only a few steps from the top.'

Armando Boito stared at Zen suspiciously.

'How did you know that?'

'I've read the file on the case, *ispettore*. Believe me, I've done my homework. What I want from you is the items that did not appear in the official report.'

Boito nodded.

'We're getting there. Forgive me, I have to take everything in order, otherwise I become confused. Signora Comai then demonstrated to the patrolman, as she did later to me, that the lift would only move as long as the control button on the arm was depressed. It must therefore have stopped when her husband, for whatever reason, lost his balance and fell forward to his death. The patrolman, who should instantly have been promoted for this thought, walked up the stairs and tried it out for himself. As the grieving widow had said, the lift moved as soon as he pushed the button. Only it moved *up*.'

He and Zen exchanged a long look.

'Those chair lifts are very simple devices,' Boito went on. 'They either go all the way up or all the way down, reversing direction at the end of their track. So Signor Comai must have been ascending and not descending the stairs when he fell, in which case his wife's version of events was obviously false.'

'What did she say to that?' asked Zen.

'She hummed and hawed for a while, then used the shock argument and suddenly remembered that she had used the lift herself to go upstairs to fetch medicines from the bathroom. She felt too weak to walk, she told me. And too frightened of the staircase. According to her, she had felt it to be a "malign force".'

Zen glanced at his watch.

'But you thought otherwise?'

'I certainly did. There was no sign of any medicines in the vicinity of the corpse, and the pathologist found no indication that any had been administered. What he did find, in addition to the expected fractures and contusions, was a deep bleeding fracture to the back of the skull.'

Boito shrugged.

'As you know, all sorts of odd things can happen when people fall to their deaths. Signor Comai might have struck his head against the edge of one of the steps, or for that matter against the banister post at the bottom, a very ornate affair with plenty of sharp edges. The problem from my point of view was that there were no traces of blood, tissue, hair or anything else on any of these places. When I remarked on this, the widow claimed that she had wiped the surfaces clean because it was too distressing for her to have to look at her husband's bloodstains. I then asked what she had used. A rag, she replied. What had she done with it? "I threw it in the fire. It made me feel unclean."'

'A fire? But this happened in August.'

'Precisely. An oppressive, sultry day with temperatures in the thirties and thunder in the air. Nevertheless, a fire was indeed smouldering in the *salone*. I inspected the fire-irons, which were of wrought iron and very heavy. They were all filthy except for the poker, which seemed to have been wiped clean. When I asked about the fire, Signora Comai blushed and replied that she had suddenly felt a chill. Perhaps it was the change of life. She was approaching that period of her life. Sometimes she felt hot, sometimes she felt cold. These were very indelicate questions. There was no law against lighting a fire in your own house, was there?'

Zen liked Armando Boito, and under normal circumstances would have been more than happy to spend the whole day arguing the toss about this long-closed case, but as it was he had become a miser with minutes.

'So you had a promising *prima facie* case totally dependent on circumstantial evidence,' he suggested.

'Just so. And what I would have liked to do, of course, was to take Signora Comai back to the Questura in Verona and submit her to a twenty-four-hour-a-day relay interrogation until she broke. But that was out of the question. The Comais did not quite belong to the cream of Verona society, of the rich and thick variety, but they weren't nobodies either. There were plenty of influential friends and acquaintances only too ready to make a public scandal out of the fact that an over-zealous police officer was not only trying to prevent Gaetano's widow from coming to terms with her tragic loss, but was virtually accusing her of having murdered him. I would never have been able to find an investigating magistrate to sign an arrest warrant. On the contrary, in the course of the one attempt I made it was made very clear to me that any further initiatives of the kind would result in me being transferred to a much less desirable posting than Verona.'

He opened his arms to embrace the bar, the village and the surrounding countryside.

'This is my home, *dottore*! I had no wish to make a martyr of myself and get shipped off to some flea-ridden cesspit in Calabria or Sicily. To what good, anyway? The case would still have come to nothing. One has to be a realist about these things.'

Zen indicated his complete understanding.

'But you still think she did it?' he asked.

Boito looked at him almost with anger.

'Do you need to ask?'

'Then how?'

Boito sighed deeply.

'My guess would be that she waited until her husband went upstairs for his afternoon nap, which he habitually did at about the time his death occurred. On some pretext she walked up alongside the chair lift in which he was seated. Near the top she somehow persuaded him to stand up, or perhaps just heaved him bodily out of the chair and down the long flight of stairs. She was much younger than him, remember, and very sturdily built. Then she ran downstairs and got the poker from the *salone*. He may already have been dead, but she wanted to make sure. She smashed in the back of the head, then lit the fire she had previously laid and wiped off the poker with a rag that she then burned. I had the cinders forensically examined and traces of cloth fibre were found, but of course that fitted in with her story.'

Zen nodded.

'All right, let's assume you're right. She killed him. Why?'

Boito made a broad, resigned gesture.

'That was the other problem I had in trying to pursue the investigation. If only there had been some clear motive, or indeed any motive at all, I might have been able to find a judge to take it on, despite the pressure from the family's friends. But on the face of it Signora Comai had nothing obvious to gain from her husband's death. She inherited, of course, but she was perfectly well provided for anyway. The Comais seemed to get along reasonably well together, like most middle-aged couples. By this point, both of them had passed the age when romantic passion could have played a part, and there were no indications that she was a psychotic. So if I'm right, and she did kill him, what could possibly have driven her to take such an incredible risk? Unfortunately I never found the answer to that question.'

Boito smiled complacently.

'But maybe you'll have better luck, *dottore*. What is the exact nature of your interest in this case, if you don't mind my asking?'

'I'm investigating the death of Signora Comai.'

Boito's reaction was one of shock. It occurred to Zen that he might well be one of those retired people who understandably feel that they have wasted enough of their lives on news about events that were either of no interest to them or beyond their control, and have decided to break the addiction and live clean for the years remaining to them.

'Like her husband, she died in a fall,' he said, rising to his feet and putting a banknote on the table to pay for their coffees. 'The official line is that it was an accident.'

They walked out into the joyless morning.

'What became of the villa?' asked Zen as he searched for the elusive new car key. 'I looked for it on the way here but I couldn't find it.'

'It's gone. Signora Comai sold it after her husband's death, citing painful memories and all the rest of it. It was torn down to make room for one of those new apartment blocks down on the main road. Not that it was any great loss, architecturally. The best aspect was always the grounds. Funnily enough, she kept a part of them.'

'How do you mean?'

'Well, the villa itself was just a nineteenth-century fantasy on Gothic and Renaissance themes, but there was an extensive walled garden reaching back to a lane behind the property. It had been well designed, and had reached full maturity back in the fifties. And in one corner, at the very end, there was a playhouse that had been built by Claudia's parents as a birthday present for her. I went down there to take a look when I was questioning her, but it was obviously of no interest to our investigation. Too small for a grown man to even stand up in. Anyway, she sold everything except for a strip at the very end, where the playhouse is, and then had a new wall built to screen it off from the new apartments. Everyone thought she was crazy. A sentimental whim, I suppose.'

Zen frowned.

'So where is it?'

'The villa was where the new block is, just opposite the AGIP filling station on the right as you drive back to Verona. But there's nothing to see.'

Zen spent some moments in thought, then breathed in deeply.

'Good air up here,' he remarked.

Boito nodded.

'In more ways than one, I would argue. San Giorgio has always been a *paese rosso*, one of the few in this priest-ridden zone. Because of the quarries, you see. This is where they mined that fine, flawless stone used for all the finishing work on the doors and windows in the area, and the quarrymen were soon organized by the PCI. So the intellectual air is also better, at least to my way of thinking.'

He smiled self-deprecatingly.

'But of course I was born here. You must judge for yourself. The church is well worth a visit. Parts of it date from 712, but the village itself is much older, at least Neolithic and probably much earlier. I'd be only too happy to show you around, if you have time.'

But time was exactly what Aurelio Zen did not have.

In the small town of Sant'Ambrogio at the foot of the hill, he parked the Fiat in the huge piazza just north of the medieval centre, and then proceeded on foot. In due course he found a grocery and a newsagent's where you could send or receive faxes. From the former he obtained a ham and cheese roll, from the latter the number of their fax machine. Then he walked back to the phone box in the piazza and called his contact at the Questura in Cremona.

'Yes, yes, we have the information you requested, *dottore*. The property you described does indeed exist, although it's now completely abandoned. Shall I give you the details now? Fax them to your hotel? Absolutely, *dottore*. At once. There's just one thing, if I may be so bold . . .'

'Well?' demanded Zen, chewing on the roll.

'When I called the land registry office, the woman there had the file we needed ready to hand. She said that this was the second time in the past few days that there had been an enquiry about the former Passarini property.'

'Who was the other caller?'

'Someone at the Ministry of Defence, she said. So I naturally wondered if there was perhaps something going on there that we should know about. We could easily send a few men out there to search the place.'

Zen almost choked on his roll.

'No, no, no! That won't be necessary. There's no interest in the property itself. It must be a ruin by now anyway. It's just a question of the deeds.'

'Ah, right. But what exactly is this concerning?'

'An on-going criminal investigation based in Rome which for obvious reasons I can't discuss. The Ministry of Defence also has an interest in the case. And to make things still more difficult, there is a civil lawsuit in progress, the evidence in which is germane to our own enquiries. One of the items regarded the ownership of this property back in the sixties. So it's purely a matter of background information relating to an affair which is of no interest whatsoever to the Provincia di Cremona. Otherwise of course I'd have alerted you.'

To his relief, the inspector in Cremona sounded convinced.

'*Perfetto, dottore*. Forgive me for bringing it up, but I thought I'd better ask. We naturally like to keep track of anything important that might be happening on our territory.'

'Of course.'

'Excellent. Well then, I'll fax the information to you right away.'

Zen left the phone booth and stood outside, smoking a cigarette and staring at the rectangular piazza lined with savagely pollarded trees. It was enormous for the size of the town, a parade ground big enough to drill a regiment. There must have been a sheep market here once upon a time, with flocks brought down from the hills above. That would explain it.

He went back into the booth and phoned Gemma. There was no answer, so he left a brief message on the answering machine, almost certainly too brief for the listeners to trace the number he was calling from. As he walked back to the newsagent's, he remembered that

Gemma had told him that she was planning to spend a couple of days visiting her son.

That gave him another idea. Having picked up the fax from the Questura in Cremona, he bought a sheet of paper – nothing came free in the Veneto – and faxed a message to his friend Giorgio De Angelis at Criminalpol, asking him to send a team of their technical people up to the apartment in Via del Fosso and remove any electronic surveillance equipment they found there. He didn't bother mentioning the spare key held by a neighbour on the floor below. The Ministry's specialists could open any door known to man while you were blowing your nose.

Back in the Fiat, he decided to take a quick look at the remains of Claudia and Gaetano Comai's country property. It was only a few kilometres away, and the nearest link road to the *autostrada* lay in that direction anyway. Following Armando Boito's instructions, he located the filling station easily enough, then turned left down a street along the side of the new apartment block. About three-quarters of the way down, what was obviously the original nineteenth-century wall of the estate replaced the modern cast-iron fence mounted on a concrete base installed by the developers. The old stone wall continued around the corner at the next cross-street, running along the rear of the property. At its mid-point, a green wooden door was inset in the wall. Stickers on the rear bumper of a battered white Toyota parked next to it exhorted people to say no to NATO genocide bombing in Serbia, save the whales, and think globally but act locally.

There was an odd, disturbing sound in the air, presumably a dog shut up here to guard the property, far from the snuffly intimacy and comforting odours of the pack. Single dogs had become the norm these days, Zen reflected as he opened the back door of the car and unlatched his suitcase. Single children too. He'd been an only child himself, of course, but things had been different back them. In the neighbourhood of Venice where Zen had grown up, there had been a community of children who played and learned together, swearing and daring and egging each other on, tussling for rank and status, inventing elaborate games for which no expensive products were necessary, exploring their territory and staging raids and mock battles with their rivals to either side. But all that had gone. Now both dogs and children had to try and make sense of life all on their own. No wonder they whined so much.

He approached the door in the wall, holding the small toolkit that he had removed from his suitcase. He had acquired this useful piece of equipment during his years as an inspector in Naples, when a petty thief had unwittingly blundered into the middle of a major operation Zen had been involved in. The burglar had gladly agreed to trade his freedom for a vow of silence and a set of his working instruments, plus a crash course in how to use them.

They had served Zen well on many occasions, but one glance at the lock told him that they would be of no use here. This was an old-fashioned barrel lock wrought by hand out of iron, contemporary with the original villa. It might have caused a slight problem even for the Ministry's technicians. Zen's bag of tricks, designed to cope with modern industrial products, would be powerless against it.

The wailing sounded out again, louder and more prolonged than before. Zen glanced at the white Toyota. It had the old-fashioned number plates starting with the two-letter code for the province where the vehicle was registered, in this case Pesaro. He grasped the handle of the garden door and pushed his shoulder against it. The door stuck for a moment on the stone ledge at the bottom, then swung open.

The remaining strip of garden consisted of dense shrubbery against the wall to either side and between the thrusting lower trunks of deciduous trees much too large for this space. A clearly-trodden path led off through this miniature glade, and Zen followed it past outcroppings of bushes and ground cover to a wall of giant cypresses where the path curved back, eventually revealing a diminutive brick house in the corner of the garden.

The wailing burst out with renewed vigour and volume, peaking in howls of grief with indecipherable words embedded in them. Zen stopped a few metres short of the little building. He knew now what he would find there, and had no wish to cause embarrassment by intruding. He could easily have slipped away unnoticed, but instead he continued to the low front door and opened it.

He looked cautiously around the tiny room before entering, knowing from experience how easily grief could find relief in violence, but there was no one there. To his left, between the windows, hung a mirror covered in black cloth. To his right, a miniaturized dresser with a central cupboard and many smaller cabinets and drawers to either side. At the far end, a table and chairs, a stove and fireplace, and another door. It was from there that the sounds were coming.

Zen stooped to clear the low beamed ceiling. The air was chill and smelt powerfully musty. He opened the door at the far end into an even smaller room. There was a chest of drawers on the same scale as the dresser in the main room. The top drawer was open. On a low wooden bed beneath the single window, Naldo Ferrero sat slumped forward and weeping uncontrollably. On his knees lay an open scrapbook of the kind in which Zen had once arranged the collection of railway tickets given to him by his father.

323

'Excuse me,' Zen said quietly.

Naldo Ferrero leapt to his feet, wiping his tears away and throwing the scrapbook down on the bed.

'How dare you come here?' he shouted furiously. 'You killed my mother! What did you say to her, you bastard? You bullied her, didn't you? You threatened her with God knows what and she threw herself off that balcony in terror and despair!'

'Control yourself, Signor Ferrero. Your mother died in Lugano. How could I have interrogated her there? The Italian police have no jurisdiction in Switzerland. Besides, her death was the result of a tragic accident. At any rate, such is the view of the Swiss authorities, who are famously efficient and neutral.'

He was almost caught off guard when Naldo suddenly lashed out with his fist, but the space was too confined and the intended blow low and wide. Zen simply moved back a step, neither doing nor saying anything. As if appalled at his own temerity, Ferrero pushed past him and ran out of the house. Zen bent over the bed and picked up the scrapbook. It opened naturally about a quarter of the way through, for a reason that was immediately obvious. Ten photographs had been glued to the facing pages at this point.

All had been taken in a large garden. The first six showed a young man, the next two a woman of about thirty. The man might almost have been as young as sixteen or seventeen, with the lean, wiry body of an athlete, close-cut black hair and a guarded gaze laden with some emotion that Zen couldn't quite read in the grainy, low-quality, black-and-white prints. In two of the shots he was wearing casual clothes with the oddly comical air of a style that is out of date but not yet classic. In three others he was in a bathing suit, in one case swimming on his back down a small pool. The remaining one presented him stretched out on the bed that Zen could see by turning his head, stark naked and apparently asleep.

The photographs of the woman had been rather more carefully composed, avoiding the amputational framing and dodgy focus evident in those of the man. The subject, however, was more problematic, despite the fact that Zen recognized her immediately. The younger Claudia had never been beautiful, so much was clear, but the look she gave the camera – as opaque in its way as the young man's – revealed her to have been as troubling as she was troubled. Hers was one of those faces where a certain combination of daring, desperation and sexual greed transforms plain, pudgy features into something far more potent than standard 'good looks'.

Her body, amply revealed by the yellow bikini she wore, provided a powerful bass to this disturbing siren song. The fact that she was slightly overweight and teetering on the brink of an early middle age added a final note. Glancing back at the shots of Leonardo, Zen realized that the look in his eyes was one of fear. This might have seemed perfectly natural under the circumstances, but the quantity and depth of the young man's emotion was somehow disproportionate to the simple fact that he was screwing his commanding officer's wife. Leonardo had been afraid of him, yes, but in some odd way he had been even more afraid of her.

By the time the last two photographs were taken, either Claudia or Leonardo must have worked out how to operate the timed shutter release function on the camera, since these showed both of them posed awkwardly in their swimsuits by the pool. These shots were the most powerfully suggestive of all. Zen vaguely remembered learning at school about certain atoms – or was it molecules? – that would 'bond' with others because they possessed a particle that the other lacked. The possibility for sniggery *doppi sensi* had been only too clear at the time, but he had never realized the wider implications until now. These photographs made it plain that Gaetano Comai's wife and Lieutenant Leonardo Ferrero had been doomed from the moment they met.

How they chose to deal with it was of course another matter, but that was in very little doubt from the moment that Zen turned back to the beginning of the scrapbook. This consisted of densely packed lines of handwriting in dark green ink, a journal of the affair evidently started shortly after it began. It would have taken at least an hour to read the whole thing, for it ran to almost seventy-five large pages, and Claudia proved to have had a prolix and evasive prose style, short on details but very long indeed on feelings, speculations, afterthoughts, commentary and rhetorical questions. Keenly aware that he could spare not hours but minutes, if that, Zen opted for a heuristic method, dipping and scanning, skipping and noting.

His initial researches told him little except for the fact, reading between the lines of loopy handwriting, that Leonardo's part had initially been passive. It was Claudia who had initiated the affair when the young lieutenant appeared at the villa one summer afternoon to return some books to his commanding officer. As it happened, Gaetano Comai was away on army business, but other business soon resulted. Before long, Lieutenant Ferrero started turning up regularly at the villa, always on days when it was known that Gaetano and the staff would be absent.

He was about to put the book down again when he noticed that the thumbed softness at the edge of the used pages continued for a further distance before reverting to the hard cut edge of the original volume.

Turning over two more blank sheets, he found the text resuming, but in what at first appeared a different hand. The pen was different too, a common blue ballpoint, and the writing tighter, harder and more slanted. There were three pages in all, and he read them very quickly.

Naldo Ferrero was standing immediately outside the front door, as if waiting for him to emerge.

'I'm sorry I lashed out at you,' he said in a contrite tone.

'Have you filed that judicial application to recover your father's body?'

'Not yet. I've been busy. But I'm still working on it.'

Zen looked him in the eyes.

'Signor Ferrero, when we met previously I promised to help you to the limits of my ability in return for your cooperation. I regret to say that I have been unsuccessful, but I will give you a word of advice which you would do well to take. Do not contact the judiciary about this. Do not make any further enquiries, either officially or unofficially. Go back to La Stalla, marry Marta if she'll have you, and try and forget the whole thing. One man has already been murdered because of his connection with this affair. A second has gone to ground under a virtual sentence of death. If you pursue this matter, you may well become the third. There are very large interests at stake, and the people concerned are both powerful and ruthless. In any case, there's nothing to be gained. I'm afraid it's virtually certain that your father's body no longer exists in any recognizable form. Put it all behind you and get on with your life.'

Back behind the wheel, Zen took out all his repressed emotion on the hapless rental car, forcing it mercilessly around the tight curves and along the infrequent straights, blasting other traffic with the horn and smashing the gears down to pass. At last he reached the *autostrada*, heading first west and then south to Cremona. When he reached the service station at Ghedi, he parked at the rear of the premises, well out of sight of the main buildings, between two huge red trailer trucks marked *Transport Miedzynarodowy* with an address in Poland. In the service area he bought a small electric torch, and then ordered coffee and a grappa and took them all to one of the stand-up tables. His hands were trembling so much that it was all he could do to get the cup and the glass to his mouth.

Some years earlier, on a return trip to his native Venice, Zen had inadvertently caused the death of a childhood friend by putting too much pressure on him at a vulnerable moment. Now it seemed to have happened again. There had been no way that he could have foreseen the consequences of his actions, but a sense of self-disgust remained. He only hoped that he might be granted an opportunity to make what amends he could.

XVIII

The first time the car passed by, Gabriele was heating up a packet of dried mushroom soup to which he'd added some fresh *porcini* from a long-remembered patch in a thicket near the river. In a minor miracle that seemed to collapse the intervening years, it had turned out still to be there. The second time, when the same car passed by in the opposite direction, he was eating the soup with some bread bought in the local town three days earlier. Dunked in the creamy brown broth, it was just about palatable.

Despite the indifferent light, he was also reading – in a very nice, tight seventh-edition copy (Hachette, 1893) – Hippolyte Taine's *Voyage en Italie*. A memory popped into his mind of a friend who had noticed one of the annual postcards of Perseus holding the Medusa's head, without of course understanding its significance, and had commented that if we could travel back to Cellini's Florence and vice versa, we would be appalled by the smells and he by the noise.

Time travel, the only kind Gabriele was still interested in, was unfortunately not yet possible, but his days here in the country had retrofitted his sense of hearing, which had become as acute as a cat's. At the *cascina,* the silence was intense, broken only by the murmur of an occasional aeroplane far above. The little *strada comunale* that passed the estate had finally been paved, but there was almost no one left with any interest in using it. So when the car drove past the first time, it was an unusual event. Gabriele tracked it, noting the specific characteristics of the engine sound. When it then returned, stopping about a hundred metres beyond the driveway, probably in that copse where the long-abandoned back entrance to a neighbouring property joined the road, he put his book and his bowl of soup aside and grabbed the pack of supplies he had prepared.

His plans had been made for a long time, and were based on a chance encounter with an elderly Chinese man in the Parco Sempione in Milan. In the midst of the usual crew of junkies, whores of both sexes and indigent homeless people, this tiny, wizened person had been tranquilly performing something that looked like art of some kind: a living statue modulating slowly but very surely between various ritualistic poses.

Gabriele had approached the man and asked what he was up to. When he replied that he was practising a form of self-defence called 't'ai chi', Gabriele had almost laughed. He associated the oriental martial arts with savage kicks, bone-breaking hand blows and a lot of screaming.

'Your silent ballet is very beautiful, but how could it help if someone tried to beat you up?'

'It would be very difficult for anyone to attack me,' the man said in a quiet, almost apologetic tone.

This time Gabriele did laugh.

'But what on earth could you do if one of the scum who hang around here went for you with his fists, or even a knife?'

The Chinese man regarded him with a gaze so dignified that it seemed a reproach.

'I would so arrange matters that I was not in the place where the blow struck.'

This was now Gabriele's strategy. He had no way of knowing whether the solemn promises in his letter to Alberto about never revealing the truth about Leonardo's death, still less Operation Medusa, had had any effect, but his last call to Fulvio had elicited the disquieting information that the window of the shop had been smashed, and that a policeman had been there making enquiries regarding his whereabouts and those of his sister. He had almost been tempted to phone Paola for further details, but her line would almost certainly be tapped.

He had decided to wait another few days before making a further appeal to Alberto. In the meantime, if anyone had managed to track him down and came looking for him, it would be almost impossible for them to approach the farm complex without him seeing or hearing them, and once they had entered he would so arrange matters that he was not in the place where they struck.

The main gates of the *cascina* were closed and locked, but he had deliberately left the door inset into them slightly ajar. When pushed, it always squeaked on its hinges. It did so now. Gabriele ran quickly downstairs and out of the rear door of the *casa padronale* into the overgrown garden where the family had sometimes taken tea in the then-fashionable English manner, past the factor's house, the laundry, the old stables and the *porcilaie* for the pigs and hens, then around the corner to the row of two-up, two-down houses formerly occupied by the workers on the estate. In through a rear window that he had left open and up to the first floor bedroom window.

'Gabriele!'

He recognized the voice immediately, but he had also been counting the footsteps ringing out on the stones of the resonant courtyard. There was only one set, so Alberto had come alone. He might of course have back-up in reserve, but that was unlikely. In a matter of this delicacy, whom could he trust? Either way, it was time to find out. He opened the window, lit one of the fireworks he had bought earlier and tossed it out.

The answer was a gunshot. The bullet came nowhere near Gabriele, but the response had been immediate and without the slightest hesitation. Alberto must already have had a pistol in his hand. In a way, this came as a relief. The terms of engagement had been established. Now he had to keep moving, rapidly, and always in the same direction. This aspect of the business he had gleaned from further explanations provided by the t'ai chi performer. The art of the thing was to hypnotize your opponent with a seemingly ineluctable pattern of movement, a process with its own rhythm and dynamics, and then, at the last moment, disappear from it.

But to do that, he first had to appear. This would inevitably be dangerous, but Gabriele's army experiences had proved that despite his seemingly infinite capacity for irrational anxieties of all kinds, he was virtually insusceptible when it came to real, solid, substantial threats. Indeed, he almost welcomed them. They took his mind off the other stuff. Nevertheless, his army experience had also amply demonstrated that his fearlessness far exceeded his competence. 'If this had been real, you'd be dead,' he'd been told more than once in the course of a training exercise. Now it was real. This still didn't scare him – as the child his imaginary fears revealed him to be, he still believed himself to be immortal – but it made him wary. He wasn't afraid to risk his life, but he would have hated to give these bastards the satisfaction of killing him.

Downstairs to the communal kitchen at the front of the house. A glance outside showed a figure prowling aimlessly about the *aia* in the rising mist, seemingly at a loss how to proceed. Now for the tricky part. Gabriele had eased the catch and hinges of the front door with olive oil, as he had those of the window upstairs, but there were no guarantees. It was strange to recall that one of the specialist courses the four of them had taken together all those years ago had been in close-quarter house-to-house combat. Nestore and Leonardo had been by far the best.

He opened the door gradually, then slipped through the gap and ran as fast as he could to his left, weaving and ducking as they'd been trained to do. Two shots in rapid succession, sounding like thunder in the well of the yard. One bullet struck the brickwork to his right. Gabriele raced up the steps of the *porcilaie* and through the trapdoor at the top, bolting it behind him. Then it was out through the ventilation aperture – barred in the traditional chequered wrought-iron fashion, but he and his brother Primo had cut down the screws, leaving only the heads in place, to create another secret exit – and on to a branch of the huge poplar just outside. By now he was ten years old again. Up the steeply curving limb to the point where it overhung the roof, from which it was an easy drop on to the terracotta tiles.

Reaching the crest of the roof, he produced another banger from his bag and launched it down into the courtyard. The explosion was satisfyingly loud, but this time there was no return shot. He worked his way along the rooftop to the slightly higher eaves of the factor's house, and then went flying as a loose tile slipped free under his weight.

By stripping his fingers on the remaining tiles he managed to save himself from going over the edge, but the net result was a twisted ankle which all but paid to his original strategy. Grunting from the pain, he worked his way along the roof to the small stone tower housing the bell whose peals, audible for kilometres over the flatlands all around, had once governed every stage of the working day of everyone on the estate.

Footsteps sounded out in the courtyard. Alberto had evidently either failed to open the trapdoor, or given up trying to find his way in the maze of buildings, a palimpsest dating from between the fifteenth and early twentieth centuries. In one of his few lighter moments, his father had once joked that even the rats must get lost sometimes.

'Stop playing these stupid games, Gabriele! We need to talk! I mean you no harm, I swear it. You startled me with that firework. Come out in the open. We just need to discuss what's happened and agree on a strategy. You must know that that's inevitable sooner or later. Let's get it over and done with now. Then you can go back to Milan and get on with your life.'

Gabriele's plan at this stage of the performance had been to drop down through the hatch at the base of the belfry, go downstairs through the factor's house, then dash across the remaining open side of the courtyard to the safety of the *barchessale*. Once there he would show himself briefly at intervals, always moving to his left. Alberto would intuitively assume that he would then proceed to the one remaining side of the rectangular structure, and would head for that to cut him off. Meanwhile Gabriele would pick up his bicycle from the niche where he had stored it and slip away through the gateway at the south-eastern corner of the *cascina*, through which the farm wagons used to enter and leave without disturbing the gentry, for whom the main entrance was reserved. While Alberto was fruitlessly searching the hayloft and byre, he could be off and away without anyone inside being any the wiser. He had done it often enough in the past.

In those days he had simply sauntered over to the open-sided sheds and spent some time chatting with old Giorgio, who was responsible for the upkeep and repair of the wagons and farm equipment stored there, before slipping out of the *porta dei carri*, but now he needed to sprint rather than saunter, and with his ankle in the state it was, that was out of the question. In short, his concept had been perfect but his perform-ance, as so often before, had let him down. Real t'ai chi masters didn't twist their ankles.

And the stakes were high. Despite the weasel words that continued to echo around the courtyard below, Alberto's three shots had left no doubt in Gabriele's mind about his intentions, and at ground level, in his present condition, he would be an easy target. As for the rear of the property, it was now overgrown with brambles at the north-east corner. That left only the roofs.

The gently sloping ridges and troughs of terracotta tiles had been familiar territory to him in his teens, but even then he had never ventured there after sunset, in misty late autumn, with a throbbing ankle and a killer ready to shoot him down the moment he presented a silhouette against the dying light. The tiles were slip-pery with moss and dead leaves, many were missing and all were loose. In one spot, the roof of the wagon shed had collapsed entirely, leaving a gaping hole. It took more time than he had ever imagined to crawl and hobble round to the hay loft on the southern side of the complex. If his memory served, there was an elm somewhere about there which jutted out over the roof.

He wasn't looking forward to shinning down it, but there was no alternative, and at least he would be in complete cover the whole time.

By now the light had almost completely gone, and he was still searching in vain for the remembered overhanging bough when the roof gave way beneath him. It was a gradual process lasting perhaps ten seconds: a gentle crack, a slow subsidence like sinking into a pile of pillows, then a deafening series of detonations and a terrifyingly quick descent.

'Gabriele!'

Alberto's booming tones recalled him to the realities of the situation. He was aching, but otherwise uninjured. The fall had been short, ending on a mound of festering hay. He was inside the raised and open loft, lying on top of the section of collapsed roof. The only exit was over the side giving on to the courtyard. Then he heard the scrape of a ladder being lifted off its metal hook and placed against the wall.

So prone to lethargy and despair in his everyday life, Gabriele showed no symptom of either now. His first thought was to fling one of the fallen tiles at his enemy the moment his head cleared the edge of the floor. Then he had an even better idea.

Alberto's torch and gun appeared before he did, the former's cold barrel of compressed light scouting out the space before coming to rest on the freshly-fallen tiles and timbers lying on the hay. It owner climbed up the remaining rungs of the ladder and stepped out on to the brickwork paving.

'Gabriele?'

There was no sound at all. Alberto walked over to the debris and inspected it with his torch, then turned and shone the powerful beam all around the floor of the loft. Then he started to search the space more carefully, pistol at the ready, obviously suspecting that his quarry was hiding under or behind one of the many pieces of agricultural detritus that littered the barn.

Perched on the main roof-beam above, Gabriele awaited his moment, gripped the knotted climbing rope as he had so many times in the past while playing the game that he and his brother had called 'flying skittles'. As Alberto returned towards the centre of the floor after overturning two casks and a wooden wheelbarrow, Gabriele launched himself into space, hurtling down and then twisting at the last moment on the rope to ram his uninjured foot into Alberto's back.

It was then that everything went out of control. Gabriele's intention had simply been to disarm and subdue his opponent, but Alberto rolled over and slipped into the *bòtola*, the aperture designed for pushing hay down to the cattle in the byre below. For a moment his fingers clung desperately to the slimy brickwork, but there was not sufficient purchase and

Gabriele could not reach him in time. There was a dull thump from below, then a scream that went on and on.

A moment later, Gabriele heard another voice in the courtyard. So Alberto had brought back-up after all. He picked up the pistol and torch, but privately he acknowledged defeat. He would go down fighting, but he had exhausted his stock of feints and dodges and had no illusions about the final outcome.

XIX

'Gabriele Passarini!'

There was a long silence, broken only by a monotonous series of muffled bellows, as of an animal in pain, emanating from the shed below the loft. But how could there be an animal there? The farm had been abandoned for decades.

Zen did not speak further, nor did he move. He just maintained his position at the centre of the former threshing floor, amid the weeds poking up between the paving slabs, as silent and immobile as the harmless if slightly dull statue in a town piazza.

At long length, a voice sounded out from inside the hay loft.

'Who are you?'

'You are Passarini?'

Another pause, interspersed by the dull howls of a third voice.

'Help me, Gabriele! My leg is broken!'

A torch beam shot out like a flick-knife, transfixing Zen.

'Drop your weapon on the ground and move away from it,' the man above said.

'I am not armed. We need to talk. I have no intention of harming you.'

A brief, caustic laugh.

'Just what Alberto said! You people from the *servizi* would lie to your mothers about your own name and the date of your birthday.'

'Please, Gabriele!' cried the other voice. 'All right, you won. Now I'm a battlefield casualty. Despite everything, we used to be comrades in arms. By your honour as a soldier, call an ambulance, for the love of God!'

Zen abandoned his imaginary plinth, switched on his torch and strode over to the shed from which these pleas were coming. He finally made out the ancient wooden door and pulled it open. Inside, the darkness was as absolute as in the military tunnels he had explored with Anton Redel. Once again, the torch acted as the presiding deity.

An overwhelming stench of damp mingled with lingering bovine odours and the acoustics of a crypt in which continual whimpers and moans reverberated like a choir of the damned. The building was all of brick. The floor was a tight herring-bone pattern, while the vaulted ceiling strengthened the ecclesiastical analogy. The design was at once sturdy, graceful and perfectly proportioned, only this was not a church but a cowshed. They did ugly things in those days too, Zen thought, but they didn't make ugly things. They just didn't know how.

'Over here, Gabriele!'

The swirling echoes cancelled out any directional help that the voice had intended to give, but the torch beam soon picked out the crumpled form lying supine on the flooring in the centre of the hall about five metres away.

'Call an ambulance! Do you have a mobile? Use mine if not. You wouldn't want my death on your conscience as well, would you? We'll just forget what's happened here. Enough is enough. No more deaths.'

Zen walked towards and then around the man, keeping the torch fixed on his head and face.

'Gabriele?' the man asked wonderingly.

'No, not Gabriele.'

The man lay breathing rapidly and shallowly. His right leg was twisted forward some thirty degrees at the knee. There was blood on his face and hands and on the brick flooring.

Zen transferred the torch to his left hand, knelt down and started to frisk the man's pockets with his right. The position was awkward, the light source too close to the subject, and he didn't see the knife until it was curving up towards his throat. But his attacker was hampered in his movements and Zen was able to roll away in time to avoid the blade. Neither man spoke. Zen stood up and kicked the hand holding the knife, which clattered away into one of the cow stalls. He retrieved it, retracted the blade and placed it in his pocket. Then he resumed his search. Having collected all the contents of the man's jacket and coat pockets, he stood examining them by the light of the torch. As he was doing so, another source of light made its presence felt as Gabriele Passarini made his way towards them, moving in the oddly aggressive manner of people with a limp. He still had the torch in one hand and the pistol in the other.

'What was I supposed to do?' Passarini asked, as if talking to himself. 'I didn't mean to hurt him. I just wanted to knock him over and take his gun away. He was trying to kill me! Only when I hit him, he fell down here from the loft.'

Zen took no notice of him. He completed his inspection of the items he had taken from the man's pockets, placed them in his own and only then looked at Passarini.

'Thirty years ago, you were a witness to the murder of Lieutenant Leonardo Ferrero in an abandoned military tunnel in the Dolomites. Tell me exactly what happened on that day.'

'Don't say anything!' the man on the floor shouted. 'He's a snooper from the Interior Ministry. They're

345

trying to disgrace the army. Shoot him and then call an ambulance for me! I'll sort it all out. I'll tell them that he was responsible for the whole thing and that you saved my life.'

'Colonel Alberto Guerrazzi was also present on that occasion,' Zen continued. 'So was Nestore Soldani, who was killed by a car bomb in Campione d'Italia a few days after the discovery of Ferrero's corpse, and one day before you fled here. The three of you, with Leonardo Ferrero, formerly constituted one unit of a conspiratorial organization code-named Operation Medusa.'

'Shoot him, Gabriele!' Guerrazzi shouted in a voice streaked with anguish. 'This man is a maverick who is being used by the Interior people to stir up trouble while remaining officially unaccountable. Whatever he has found out remains for the moment his private knowledge. It has not been communicated to Rome. I would know if it had. The risk is therefore containable, just as it was with Ferrero. Like him, this individual represents an Alpha-grade threat to national security. I now outrank you, and as the senior officer in this emergency situation I am ordering you to eliminate him immediately. You have the means at your disposal and I will take full responsibility. Failure to obey my order would be tantamount to treason.'

Gabriele Passarini sighed.

'Fuck off, Alberto,' he said.

There was a strangled sound from the floor.

'Guerrazzi was the leader of the cell,' Zen continued in an utterly bored tone, 'the only one with access to higher levels of command within the organization. At a certain point, he informed the rest of you that he had been ordered to take you all up to an abandoned system of military tunnels in the Dolomites to undergo a series of ritual ordeals. The reason given, I imagine, was both to bond the cell together – you were all very new recruits to Medusa – and also to bind that organization in a mystical *Blutbruderschaft* union with the glorious dead of the regiment who fell there during the First World War.'

'All honour to them!' cried the injured man.

'I entirely agree. All honour to them. All pity too, the poor bastards. At any rate, this is what you were told, and of course you all leapt at the chance to get out of the barracks for a laddish weekend in the mountains, just as you had at the invitation to be inducted into an elite club like Medusa in the first place. Guerrazzi here was the only one to know the real purpose of the expedition. Colonel Gaetano Comai, his commanding officer and Medusa contact, had informed him that Leonardo Ferrero had contacted a radical Communist investigative journalist named Luca Brandelli with a view to disclosing details about Operation Medusa.

347

Comai no doubt showed him photographs taken covertly during their meeting at a pizzeria in Piazza Bra. Guerrazzi's mission now was to find out how many other times Ferrero had talked to Brandelli and exactly how much he had revealed, and then eliminate him. I don't know how he put it to you and Soldani, Signor Passarini, but it may well have been in terms very similar to those he used when he tried to persuade you to shoot me a moment ago.'

'Alberto told us . . .' Gabriele began.

'Shut up!' yelled Guerrazzi. 'If you won't do your duty, at least hold your tongue.'

There was a brief silence.

'Would you by any chance have any paper here?' Zen asked Passarini.

'Paper?'

'Typing paper, preferably, but anything will do. I know that you are a man of books, so I thought maybe . . .'

'I've got some at the house.'

'Would you be good enough to bring a few sheets over here?'

'But why?'

'Five or six sheets would be perfect. Oh, and please don't think of just running off and disappearing, tempting though that obviously is. If you do, I'll have to call headquarters and have them issue an arrest warrant for the attempted murder of Colonel Alberto Guerrazzi.'

'It was an accident!'

'That would be for the courts to decide, but the case would take at least three years to come to trial, should you be lucky enough to survive that long. I'm sure that the colonel and his friends would take steps to ensure that your time in prison was as unpleasant as possible, if not indeed fatal.'

Gabriele's fear was evident even in the wavering torchlight. He nodded once and limped away.

'I knew you'd be trouble as soon as I heard about you, Zen,' said Guerrazzi. 'Yes, I've guessed your identity, although I hope you noticed that I didn't reveal it to our little bookworm. So we can put all this behind us. I know I can count on you to keep your silence. You're a patriot, just as Brandelli was in his own way. He was our sworn enemy thirty years ago, of course, like all the PCI crowd, but times have changed. When I see the shallow consumerist trash running around these days I almost begin to feel nostalgic for enemies like that.'

'I imagine that Ferrero was tortured before you threw him into that pit,' Zen said.

Guerrazzi sighed wearily.

'We naturally tried to extract whatever information we could about what he had divulged. Don't think that we enjoyed it. We were acting under orders. It was out duty to obey, just as it is your duty to summon an ambulance and have me taken to hospital immediately.'

'And then a few days later a military aircraft with Leonardo Ferrero supposedly aboard conveniently went missing over the Adriatic following a mid-air explosion.'

'Many of your guesses so far have been very clever and correct, Zen, but you are mistaken if you believe that I had anything to do with that.'

'How many men were on board the plane?'

'In theory, two.'

'But in practice one. An innocent serviceman.'

'It was a historic moment, Zen! The whole of Europe was teetering on the brink of armed revolution. The fate of the nation hung in the balance. In the end, the Maoists and Stalinists and anarchists were defeated, but it was a war, albeit secret and undeclared, and in any war there will be casualties. All the liberties and privileges that we take for granted today were won through struggle, sacrifice and suffering, yet how quick we are to forget! And even quicker to condemn.'

'And to panic, as when Ferrero's body unexpectedly turned up after all these years. What has become of it, incidentally?'

'It was cremated last week under a false name and death certificate. I myself scattered the ashes in the

Tiber.' Guerrazzi managed a laugh. 'One of the *vigili* noticed what I was doing and threatened me with a fine for polluting the environment. I took his name and number and told him that if he didn't bugger off he would be in the next urn.'

The light increased perceptibly as Gabriele Passarini returned, holding a sheaf of paper. Zen carefully extracted a slim pile of sheets from the inside of the pack.

'Thank you. Now then, we're going to need to leave soon, and it's vital that you leave no traces of your occupancy here. Go back to the house, pack up whatever you brought with you and try and make the place look as it did when you arrived. Then wait for me in the courtyard. Oh, and leave the pistol here.'

'Don't give it to him!' Guerrazzi shouted, sounding genuinely panicked for the first time. 'Give it to me! I'll cover him while you call an ambulance!'

Ignoring him, Gabriele addressed Zen.

'Why do you want the gun?'

'It's government property. Now it's one thing for you to have critically injured Colonel Guerrazzi . . .'

'It was an accident, I tell you!'

'Exactly my point. But if you take the pistol, that's theft. It's the property of the state and must be returned to its assigned user.'

He pointed to the low wall of the nearest stall.

'Just leave it there and go and pack. I'll be with you as soon as I've discussed a few remaining issues with the colonel.'

Gabriele did as he had been told and walked off. The door at the end of the byre grated on its hinges as he went out.

'Well, you've certainly got Passarini eating out of your hand,' Guerrazzi commented sarcastically. 'As a matter of interest, are you planning to shoot me?'

Zen did not reply. He took out a pen and held it out at arm's length to Guerrazzi along with the sheaf of papers.

'Sign each of these at the bottom, in order, printing your full name and title underneath.'

Guerrazzi regarded him spitefully.

'Why?'

'I want your autograph. A keepsake for my children's children.'

'You have no children, Zen. I checked your file.'

'Sign anyway.'

'Do you take me for an idiot? I'm not signing some blank sheets of paper that could be used to forge a statement or a confession. Never!'

Zen straightened up and consulted his watch. Then he took a step forward and very deliberately rearranged the position of Guerrazzi's broken leg. He paid no attention to the resulting clamour. He did not even look at Guerrazzi, only at his watch. When a minute had passed, he repeated the procedure.

'All right, all right!' barked Guerrazzi when he could speak again. 'My heart is weak. You'll kill me.'

'Then sign.'

And Alberto did. Zen supervised the process carefully, then retrieved the pages and the pen and placed them in his pocket.

'Thank you, *colonnello*,' he said. 'We're almost finished. It only remains for me to tell you why Leonardo Ferrero was killed.'

'We've already discussed that.'

'We've discussed the reasons that your commanding officer gave you. They were in fact false.'

'For Christ's sake, Zen, call an ambulance! This pain is unbearable.'

'I fear that the truth will be even more painful. Indeed, it seems to me almost the cruellest aspect of this little miserable affair.'

'Don't lecture me about the truth! I was there. I know what happened.'

'No, you don't. And even the version you did believe must have provided little comfort as the years went by. You believed that you had been ordered to eliminate a traitor who was threatening to expose a clandestine organization essential to the future stability of the country. But as time passed it surely became clear that if that stability had ever been under any real threat in the first place, it would have been from people like you. There was never the slightest prospect of the armed left-wing uprising. You had not only underestimated the common sense and decency of the Italian people, but committed an atrocious act in their name and without their consent.'

'It's easy to be wise with hindsight.'

'The three of you have had to live with that knowledge ever since, and each dealt with it in his own characteristic style. Nestore Soldani emigrated to Venezuela and made a fortune in various shady ways. Signor Passarini became a recluse and retreated into the world of antiquarian book dealing. You transferred to the secret service and used your power to terrify and if necessary eliminate anyone who threatened you. Soldani's dead, and I shall spare Passarini, but your case is different. The other two were accomplices to Ferrero's murder, but you were in charge. In charge of everything – the details, the duration, the *durezza*. You decided exactly how much Ferrero had to suffer before you threw him into that blast pit. It's only right that you at least should know the truth.'

Alberto Guerrazzi managed a scornful laugh.

'I have always known it, and I am neither proud nor ashamed of what I did.'

Zen ignored him.

'In the course of the interrogation to which you sub-jected him, Leonardo Ferrero must have claimed that he had been ordered to contact the journalist Luca Brandelli by your commanding officer, Colonel Comai.'

'He said a lot of things.'

'People under torture do. They will say anything to stop the pain.'

'Just as I signed those sheets of paper. What do you plan to do with them, incidentally?'

'But in this case what Ferrero said was true. There's no doubt about that, because he said exactly the same thing to the journalist when they met. He told Brandelli that his commanding officer had recently discovered the existence of Operation Medusa and was very con-cerned about the implications for democracy. He had therefore instructed Ferrero to arrange for selected details to be leaked to the press so that the whole matter would come to light.'

'That's absurd! Comai personally inducted me into Medusa. As cell leader, I recruited the other three. They reported to me and I reported to Comai. If he had doubts about the organization, why would he do all that?'

Zen nodded. 'That's an interesting point. Another is the cellular structure of Medusa. The idea of course is to protect the organization from external scrutiny in the event of a breakdown in security. Since each cell is discrete, its members cannot betray anything more than their own limited knowledge. By the same token, however, they cannot know anything more either. They cannot know, for example, whether the organization actually exists at all.'

He shone the torch beam at Guerrazzi's face.

'Your induction occurred during the three-month period preceding Lieutenant Ferrero's death, right?'

'How can you know?'

'Because the beginning of that period is when Colonel Comai discovered that Ferrero had been having an affair with his wife Claudia. Or rather, that's when she told him.'

'What are you talking about?'

'Ferrero had broken off the affair a few months earlier, and he chose the cruellest way, a wall of silence. The coward's way, she calls it in her journal. It was very difficult and dangerous for Claudia to contact her young lover, and on the few occasions when she tried he simply refused to respond. In a word, he had tired of her, and was no doubt also worried about the effect on his career if her husband found out. Anyway, he dropped her.'

'This is all . . .'

'Shortly afterwards, Claudia discovered that she was pregnant. She broke both the good news and the bad to her husband. She was going to be a mother at last, and he a father. It was a new beginning for their marriage, and in order that love and trust might henceforth be abounding there was one past peccadillo that she wanted to confess to, just so as to clear the air. She backdated the end of the affair with Ferrero by about a year, so that her husband would have no suspicion that the child was not his, and indeed it seems that he never did.'

Guerrazzi looked completely dazed, and not just by pain or the light.

'Signora Comai's object in all this was to protect herself against possible future indiscretions by her ex-lover, and more importantly to get her own back. She knew exactly how ambitious Ferrero was, and in his military career he would soon be facing the same wall of silence to which he had treated her. It was a just punishment that would hurt him just as he had hurt her. Colonel Comai had other ideas, however. It was he, no doubt, who suggested that Leonardo Ferrero would be an excellent choice for one of the other three members of the newly formed Medusa cell.'

'He mentioned his name.'

Zen murmured indulgently.

'The idea was a stroke of genius on his part, I must admit. A stupid man would have made do with one assassin, or even have done it himself. But Comai couldn't know how many other people knew about Ferrero's liaison with his wife. If the young lieutenant turned up dead in an alley somewhere then tongues might have started to wag. Besides, an individual might have betrayed him, but a group like yours was bound together by a sense of shared responsibility and guilt. To reveal the truth would have been to betray your comrades in arms, not to mention a patriotic conspiracy of the highest secrecy and significance.'

'This is all bluff, Zen! You have no proof.'

'Proof exists, in the form of Claudia Comai's journal. I read it earlier today, although apart from a few details it merely confirmed what I already knew or had guessed. And I could easily have brought it with me, had I been interested in collecting evidence. But this case is never going to come to court. Apart from anything else, the principals are all dead. Colonel Comai was almost certainly murdered by his wife, by the way. At the time of Ferrero's death, Claudia assumed that he had been killed by accident in that plane crash. It was another fifteen years before her husband finally revealed the truth in the course of a marital row. A short time later he fell, or more likely was pushed, to his death. And his widow Claudia herself ended her life at a hotel in Lugano.'

He paused for a moment.

'Which leaves only you, Guerrazzi.'

He went over to the wall where Passarini had left the pistol and carefully wiped the weapon clean of fingerprints on his scarf before setting it down on the floor about two metres beyond the furthest reach of the injured man.

'You should be able to reach that in due course. It will be totally dark in here, of course, and moving will be painful. But under the circumstances you may well decide that the alternatives are even less desirable.'

Zen got out Guerrazzi's SISMI identification and checked that the signature on the blank sheets of paper corresponded to that on the card. He then went through the rest of the other man's belongings. The keys he retained and the knife he tossed into a corner. Lastly he removed the battery from the mobile phone and then threw them separately to different ends of the shed.

'So you're appointing yourself judge, jury and executioner,' Guerrazzi commented with a certain bitter satisfaction.

'Just the first two, *colonnello*, and then only after conducting a full investigation. Unlike you, who took on all three roles on nothing but the unsupported word of a vengeful husband.'

'I was a soldier obeying the orders of my commanding officer!'

'What you were was a fool, Guerrazzi. Take these tattoos with the face of the Gorgon, for example.

Ferrero and Soldani both had them. I imagine that you and Passarini did too.'

'It was part of the induction ceremony.'

'To make life easy for the opposition, no doubt. No need for lengthy interrogations or the third degree. To identify you as a member, all they had to do was roll up your sleeve. And it wasn't as if Colonel Comai didn't know any better. He regularly used to smuggle in huge amounts of cash through Switzerland, using the casino at Campione as his clearing house. You can't do that without powerful friends, and Comai was almost certainly paymaster to one of the real extreme right-wing conspiratorial organizations that were oper-ating at the time. But he knew that the real thing wouldn't be colourful enough to attract young idiots like you, so he dreamt up this fantasy secret society complete with tattoos and passwords and induction ceremonies and bonding rituals and all the rest of it. And you fell for the hoax, and on the strength of it you have committed two murders and were planning a third.'

'It's not true! It can't be true!'

'It is true, *colonnello*. Your entire career has been predicated on a lie. You are evidently a great admirer of military discipline and traditions. So am I, in my way, so I shall now leave you to reflect on the situation and then do as you see fit.'

Zen walked down the alley and out of the building, closing the heavy door behind him and wiping off the handle. After the damp, fetid atmosphere inside the *stalla*, the night air smelt wonderful.

Gabriele Passarini was waiting with his bags in the courtyard.

'Right, let's be off!' said Zen briskly. 'Got all your stuff?'

'Everything except my bicycle.'

'Is there anything about it to link it to you?'

'No.'

Passarini hesitated.

'In fact it's a ladies' model.'

'Then forget it. We must leave immediately.'

'But what about him?'

He gestured to the cowshed.

'Oh, that's all sorted out,' Zen replied, picking up one of Passarini's bags and leading the way to the gate. 'Colonel Guerrazzi and I have come to an understanding and he's given me full instructions. As soon as we're clear of the area, I'll call a number he provided and dispatch a military ambulance to come and pick him up. We couldn't use the civilian service, of course. They'd want to know what he'd been doing here and how it happened and who we were and all the rest of it. This way, the whole incident will just be forgotten.'

They passed through the little door and Zen closed it behind them.

'But what about me?' Passarini whined. 'He'll come after me again, or send someone else.'

'No, he won't,' Zen told him as he unlocked his car. 'Part of our understanding is that he's made a written statement on those sheets of paper you brought me. I'll ensure that it's forwarded to the appropriate quarters. Soon everyone will know about Operation Medusa, so your knowledge will be of no significance.'

'But there'll be an enquiry. I'll have to testify in court.'

'Your name is not mentioned in Colonel Guerrazzi's statement. Anyway, no one's interests would be served by holding a public enquiry. The whole thing will be brushed under the carpet as yesterday's news. Apparently he's planning to put out a disinformation story to account for his injuries and allow adequate time for recuperation. But the success of this plan depends absolutely on neither of us disclosing anything about what has happened. Now then, where did he leave his car?'

Passarini looked at Zen doubtfully.

'Didn't he tell you?'

'We overlooked that detail.'

'It's in a thicket just a little way along the road. I heard him arrive.'

'Right. There are apparently sensitive documents in the vehicle and he wants it disposed of safely. He's given me full instructions. Can you drive with your ankle in that state?'

'I'm not incapacitated. It'll hurt a bit, but that kind of pain I can deal with.'

Zen started the engine and turned round.

'Then you take this car and I'll drive his. Stay behind me all the way to the place where he wants it dropped off, and then I'll drive you back to Milan.'

'I still don't understand,' said Passarini as they bumped down the drive leading from the *cascina* to the paved road. 'I don't understand who you are and I don't understand what you're doing.'

'It's not so much what I'm doing, it's what I'm undoing. And you don't need to understand. All you need do is to forget that this ever happened. If you do that, I guarantee that you will be left in peace.'

It was this last phrase that finally persuaded Gabriele. Left in peace! That was all he had ever wanted to be.

XX

Two days later, shortly after seven o'clock in the morning, Aurelio Zen stepped out of the front door of the apartment that he shared with Gemma Santini and ran lightly downstairs and out into the hazy sunlight, heading for the Piazza del'Anfiteatro. It was a short walk to the archway into the oval space that never failed to move him at any hour of the day or night, its perfect proportions balanced by the variegated façade of medieval houses quarried out of and built on to the original Roman walls.

The only café open offered *La Nazione, La Stampa* and *La Gazzetta dello Sport* by way of national newspapers. Lucca was the inverse of San Giorgio di Valpolicella, a 'white' town in the midst of traditionally Communist Tuscany. Zen ordered a double espresso and glanced through the first two papers, but there was no reference to the matter in which he was interested. Nor had there been a word about it on the news he had listened to before leaving the apartment. It had of course occurred to him that this might well not work out. It was like patience, the only game Zen enjoyed playing, apart from professional ones. Sometimes the cards came out right, sometimes they didn't. All you could do was to arrange them as best you could and leave the rest to chance.

He had arranged the cards he had been holding as best he could during the intervening days. After locating Guerrazzi's car, he and Gabriele Passarini had driven in tandem up the A21 to Brescia, where Zen had parked on a side street in one of the tough *borgate* on the fringes of the city. He had left the key in the ignition and the window open. The vehicle would be stolen within hours, if not minutes. He had then taken over the wheel of the rental car from Passarini and driven to Milan, dropping his passenger off at a metro stop in the suburbs before proceeding to one of the ubiquitous Jolly Hotels, where he had rented himself a hutch for the night and gone straight to sleep. But only for a few hours. There was still work to be done, and no time to be lost.

He awoke around three, and spent much of the morning composing and correcting a total of six drafts of text on his notepad. Then he checked out, drove to Linate airport and returned the rental car. From there it was a forty-five-minute cab ride to the central Questura, where he identified himself and requested the use of a photocopier and an office with a secure telephone and a typewriter. The latter item of obsolete technology initially proved to be a problem, but in the end someone located a functioning model in the basement. Zen then prepared the document, and contacted the recipient about arrangements for handing it over. By early evening he was back in Lucca, in good time for the dinner of bean soup and a massive *fiorentina* steak that Gemma had prepared.

But now was the moment of truth. He told the barman that he would be back in a moment and went outside. At the corner of the main street beyond the piazza was a newsagent's kiosk. Zen bought *La Repubblica* and *Il Manifesto* and returned to the café without even glancing at the headlines. His coffee was still steaming on the bar. Zen took it over to one of the more remote tables together with the papers he had bought.

There had been nothing to worry about. *La Repubblica* had not only printed Luca Brandelli's piece, it had done him proud. There was a panel headline and brief introduction on the front cover, with the full story in the '*Politica Interna*' section as well as a typically mordant editorial on the subject by Eugenio Scalfari.

The main article was a two-page spread featuring photographs of the signed statement that Zen had typed above Guerrazzi's signature at the Questura in Milan and of the photocopy he had taken of the colonel's SISMI identification card, accompanied by a full transcript of the text which Zen had concocted earlier at the Jolly Hotel. This was basically an edited version of the account of Leonardo Ferrero's murder that Alberto Guerrazzi had given at the *cascina*, omitting all mention of Gabriele Passarini but stressing the involvement of the late Nestore Soldani, alias Nestor Machado Solorzano, of the even later Gaetano Comai, and above all the crucial significance of the Operation Medusa conspiracy. Alberto Guerrazzi admitted his own full responsibility for Ferrero's death, which he now deeply regretted, but argued that he had acted in the best interests of the country as he had perceived them at the time. He further stated that following the recent discovery of Ferrero's body he had realized that it was only a matter of time before the truth came out, and that he preferred to avoid the shame and scandal that would inevitably follow by leaving the country for some time.

The rest of the article consisted of Brandelli's lengthy and subtly self-inflating commentary. The document, he claimed, had appeared in his letter-box the day before. He had no idea as to its provenance, but sources at SISMI had apparently indicated on condition of anonymity that the signature was indeed that of Colonel Alberto Guerrazzi. What he did know was that Leonardo Ferrero had approached him over thirty years earlier, at the time of the events described in the document, and indicated the existence of a clandestine

military organization known as Medusa. His informant had then disappeared before being able to furnish
further details.

Brandelli went on to give a colourful and detailed
account of his original meeting with Ferrero, including
much retrospectively corroborative material that he had
not mentioned to Zen and had quite possibly invented.
He also noted that the conspiracy described in Guerrazzi's
statement accorded fully with what was now known of
other similar organizations of the period, and further
remarked upon the fact that Nestore Soldani had been
murdered in a car bomb explosion near his home in
Campione d'Italia a few days after the discovery of
Ferrero's body. He did not directly speculate on the
identity of the latter's killers, but the implications were
clear. As for Alberto Guerrazzi, all Brandelli's attempts
to reach him had failed and his whereabouts appeared to
be unknown even to his most intimate colleagues. The
reader was left to draw his own conclusions.

Zen paid for his coffee, walked around to the bakery
that he and Gemma favoured and ordered an assort-
ment of goodies which they boxed up for him. No
wonder there had been nothing in the other papers or
on the radio or TV. *La Repubblica* had understandably
wanted to keep this exclusive scoop secret until its own
edition hit the streets. But by lunchtime it would be
one of the top news stories in the country.

When Zen delivered the faked statement to Luca Brandelli, he had assured the journalist that Guerrazzi's signature was genuine and that the text represented a fair summary of his views, all of which was substantially true. He had however declined to say anything about how he had obtained the document, implying that the interests involved were so powerful and the situation so dangerous that such knowledge would compromise both of them. This too was substantially true. Given Brandelli's reputation as a fearless investigative journalist whose livelihood depended on protecting his sources, there seemed every reason to suppose that he would do so in this case. As for Gabriele Passarini, Zen felt reasonably sure that his discretion and common sense could be counted on.

There had been little talk between the two men during the drive from Brescia back to Milan, but as they neared their destination Passarini had finally broken the silence.

'There's something Leonardo said once that I've never understood.'

Zen knew that his companion wanted to be prompted, but he was too exhausted to bother. In the end they drove on for another two kilometres before Passarini continued of his own volition.

'When we were told about Operation Medusa . . .'

Another breakdown, another kilometre.

'I asked Leonardo why they had given it that name. He said that Colonel Comai had told him that it was based on the bronze statue by Cellini in Florence, a flattering justification of the autocratic rule of the Medici family, Cellini's patrons. The snakes that were Medusa's hair symbolized the squabbling factions of Guelphs and Ghibellines which had brought Florentine democracy to its knees, but had now been eradicated by the Medicis' tyranny, symbolized in turn by Perseus's single sharp sword blow severing the Gorgon's head. I could see the parallel with the situation here in Italy in the seventies, but then . . .'

More silence, this time for two kilometres.

'Then Leonardo said something very strange, something I've never forgotten but never understood. He said, "Every woman is Medusa. When you look into her eyes, you see the entire history of the human race. That's enough to turn anyone to stone."'

Halfway back to the house, Zen's *telefonino* shrilled. It was probably Gemma, he thought, wondering aloud in her charmingly stroppy way how much longer she would have to wait for her breakfast. But he was wrong.

'This is Brugnoli. You've seen *La Repubblica*?'

'I glanced at it.'

And then the question Zen had been dreading.

'Did you by any chance have anything to do with this?'

'Well, to an extent. The wheels were already turning, but I gave them the odd push here and there. Let's say that I acted as a "facilitator". Like you, Dottor Brugnoli, if you'll forgive the comparison.'

To Zen's surprise and relief, his superior laughed quietly.

'On the contrary! If there's any comparison to be drawn, it's I who should feel flattered by it. For obvious reasons, I'm not going to ask what you did or how you did it, Zen, but let me assure you that the powers that be here at the Ministry are well pleased with the outcome. Our neighbours up the street are going to be covered in shit of the deepest hue for the foreseeable future, and no matter what specious excuses, denials and cover stories they come up with, a lot of it is going to stick. In short, you're a star. Take the rest of the month off, keep your head down and needless to say don't breathe a word about this to anyone. Speaking of which, in response to your request, some of our technical people called in to do an electronic sweep of the apartment that you share with Signora Santini. She was away at the time and is unaware of the intrusion. The whole place had been bugged up one side and down the other. Anyway, that's all taken care of now and you can resume your normal life until further notice. And once again, congratulations.'

Zen walked back along the deserted street. From a government building opposite the national flag was flying at halfmast in honour of a politician of former notoriety who had died the day before. Zen regarded it with an irony not unmixed with pride. I too have done my duty, he thought.

Gemma was prowling around the kitchen in a silk dressing-gown which Zen had bought her shortly after moving in.

'God, that took long enough!' she said with mild exasperation, opening the box of pastries. 'Never mind. The milk's still warm and I'll make another pot of coffee. Oh, I forgot to tell you, that friend of yours came round.'

'What friend?'

'Some Sardinian name.'

'Gilberto Nieddu?'

'That's him. He sent me an email saying that he was going to be in the area and could he drop by. I told him you were away, but he said he wanted to see me. It turns out that he's importing generic copies of patented medicines manufactured illegally in India and the Far East, repackaging them here to resemble the original and then offering them to pharmacists at a large discount to pass off as the full-price brandname product.'

'And what did you say?'

'No, basically. It was a bit awkward, what with him being your friend and all. But I'm doing all right as it is, and I just want to feel decent, you know?'

'I certainly do.'

'Anyway, tell me all about this case you've been working on up north. I didn't ask last night. You were just too tired.'

Zen grimaced.

'There's really nothing much to say. Just a nasty little domestic drama of no significance. The wife had an affair, the husband found out and killed the lover, then the wife found out about that and killed the husband.'

'How sordid.'

'Exactly. But who cares? It's got nothing to do with us.'

He kissed her on the lips.

'I love you madly.'

'*Carissimo!* And I love you sanely. A winning combination, don't you think?'

Zen kissed her again as the coffee started to gurgle up into the pot. He smiled for what felt like the first time in days.

'It could be worse,' he said. 'It could be a lot worse.'

The Zen Series from Michael Dibdin

Ratking
Zen is unexpectedly transferred to Perugia to take over an explosive kidnapping case involving one of Italy's most powerful families.

Vendetta
An impossible murder in a top-security Sardinian fortress leads Zen to a menacing and violent world where his own life is soon at risk.

Cabal
When a man falls to his death in a chapel in St Peter's, Zen must crack the secret of the Vatican to solve the crime.

Dead Lagoon
Zen returns to his native Venice to investigate the disappearance of a rich American resident, while confronting disturbing revelations about his own life.

Così Fan Tutti

Zen finds himself in Naples, a city trying to clean up its act – perhaps too literally, as politicians, businessmen and mafiosi begin to disappear off the streets.

A Long Finish

Back in Rome, Zen is given an unorthodox assignment: to release the jailed scion of an important wine-growing family who is accused of a brutal murder.

Blood Rain

The gruesome discovery of an unidentified corpse in a railway carriage in Sicily marks the beginning of Zen's most difficult and dangerous case.

And Then You Die

After months in hospital recovering from a bomb attack on his car, Zen is trying to lie low at a beach resort on the Tuscan coast, but an alarming number of people are dropping dead around him.

Medusa

When human remains are found in abandoned military tunnels, the case leads Zen back into the murky history of post-war Italy.

Back to Bologna
Zen is called to Bologna to investigate the murder
of the shady industrialist who owns the local football
team.

End Games
After a brutal murder in the heart of a tight-knit
traditional community in Calabria, Zen is determined
to find a way to penetrate the code of silence and
uncover the truth.